SHRINKING
THE
TRUTH

a mystery by
Marc Darrow

OTTER B BOOKS
Santa Cruz
California

12/8

Shrinking the Truth is a paperback original mystery published by OTTER B BOOKS, March1997. Information concerning rights to reprint this book or portions thereof in any form except as provided by the U.S. copyright law may be obtained by contacting the publisher at 1891-16th Avenue, Santa Cruz, CA 95062; (408) 476-5334.

Printed by arrangement with the author.

Manufactured in the United States of America.

ISBN 0-9617681-9-3

The cover design is by Amanda Tennant .

Cover is based on a photo of the Fall Creek lime kilns provided by Frank Perry.

Author photo by Paul Coenen.

To Jill Schettler,
my wife and editor.

Author's Note

Since I'm a psychotherapist myself and I've chosen to tell this story from the point of view of a character who's also a psychotherapist, I believe it's extremely important for me to clarify the question of what's real and what's fiction in this book.

It's all fiction.

Every word.

Not a single actual client or composite drawn from actual clients appears in these pages. None of the behaviors, syndromes, or behaviors of clients or colleagues depicted here are drawn from my experiences either.

Also, I am *not* the protagonist and I don't share his point of view, about *anything*. The only similarity between the main character and myself is that we're both tall. Honest. I've taken great pains to ensure that I can accurately state this fact since the confidentiality of past, present, and future clients is paramount in my line of work.

Basically, I made all this up and then took the extra step of carefully crossing-off anything that looked suspiciously like my version of reality in case my subconscious was playing any tricks.

I hope that this book *seems* real and I'll be well-satisfied if at some point you wonder if maybe I'm just a big liar about all this fiction business. But the bottom line is that no one I know need fear that they're in here and the first person format is merely a device to create an *illusion* of autobiography.

If you refuse to believe me after reading the book in its entirety, then I'll be forced to come over to your house and diagnose you and we wouldn't want that, would we?

— Marc

Chapter 1

Once I saw a male penguin courting on television. He selected a small black rock that he imagined the female might like, transported it with his long thin beak across a desolate shore, and then laid it gently at the feet of his beloved. The female, however, was fussy and this first offering failed to warm her heart. Second and third efforts fared no better and a pile of smooth black stones accumulated, each studiously chosen and painstakingly hauled into place. Finally one of the gifts pleased the female and the birds mated offscreen, their hot penguin love presumably too provocative for public viewing.

Did the rocks vary in any significant way? Not to my eye. Had the male proved his commitment by bringing over a certain *number* of rocks? Was the female helping her future mate understand the essential capriciousness of sexual relationship? I don't know.

I feel as though this snippet of bird courtship lore is the core metaphor of my life, except that unlike the male penguin I've never selected a rock that worked. I don't mean just with women. It's as though everyone else knows something I don't, or at least they all pretend they do, perhaps following a set of conventions that no one's told me about.

When you lack basic values and tools to guide decision-making, life can be a tiring exercise, a series of events which may or may not hold meaning.

I can remember two occasions, though, when I felt completely free of this burden. The common denominator of these anomalous episodes was a temporary loss of self. I'll explain.

When I was eleven, I fell out of a willow tree and landed on the back of my head. That's what they tell me, at any rate. I remember inching out onto a sturdy-looking branch and then I remember lying in a bed wondering who I was. The anxious woman hovering nearby was also a total stranger and the room was unfamiliar. It was sublime. With no one minding the store, I was free to marvel and the world was nothing but wondrous. Another way to describe it is that I was so devoid of content that I became a process — a process of experiencing. After a couple of hours everything gradually seeped back in, coagulating in familiar clumps. I was me again and my mom was my mom. This glimpse into an alternative way of being has dogged me, transforming hard-earned satisfactions into sour disappointments.

I was blessed by another bout of bittersweet amnesia years later as an adult. Prone on a gloriously comfortable sofa after a hard day's work, I slipped into a deep sleep — a truly epic stint of unconsciousness. Some time later the doorbell rang and I awoke, or at least part of me did. I imagine we've all experienced a moment or two of confusion upon an abrupt awakening. This was more than that. For several minutes I lay and gazed about me with absolutely no clue as to who or where I was. My peace of mind was so complete that everything seemed perfectly matter-of-fact. While it would've been an odd or intriguing experience were I capable of conceptualizing, it simply was what it was, and nothing more. Finally the doorbell rang again, followed by someone knocking, which I somehow understood to be an event which required a response. I lurched to my feet and wobbled to the door, opening it with no expectations. It could've been a herd of wildebeest on the doorstep for all I knew.

There were two small demons. One resembled a traditional devil, replete with a bony red face and milky white horns. The other's features were contorted in a fierce snarl and huge black fangs overhung its bulbous pink lips. I wasn't scared; I wasn't anything.

"Trick or treat!" two high-pitched voices called.

"Oh. Halloween. Oh… just a minute."

This time it all rushed back in a millisecond. I was me. I needed to get the candy from the kitchen table. The kids would not rip me apart and eat me.

Less profound than my hours of amnesia, the episode nonetheless reminded me of how much I didn't want to be who I was — in this world in which I found it so hard to live.

*   *   *   *   *

So what profession does a confused-by-penguins-and-likes-amnesia kind of guy ultimately select? Psychotherapy, of course — where all the higher-functioning crazies accrete. 'It takes one to know one,' my aunt liked to chant. She also was fond of declaring, 'to each his own, said the lady as she kissed the cow,' so perhaps we shouldn't rely too heavily on her folk wisdom. But there is certainly truth in the notion that therapists in all the standard flavors — psychiatrists, psychologists, social workers, and counselors (listed in descending order of status and average fee) — tend to be at least odd. I believe that most practitioners are drawn to their livelihood by an unconscious sense that healing is omnidirectional. Thus the client and the therapist both mend in their sessions, and sometimes elderly psychologists are hardly even crazy anymore.

As for me, at age forty-four after twelve years in private practice, the process was still ongoing. I was nowhere near as depressed and anxious as when I began, yet no one would nominate me as a poster boy for American mental health either.

It was difficult to ascertain how my open door policy affected my long-term healing. Unlike virtually every other therapist in Santa Cruz, I saw absolutely any client, no matter how bizarre, obnoxious, or hopeless. By weathering the entire available continuum, I hoped to expose myself to the maximum dose of reciprocal healing. Sometimes, though, severe pathology and aberrant personality disorders functioned purely as corrosive solvents, attacking the structural integrity of everyone in the room.

It was rarely dull — that's one thing I can state with certainty. California is simply a lively place to practice; it's chock full of offbeat psyches. Some of my all-time favorites: a man deathly afraid of spontaneous combustion, a couple who could only make satisfying love in pick-up trucks, and a young girl who believed she was the reincarnation of a rock star who wasn't dead. Usually I heard "I can't sleep," "I'm anxious at work," or "There's nothing wrong with me — I'm just here to make my wife/husband/boss happy." These are merely prologues to the work, of course. The real task is uncovering what lies beneath such presentations. It's a bit like being a detective except that the suspect has already turned himself in.

Despite this advantage, clients can be even less cooperative than criminals. For one thing, they aren't necessarily consciously aware of their hidden material. For another, most people work at least as hard on maintaining the status quo as they do on changing, regardless of whose office they've dragged themselves into. The therapist is compelled, then, to work with the client's unconscious psyche, which often embodies a completely alien agenda. Sometimes I felt as if there were a secret race from some other world that lived deep inside us all. An alliance between these strangers and our conscious selves was not a simple matter to negotiate.

At any rate, George Arundel was something new and by now this was rare. I met him at my downtown office on a Tuesday afternoon in late April. My first impression was of a tall, overweight fifty-year-old white man who couldn't accept his baldness. Arundel's combing-forward strategy lent his forehead a comic-strip character effect, as if a lazy illustrator hadn't bothered to sketch in all the details. His facial features were reasonably regular, although his mouth was a bit oversized and his teeth were worn and rounded, as though his diet included rocks or something else much harder than ordinary food. He was pale and freckled and he wore a white dress shirt and brown wool pants.

"Tom Dalziel?" he asked, extending a large pink hand as he hovered in my doorway. The tone of his question implied an uncertainty beyond a first meeting's customary hesitancy. Could he be seriously wondering if I was an imposter?

"That's me," I responded. "And you're George Arundel?" I was conscious of an odd feeling as I shook his hand. Before I could process it, my prospective client had nodded and asked another question.

"This is your office?"

"Yes. Please come in."

He hesitated, as if unsure whether to believe me or not.

"Is there a particular concern I can help you with right now?" I asked in my fragile-client voice.

"Well, I expected something rather different," he answered, still frozen in the doorway. His voice betrayed no anxiety, just mild surprise. Apparently this was sufficient to immobilize him.

"Would you like to sit down and talk about it?"

"Of course, of course," Arundel sing-songed, striding forward with great energy. This behavior was completely incongruous with my sense of the man thus far. He plopped down in the green armchair that was obviously mine and peered around with no apparent interest. That is, his eyes surveyed the contents of the room — the antique wooden furniture, the floral watercolors on the walls, the one large window — yet there was no impression that anyone saw them. His face was a mask, and his eyes seemed to be sending signals by rote that never reached Arundel Central.

So far, I'd observed enough pathology to justify a dozen different diagnoses. I tried to ignore all that and focus on the matter at hand as I seated myself across from Arundel. It was distracting, though, to see the room from the perspective of the client's chair. The desk and coffee table really didn't match the way they appeared to from my usual seat. And the gray carpet bulged in two spots in front of the window as though it covered some embarrassing secrets. Dead rats? God knows why I thought of that.

"So you had particular expectations?" I blurted out.

"Yes." The brain and the eyes were back on line.

We stared at one another for a moment. All I knew about Arundel before that day was that he'd been referred by a local psychotherapist who had described him as 'a substantial challenge.' This was standard inter-therapist code for 'a big pain in the ass.'

"I had a dream," he told me. Now his voice was soft — a loud whisper.

"A dream?"

"Right. You were smaller and younger and your office was like a washroom in an old train station."

"Are you disappointed?"

"No. Should I be?"

I shrugged in lieu of explaining my strong feelings about the word 'should.' I wish we could just exorcise the whole concept from our language.

"I can feel myself adjusting," Arundel reported.

This struck me as worth investigating. "What does it feel like?"

"Like adjusting."

"I'm not sure I know what you mean."

"So?"

"You don't care?"

"Should I?"

Here we were again; I didn't respond. Arundel began cleaning one of his ears with his index finger. After a long pause I decided to start from scratch.

"What brings you here?" I asked, my standard opening line when I haven't been preempted by a client's idiosyncrasies.

"I need help," he announced.

"Why do you say that?"

"I cannot fulfill my mission without help."

"Your mission?"

"That's right." Arundel began cleaning his other ear.

"What do you mean?"

"Surely you know the meaning of the word 'mission'?" He was smiling now, but it was a cold, creepy smile.

"I'm interested in what *your* idea of the word is," I explained.

"My personal definition is no different than the one in a dictionary."

"And what would that be?"

"A series of tasks designed to achieve certain goals." Finished with his ears, he laid his hands on his expansive belly, one on top of the other.

I was struck by Arundel's ability to provide a concise, accurate definition of a fairly complex term. It's been my experience that the average person can't muster such information.

"So you need my help but you'd prefer not to tell me why at this point?" I tried.

"I have told you why."

"But how can I help you fulfill your mission if you won't tell me what the mission is?"

"'Won't' is not the proper word. 'Won't' implies a willful disobedience over the course of time. As yet, I haven't told you what you want to know, but that doesn't mean I 'won't.'" He smiled briefly and then looked down at his hands. For some reason my gaze fell even lower and I found myself studying his shoes. They were unremarkable low-tech running shoes, except for the large letter K scrawled above the heels in black magic marker. A team insignia? Borrowed shoes? Was Arundel his real name?

I looked up quickly, expecting to be caught out; it seems as though clients always know when their therapist has become distracted. George Arundel, though, was still gazing serenely at the pile of fingers on his gut.

"So are you ready to tell me?" I asked.

"No. It will work out best if I don't go into that now. But the time will come when it will be appropriate."

I was struck, once again, by the formality of the man's language, and also by the literal quality of most of his responses. Technically, he always answered my questions, yet no information beyond the bare minimum was ever transmitted. What did I know so far? Not a hell of a lot.

Belatedly, I was aware that Arundel had thoroughly wrested control of the session away from me. By sitting in my chair, playing games instead of providing useful answers to my questions, and then lecturing me on word usage, he had successfully created a context in which he was comfortable. That it might have come at my expense didn't seem important to him. I was impressed by the efficacy of this feat, but also disconcerted by the way *this* Arundel varied so drastically from the confused soul who had loitered in my doorway minutes before.

"Perhaps you'd like to tell me something else about yourself?" I suggested.

"What would you like to know?" He crossed his legs and jiggled his foot frenetically. The movement implied an urgency that he hadn't exhibited thus far. I was perversely pleased to see it.

"What do you feel would be relevant to our work here?" I asked. I was trying hard to remain non-directive. On the one hand, continuing to ask him to supply an agenda was playing into his game of holding the power by refusing me, but on the other hand I wasn't ready to abandon one of my key principles yet. I firmly believe that the work has to emerge from the client, and that what clients choose to share is a vital piece in the therapeutic jigsaw puzzle.

"I have no idea at this time," Arundel finally pronounced. "Do you?"

"Well, there are certain areas that are customarily discussed."

As soon as these words crossed my lips, I regretted them. They were nothing more than an announcement that I would indeed collude with Arundel in the business of my own manipulation. It was one thing to choose that course of action consciously but I had simply spoken carelessly and now there we were.

Arundel frowned, perhaps disappointed that I didn't represent a more formidable challenge.

"What?" he asked sweetly.

What the hell, I thought. "Let's see. Occupation, family of origin, current domestic situation — that sort of thing. I can't help you unless I understand your life context."

"Administrator, a mother, father, and brother, and I live alone," he reported.

"Are you uncomfortable letting me know you? Do you distrust me?"

"No. Not at all." He held his foot still and made an obvious, concerted effort to physically relax. "Do I look uncomfortable?" he asked.

"Not now," I replied, smiling.

He ignored this, waiting expectantly for me to continue. I thought about making a stand by remaining silent or saying something like 'that's my answer,' but I decided to raise the stakes even higher.

"Look," I began, "talking with you feels like pulling teeth. You've systematically refused to cooperate with me and frankly I'm feeling very frustrated. If we can't deal with any meaningful content, then at least let's talk about *why* we can't. You must have some reason for your reticence."

I figured I'd either lose Arundel entirely or else jar him into loosening up. If he wouldn't give a little, I didn't care to work with him anyway, so I wasn't anxious about which it would be. I didn't consider that he'd find a way to deflect the substantive portion of my diatribe, rendering the choice irrelevant.

"So everything that happens has a reason?"

I sighed. "That's my belief. Yes."

"Such an attitude inevitably generates frustration," he told me.

"Do you have an alternate point of view?"

"Yes."

"Would you tell me about it?"

"No."

I wondered if he was this way with everyone. It would certainly explain why he had problems and needed therapy.

Suddenly, he stiffened. I can't think of any better way to describe it. He just became rigid. It wasn't a convulsion or a cramp or anything else I was familiar with. A second later, he was supple again, blinking furiously and poking his tongue out of his rounded mouth.

"Are you all right?" I asked, seriously concerned.

"I'm fine," he boomed. His voice was now low and loud. "But I have to go."

"We're almost out of time but we haven't decided if we can work with each other," I pointed out.

"Yes!" he shouted.

"Yes?"

"Yes, we can!"

"I'm not so sure. Why should I help you?"

"It's your job!" he roared. My ears were beginning to hurt and his verbal assault was exacting a toll on my nerves as well.

"That doesn't mean I have to accept every potential client I meet. I don't have the impression that you're interested in the sort of work I do."

After a pause, Arundel responded in a much quieter, gentler voice. "I believe that a friend of mine is actually an angel."

I stared. "Is the same time next week convenient for you?"

"Yes." Arundel rose and strode out of the room.

Chapter 2

There were still fifteen minutes remaining in the fifty-minute session; I sat and tried to make sense out of my experience. An angel? Was that another ploy or a sincere belief? If it was just an attempt to ensure that I'd see him again, it had certainly worked. My interest was piqued. Sincere or not, mentioning it the way he had, after all the verbal jousting, was strange, too. Strange enough to engage me long-term? Perhaps. As far as I was concerned, though, the strangeness ran a great deal deeper than that.

Usually, people manifest a certain kind of internal integrity. That is, they may be composed of various parts and some of these parts might, at first glance, appear to be odd bedfellows or even paradoxical, but at a deeper level the composite mosaic of personality traits *makes sense.* The sense may be idiosyncratic, bizarrely twisted, or impossible to understand. But when I meet people, I can usually intuit that their way of being is in fact a way of being, not a random assortment of attributes. In total, then, the collection of parts — the personality — is organized around *something,* however vague or impractical.

I received no sense of this from George Arundel. For short stretches his reactions had been consistent, but there seemed to be no unifying theme underlying the behaviors that he'd demonstrated so far. It was more of an intuition than something I can describe well in words. I guess another way to say it is that I didn't experience the continuity I've come to associate with personhood.

Were I a fledgling therapist, I would have undoubtedly attributed the phenomenon to a lack of perception on my part.

After twelve years, I interpreted it as evidence that I had been chatting with a truly weird character.

I didn't have time to think about George Arundel for the rest of the week, but as the hour of his second session neared I found myself eagerly anticipating the event. I was puzzled by this. Had I enjoyed the first session? No. Did I have some special interest in angels? No. Perhaps I'd developed a hitherto unknown fascination with delusional disorders? Another no.

I finally realized (on poor Alice Loomis' time) that I was looking forward to finding out what made Arundel tick. I use the vernacular since the attitude harkens back to my original, pre-jargon motivation for entering the field. I'm simply someone who wants to understand people. I guess I keep hoping that if I figure everybody else out I might be able to help myself. The reality is that I probably know too much, not too little, to elude my cyclic depression.

*   *   *   *   *

Arundel wore a black polo shirt and well-worn jeans this time. I nabbed my chair; he didn't seem to care. He opened his arms as he sat across from me, as if he were demonstrating how big a fish he'd caught.

"I'm prepared to answer more questions today," he told me.

"Great. Shall I get right to it, then?"

"By all means." This time he gestured with one arm, moving it horizontally across his body as though he were scattering seed. I couldn't discern any correlation between his words and his movements.

"You mentioned last week that you were an administrator. Who do you work for? What exactly do you do?"

"Once again I'm afraid it would be best not to go into great detail. I am the number two man in an organization. I do what's needed, which varies a great deal."

"I'm getting an image of you smoking a cigar in an Italian restaurant, surrounded by burly men with machine guns."

Arundel held up a hand, although he presented the back of his hand rather than his palm. "Rest assured. It's not a criminal organization."

"I didn't think it actually was. I just wanted you to understand how my mind fills in the blanks you leave."

"That's fine. The way your mind works is a topic in which I have a great deal of interest."

"Why is that?"

"I'd rather not answer that."

We were both silent then. I watched Arundel as he surveyed the room carefully, never looking at me. After a few minutes he spoke.

"I like the paintings," he said.

"You do?"

"Yes."

"Why?" This is a question that therapists are taught to avoid. I break this rule regularly.

"I don't know. Perhaps because the patterns resonate with something within me."

"That's an elegant thought," I commented. "I admire the way you use words."

"Thank you. At one time I was a professor of English literature."

"Really. Where was that?"

Arundel waved an arm vaguely toward the office window. "Back East," he replied.

I was encouraged; we were almost having a conversation. Perhaps if I could keep addressing the qualities embodied in his responses, instead of the stingy content itself, we could make some headway.

"That's an interesting phrase, isn't it?" I tried. "Back East. It seems to refer to more than geography."

Arundel nodded. "It certainly has cultural and sociological implications as well."

"There's a certain duality to it too."

"There's no east without a west. That's true enough. But is this really duality?"

"What do you mean?"

"Is hot the opposite of cold or are they just arbitrary labels for certain ranges on a continuum of temperature? On our planet — and some say in the entire universe — travelling either east or west will eventually bring you to the same place. Where is the duality?"

"I don't know," I confessed. "Obviously you've put a lot more thought into this than I have. Do you have an interest in philosophy?"

"In a way."

Back to silence. Apparently that question had been too personal. I wanted to build on what we'd managed to eke out thus far, so I broke the silence this time.

"Is there anything else you're willing to tell me about yourself?" I asked.

"I am a careful man."

"What do you mean?"

"In this context it means that there must be an exchange of information between us. I need to know who you are."

This was very interesting. In effect, he was saying, 'Let's reverse our roles,' which provided me with a lovely opportunity to model behavior for him. Ordinarily, I wouldn't allow myself to abdicate the therapist role while in session. With Arundel, it felt perfectly appropriate to show him how to safely reveal himself. I couldn't resist one quick retaliatory response, though.

"What would you like to know?" I asked in true Arundel fashion.

"What theoretical school of therapy do you espouse?"

He liked it. Oh well. "None. My work is eclectic."

"Were you born with the last name of Dalziel?"

"Yes."

"Do you have a family?"

"I'm divorced and there were no children. I'm close to my mother and an older sister, though."

So far, so good. I was hoping he'd ask something inappropriate so I could demonstrate how to set limits.

"Are you right-handed?"

"Yes."

"Do you drive a foreign car?"

"Yes."

None of these questions were truly inappropriate, but they certainly didn't seem germane to our work or even related to one another.

"Why is your face scarred?"

"An automobile accident."

One of my cheeks was badly burned and a network of thin white scar tissue encircled the eye on the other side of my face. I was lucky to retain my vision, but unlucky in that I couldn't afford plastic surgery, which my insurance company termed 'elective.' Later, when I had the money, I found that I'd become accustomed to my face. I'd always been a bit of a brute physically; now I had an obvious excuse to be ugly. It made things easier somehow. I hadn't had an urge to repair the damage in a long time.

"Have you ever travelled to Asia?" Arundel asked next.

"No. Just Hawaii."

"What did you do before you became a therapist?"

"A variety of things. Just before, I was a private detective, actually."

"Was it fun?"

"Fun? No, not really. It was usually boring and occasionally depressing. I mostly handled employee theft and divorce cases — accounts that my uncle passed on to me when he retired. And I wasn't particularly good at it."

"It's more exciting in the movies, eh?"

"Absolutely."

"Are you a picky eater?" Arundel asked next.

"No."

"Have house pets played an important role in your personal history?"

I had to think about that one. "I'd say yes," I replied.

"If you had to be an inanimate object, what would you be?"

"I can't imagine why you feel you need to know that, but in the interest of getting acquainted, I'll give it a try." I was obviously stalling. "Hmmm...you have to get into an odd frame of mind to even think about it. I'd say...a Mayan pyramid."

"And what would your favorite color be?"

"Blue."

"Okay. That's it."

"It?"

"We're done. I'm satisfied." Arundel leaned back in his chair and tried to assume a posture and expression of satisfaction. He looked constipated. The man had a lot to learn about congruent behavior.

I still couldn't sense any pattern to the series of questions. Once again I doubted my client's sincerity. Could these really be the facts he needed to know to trust me? Had I misunderstood his motives? Was he toying with me again?

"Will you tell me about your friend now?" I asked. I reasoned that this would serve as a gauge of the exercise's effectiveness.

"What friend?"

"Your friend who's an angel."

It was as if I'd goosed him. He jumped up, clearly alarmed. "Who told you that?" he demanded. "Have you been following me? There are laws against that, you know."

His fists were balled up and his face was red. Some of his plastered hair had even unplastered itself somehow.

"You told me, George. Last week."

"I did not!"

"It was at the end of that session. That's why I agreed to meet again. Remember?"

"Oh. I see." He sat down and replastered his hair. "That's all right, then."

"I'm sorry I upset you."

"I can see it was all a misunderstanding. Just one of those things. Don't mention it. It's fine, really."

He was stringing all this together in an abstracted tone of voice as he studied my face. After a long moment in which he seemed to focus on my mouth, he stood again.

"I have to go," he announced in that deafening voice he'd used the week before.

"Right now?"

"Yes. Right now!"

"Will I see you next week?" I asked.

"I'll call!" he shouted. If anything, he was even louder than last week.

Before I could say good-bye, he was gone.

This week I used the leftover time to buy an ice cream cone from the kiosk around the corner.

Chapter 3

Santa Cruz is situated on the northernmost tip of Monterey Bay, about seventy-five miles south of San Francisco. By virtue of the horseshoe shape of the bay, the Pacific Ocean is actually south of town instead of west, while inland lies to the north. For me, this is typical of the place; everything is rotated at least a quarter-turn sideways. Culturally, politically, artistically, and even sexually, Santa Cruz dances to its own drum ensemble, composed of motley, offbeat musicians. In a town of fifty-thousand people, there are eight health-food restaurants, eleven organic grocery stores, and eighteen coffee houses. There are eateries specializing in Ethiopian, Brazilian, New Orleans, Caribbean, and Korean cuisine, as well as all the traditional ethnic fare.

A boardwalk and amusement park attract tourists, the University of California campus on the northeast edge of town draws local and international students, and the beaches, redwood forests, and marvelous weather are a magnet to a variety of residents. By and large this diverse cast of characters, while electing not to fraternize a great deal, interacted amicably enough. Old-timers resented the university population and everyone experienced the tourists as rather grotesque accoutrements to the natural beauty, but there was a balance maintained in the economic sector that no one was anxious to upset.

One unfortunate side-effect of such an intensely heterogeneous population seems to be a high crime rate, especially violent crime, and lately a serial killer had been stabbing his way into the headlines. The victims were an elderly retired man, a U.C. Santa Cruz coed, and Denise Hellman, a colleague I knew quite well. At breakfast the morning before I was to see Arundel again, the local newspaper reported the details of this latest murder.

Denise was a wonderful person. I first met her at a workshop on narrative therapy, in which the therapist helps the client rewrite the story of his life. It was a fascinating weekend, all the more so for Denise's presence. By chance, we were paired off for a practice session, and despite very different backgrounds, we hit it off immediately.

Poor Stuart. Her husband had been completely devoted to her. He was the type of man who glowed when he was with his partner, becoming more than the sum of his parts somehow. He must be devastated, I thought. I wrote myself a note to give him a call soon.

Denise had been a hypnotherapist with an office on the west side of town about a mile and a half from my own. After seeing her last client the evening before, she'd been stabbed seven times in the chest as she was unlocking her Volvo — the same type of car I own.

The parallels personalized the tragedy even more. I don't have a problem with death, per se. In fact, part of me looks forward to this whole messy business of life finally ending. But Denise was young and had a family. What purpose could such a sudden, horrible death serve? To warn us all to live as though this were our last day? To instruct us to park under streetlights? To carry weapons? To trust no one? To move to Sweden?

This was how I tormented myself — this endless, futile attempt to make sense out of everything. If I could've just thrown a switch and thought half — no, a third — as much, I would've been better off. Accepting reality without processing it — the very idea smacked of irresponsibility to my mind, which was always wrangling to become even more indispensable.

Despite my best efforts to fend it off, I now found myself remembering a very intense experience. In an earlier era of my life, I'd worked as a private investigator for my uncle's agency. One morning I was following a young man whose family believed he'd joined a cult. He'd suddenly cut himself off from everyone and had taken to wearing baggy white clothes. At the time, I'd joked that this body of evidence could also be used to condemn unfriendly baseball players, undersized Good Humor men, or a good percentage of doctors. My uncle's sense of

humor was not well-developed and he patiently explained that
the man's parents and siblings had a right to be concerned. In
addition, he conceded, the man — his name was Levine —
happened to control a hefty family trust fund. This was typical. In those days, if it wasn't cherchez la
femme, it was cherchez les bucks. So one sunny morning I was
following Levine to see whether he was in a cult, just behaving
oddly on his own, or if there was anything else going on that
would enable his relatives to wrest away his money. Despite
my misgivings surrounding this venal motive, I recall feeling
fairly centered as I sidled down a steeply inclined sidewalk
near the boardwalk. Perhaps I'd eaten a satisfying breakfast or
I'd just seen a puppy; I don't remember. Levine — a slightly
chubby twenty-four year old — strolled about half a block
ahead of me, apparently heading for the beach. Along with his
baggy white outfit, he sported a cheap straw hat on his
oversized head and an orange beach towel over his shoulder.
I'd been tagging along with him for two and a half days and so
far all he'd done was eat, sleep, and meditate on the beach.
While his regimen might've been a tad dull, it struck me as
being several cuts above watching someone *else* eat, sleep, and
meditate.

A light blue pick-up truck edged past me as if it were
trolling for a parking space. In the back bed, two young women
in brightly-colored work-out clothes sat stiffly against the side
wall. One was a slim blonde with a long, tight braid. The other
one was darker and built more along the lines of Levine.
Neither one was particularly good-looking nor were their
outfits especially remarkable. If what happened next hadn't
happened, I'm sure I wouldn't have remembered them at all.

The driver, a shaggy-haired man wearing a black tee
shirt, guided the truck to the curb ahead of me, just behind
Levine, and the blond woman lithely leapt out. She held
something in her hand but I couldn't see what it was. Before I
could move, she'd raced to her victim and buried a hatchet in
the back of his head. I vomited — violently and profusely.
When I regained my senses, the woman was back in the truck
and it was speeding around the corner.

Levine lay on the concrete ahead of me, a halo of blood
framing the mess that was his head. I ran to him to help but
he was already dead. I shouted for someone to call 911 and

then I sat down, which made me sick again. By the time the cops arrived, I was sicker yet, dry-heaving every few seconds.

For days, I couldn't sleep at all and it was only after several years of counseling that I began to let go of the pantheon of my maladaptive responses. My career as a private eye was over, of course. In a sense, Levine's death was the demarcation between the old me and the guy who was now a psychologist.

The murder investigation was very frustrating for everyone concerned, except the killer, I suppose. The truck was never found, nor were any vehicles missing that matched its description. Although two other witnesses described the young women and the driver in much the same terms as I had, they disappeared just as thoroughly. No suspects ever emerged and no one was ever arrested. There wasn't any evidence of a cult involvement either and all of Levine's relatives were eventually cleared. For all intents and purposes, I had witnessed a truly arbitrary killing — one with no known motive, no suspects, and no resolution — even sixteen years later.

To this day, I wonder if I didn't unknowingly finger the victim by following him. Maybe I should've been more alert too. Someone else might've picked-up an earlier cue and prevented the murder. I don't know. I do know that what has haunted me the most was the suddenness of the event. At any moment, from any direction, anything can happen. This was what I learned and I hated learning it.

*   *   *   *   *

The next session began with silence. George Arundel had wandered in as though he still wasn't sure if my office was where he was supposed to be. There was no eye contact and all his movements were tentative.

Silence can be a powerful tool in therapy. This particular silence had an unusual quality to it; it was definitely not a waste of time. I was curious to see what emerged out of it, speculating at various points that Arundel would erupt in anger, intellectualize about the silence itself, or never speak the entire session. This happened sometimes and was usually the prelude to deep work.

After eight minutes, he spoke. "People pay you for this?" His voice was completely different this time — high-pitched, casual, and soft.

I nodded, puzzling over the new voice.

"That doesn't bother you?" he asked.

"No. It's a hard job, believe me. I earn my fee."

"Oh, I guess I believe you, all right. Crazy people give me the heebie-jeebies," Arundel told me, rolling his eyes and flashing a broad, earthy grin.

I was beginning to understand. As I smiled back at him, he continued without prompting.

"Heck, I give *myself* the heebie-jeebies sometimes."

"How's that?"

"I don't know. I guess sometimes the way I am or the things I do seem kinda drastic." He wrinkled his brow and frowned.

"Drastic?"

"Yeah, the kinda thing you can't even say out loud 'cuz you know ahead of time that anyone hearing you would freak out."

"Can you give me an example?"

"Do you promise not to freak out?"

"I promise."

"Well, you already know one — the angel."

"Oh yes. Can you tell me more about that?" I asked.

"Of course I can. You mean will I." The professor was back. The voice, the demeanor, even the gleam in his eye was now familiar to me. It was like a separate, distinct personality.

"May I speak with the other guy?" I asked.

"No," the professor replied. "I'm the one you'll deal with. That was a mistake."

I was facing my first client with a clearly defined multiple personality disorder. I'd worked with several highly dissociated women who may or may not have split into actual personalities, as opposed to ego-states. And since, on the average, MPDs are in therapy for seven years before they're correctly diagnosed, I may have seen a few without knowing it. But here was one — a classic example — basically admitting his situation in the third session. This was an extremely rare event in the therapy world.

"How many of you are there?" I asked.

"Quite a few. Let's leave it at that."

I constructed my next question as carefully as I could. The exact wording seemed important. "Why are you the one who can best profit from this experience?"

"Your inquiry is unanswerable due to several assumptions that are subsumed within it."

"Subsumed?" I'd never heard anyone use that word in conversation.

He nodded primly.

"All right," I conceded. "Let me try again. Why are you here with me instead of one of the others?"

"That's a much better question. You see how your initial query wasn't sufficiently open-ended? This one gives me an opportunity to really explain."

"Go ahead."

"I choose not to at this time."

I checked to see if Arundel was wearing his creepy 'gotcha' smile. He actually appeared chagrined that he needed to withhold information from me. This must be that warm slushy bond that was supposed to happen in therapy — Arundel's version, anyway.

"Will I at least get to meet the others?" While he was feeling merciful I thought I'd press him a bit.

"We'll see." The grin was back.

"Is your friend who's an angel one of the others?"

"No. She is an independent entity."

"Do you recall any of the early childhood trauma that you've suffered?" All MPD cases are created by the need to escape experiencing intense, repeated abuse before a certain age. It used to be four, now they've made it six. Don't ask me how they can change diagnostic criteria so facilely and expect us all to buy it.

"I wasn't there, so I don't remember it, but I am familiar with the general details."

"May I speak to someone who was there?"

"No. It was the usual sort of thing. Their parents were members of a Satanic cult. There was a pattern of ritualistic sexual and physical abuse."

This was told to me with completely flat affect. Arundel could've been reading an actuarial table aloud.

"It seems as though you have no feelings about it," I pointed out.

"Why should I?"

"Most people would be horrified or disgusted. I am."

Arundel shrugged. "Such is life. I am interested in the current ramifications of the trauma in terms of how we're organized, but other than that...it was a long time ago."

I paused before continuing, reminding myself that for all intents and purposes I was only talking to a cautious English professor.

"Have you ever been diagnosed as MPD?" I asked.

"No. I've known, of course. I'm not like some of the others with their heads in the sand. But you're the first therapist I've seen more than once."

"I'm not surprised," I admitted.

"Why is that?"

"You're rather difficult to work with." Surely he knew that. Who could be such a pain by accident?

"Yes, I see. Actually I was the one who ended my relationships with other therapists," he told me.

"Why was that?"

Arundel shook his head slowly and began to answer.

"Don't tell me," I interrupted. "It would work out better if you don't reveal that now, right?"

"Yes."

I tried a new tack. "How old are you, Mr. Arundel?"

"Forty-eight."

"Your way of being has worked for you all these years?"

"By and large. As you can imagine, our sex life hasn't been satisfactory, and I, for one, never watch certain types of movies. But basically — yes."

"Any sleep disruption?"

"Nightmares that wake me up, yes. And headaches that worsen at night. But it's a small price to pay."

"Does everyone in there agree with you?"

"Of course not. There is probably nothing in the universe that we all agree on. But I assure you that the side-effects really are a small price to pay."

"What do you mean?"

"The array of personalities works." He sat back and assumed his constipated pose. I could no longer remember what it was supposed to represent.

"Then why are you here?" This was a wonderful arrow to shoot at self-satisfied clients in need of deflation. Why indeed, if they're truly perfectly happy with themselves?

"For another reason entirely which I'm not going to discuss today," he informed me.

I felt like giving him a Bronx cheer or a cuff on the ear. Unfortunately, my scope of practice didn't encompass such satisfying spontaneous displays.

"Will you tell me how your way of being works for you?" I asked.

"Certainly. One of us is a virtual genius with money. Thus, we are rich. I don't care for social gatherings — parties and the like — so others attend them and I am spared the experience. And so on."

I was reminded of a story my own therapist had told me once; I decided to share it.

"Have you heard about the man who learned to walk on water? It took him twenty years and all sorts of self-discipline and practice, but he finally did it. Then a wise old man came along and asked him why he didn't just pay his dollar to the ferryman."

"I don't like stories," Arundel replied.

"So you understand that one?"

"Of course, although you told it wrong. It's an old Buddhist parable."

"Is that right?"

"Yes. Your version eliminates the whole guru-disciple relationship and the questions of spiritual ambition, pride, and self-satisfaction. It's been gutted, or let's just say Westernized, eh?"

"Fine, but back up a minute. You said you dislike parties. Couldn't you just not go? Isn't the simplest solution usually the best?"

"Sometimes it's necessary to attend. I'm not interested in your hierarchy of values. That's another topic entirely. My point is that everyone has strengths and weaknesses, likes and dislikes. Our system matches these qualities with the appropriate circumstances."

It was time to try another approach (again).

"If I tortured you, who would experience it?" I asked.

"There is an early personality named Gooey who can experience such things without suffering."

"How is that?"

"Gooey doesn't have feelings."

"Do you?"

"Oh yes. They're under control, of course, but there's a world of difference between Gooey and myself."

"Can I talk to him?"

"No. He's pre-verbal."

I was fascinated, but concerned that my fascination would interfere with the business at hand — Arundel's therapy. In other words, was I interrogating my client in response to my own curiosity or did it serve a true therapeutic purpose? To be on the safe side, I decided to refocus on Arundel in the here and now.

"What are you feeling right now?" I asked him.

"Slight discomfort."

Bingo. I'd tapped into something non-mental for a change.

"Tell me about it."

"My foot has fallen asleep. I have a tendency to stay in one position too long."

"Could that be metaphorical for the rest of your life as well?"

"I guess it is. That was astute."

Suddenly Arundel's demeanor dramatically shifted. His features softened and re-formed into someone younger.

"Who are you?" I asked.

"Jeff." The voice was unsure of itself. "Who are you? You're awful big."

I'm six-foot five and I weigh about two-hundred and thirty pounds. "I'm ugly too, aren't I? My name is Tom Dalziel and you're in my office. How old are you?"

"Fourteen."

"Do you know why you're here?"

"No. Did I do something wrong?"

"Not at all. It's a little hard to...."

"That's enough. I'm back," the professor interrupted. "Sorry about that. We don't have all the bugs worked out in this context yet. When something unexpected happens, well, you see the result."

"What was unexpected?"

"Actually, that you would generate a useful insight." He had the decency to appear sheepish, shifting his weight and fussily crossing his legs.

"Thanks a lot," I responded.

"I didn't select you because of your therapeutic skills," Arundel informed me.

"Why then?"

He smiled his creepiest smile yet and held my eyes for a few seconds. "Not yet," he cautioned. "Be patient."

I squelched my irritation. With most clients I am quite content to pace the work around their readiness. After all, three sessions into a course of therapy is still a very preliminary stage. Why should a client trust me? I'm still a virtual stranger and it's healthy to need to feel safe before opening up. In some cases, I slow people down who don't know how to take care of themselves around safety and trust.

But Arundel's behavior smacked of gamesmanship and I've found that the more I do this work, the more intolerant I grow of game playing. Intellectually, I knew that as a survivor of very serious abuse, my client was doing remarkably well simply to be walking and talking. In a sense, his history gave him dispensation to use any means necessary to protect himself. But nonetheless I experienced my compassion stretching particularly thin at that moment in our session.

"So I gather you don't normally slip-up and change personalities like that?" I tried.

"Absolutely not. As I said, certain circumstances demand certain personalities. I'm in charge of all that, actually."

"Really? That sounds like an important job."

"Oh it is. Without me, the whole thing would fall apart."

"Do the others recognize that?"

"Some do. Some don't even know about me, let alone appreciate what I do."

"So there's a real variety of folks in there?"

"Oh yes. Men, women, children — even a dog."

"A dog?"

Arundel nodded. "I'd let you meet her but she isn't house-trained and she's likely to get excited and urinate on your rug."

I smiled, sure that he was pulling my leg. "That's very hard to believe," I told him.

"I've researched it. It's actually quite common in full-blown MPD."

"You're serious?"

"Yes."

"Well in that case, can you direct me to some up-to-date literature? I see that I need to do some catching-up on this."

"Of course." Arundel produced a list from a back pocket. "I anticipated your request. And do try to avoid the popular material — *The Three Faces of Eve* and all that — it's terribly distorted."

"Sure. You're the expert."

I checked the clock, saw that we needed to stop, and informed Arundel. "Same time next week?" I asked.

"Yes. See you then. Perhaps I'll bring the angel."

"Really?"

"We'll see."

Chapter 4

I had a chance to read quite a bit about MPD in the following week, which was a mixed blessing. In my business, cancellations, vacations, and no-shows cut into one's schedule much too regularly. For 'schedule,' substitute the word 'remuneration' and the problem becomes clearer. Worse yet, actual success can be measured by a client's move from dependence to independence. In this case, translate these terms to 'showing up and paying eighty dollars a week' versus 'maybe sending a Christmas card someday with no check enclosed.' The better I do my job, the sooner my clients disappear.

That week, I had five cancellations, two no-shows, and one termination. 'Termination' — that's the actual preferred professional term for ending therapy. Isn't that amazing? "My client was uncooperative so I terminated him." The word is so final, so radical. And it's employed for completing the full course of therapy or simply dropping out. A lot of therapists demand a 'termination session' too, even if the client is quitting because they don't want to continue seeing that particular person. I suppose every profession has its nonsensical elements, but obviously this type of thing peeves me.

So during my unsolicited light week, I discovered that MPDs really did develop animal personalities, among other things. The material was a testament to the flexibility and imagination of the human psyche. Isn't it astonishing that a three-year-old child can produce 'alters' as a coping strategy — entirely independent personalities that even react differently to drugs?

Hard to believe in another way were some of the histories of abuse detailed in the case studies. Hitler gassed the Jews, but they weren't his own children. I honestly find the data too horrific to describe here. That adult survivors function at all after the incredible pain they've endured — thank God for MPD. It's saved a lot of them.

*   *   *   *   *

Arundel escorted an unlikely-looking angel to our next session. She was a raggedy young woman, barefoot, with long black hair that was tangled and matted. She wore faded blue denim overalls over a dingy white tee shirt. Her loose clothes accentuated her slight build and short stature, suggesting a child playing dress-up. Dark-complected, her delicate features didn't hint at any particular ethnicity, but the effect was quite attractive, I thought. She could have been twenty-two or twenty-three.

"This is Zig-Zag," Arundel told me. "Zee," he said to the girl, "this is Tom Dalziel."

Zig-Zag extended her slender hand and I shook it. Her grip was surprisingly strong and she flashed dazzling white teeth at me.

"Let me just rearrange the chairs," I told them, placing two seats about four feet in front of my own. When everyone was comfortable, I spoke first.

"Mr. Arundel tells me that you're an angel," I began. A direct approach seemed worth trying, despite my track record with the young woman's companion.

"I'm not," she replied quickly in an unaccented, educated voice. "What I am is an environmental crusader."

"Crusader?"

"Activist. I'm saving your goddamn planet." Her fierce expression suggested that I didn't deserve saving, and not only that but I probably threw away bottles and cans as well. I was tempted to thank her — after all, who doesn't want their planet saved? — but I settled on a continuation of my direct questioning. Arundel, by the way, seemed to be enjoying the interaction so far. He was smiling and alternately scanning our faces.

"Why do you think Mr. Arundel believes you're an angel?" I asked.

"Ask him. He's sitting right here, isn't he?"

Arundel spoke. "There are numerous clues. I've delineated them to Zig-Zag but she is very resistant to her destiny."

The young woman snorted and rearranged herself, moving each limb in turn so that the maneuver took several seconds.

Arundel continued. "First of all, my friend here is the illegitimate daughter of Krishnanda."

"The Indian guru?"

"Exactly. He was no ordinary man and she is his only offspring. Next we have the fact that her mother's last name is Cassiel, which is an angel name. Then there's the fact that without any training whatsoever, Zee here sees people's auras."

"Really?"

Zig-Zag and Arundel nodded in unison.

"What does mine look like?" I asked.

"Mostly purple with a gold glow around your throat," she reported.

I began to feel as if I were in a surrealistic film. One week it was multiple personality disorder, the next we've got guru offspring seeing auras. I yearned for a nice obsessive-compulsive who just washed his hands too much.

"Have you always had this ability?" I asked.

"Sure," Zig-Zag replied. "It's no big thing."

"Next," Arundel continued, "there are the prophetic dreams, the sensitivity to ethereal energy, and the moles."

"The moles?" Now I felt like a straightman in a comedy team — feeding lines to an unpredictable partner.

"The moles on her back," Arundel explained. "They trace a pattern — wings."

"You mean if you played connect-the-dots with them that would be the picture you'd end up with?" I asked.

"Exactly. And there's more...but this is all I'm at liberty to say at this time."

I looked at Zig-Zag and she looked back at me — no help there. I thought things over for a moment and then spoke to Arundel.

"I don't understand why you're telling me all this. I'm not qualified to adjudicate any spiritual matters, and if you don't have a psychological problem with your beliefs, then I don't either."

Arundel paused, pursing his lips and wrinkling his brow. It was a stage actor's version of deep thought. "It's time to lay some of my cards on the table," he finally told me. "Can you name any angels, Thomas — from the Bible or folklore?"

"Well, let's see. There's Gabriel and Raphael. Uh...that's all I can remember." I had no clue as to what Arundel was up to. Was he trying to seize control of the session by playing teacher again?

"How about Michael, Gaddiel, or Adriel?" he prompted.

"Michael I know, of course. I'm not sure about the others."

"Put your detective skills to work," Arundel instructed. "What do all those names have in common?"

"Well, the endings are similar phonetically."

The man actually clasped his hands in delight. "And...?" He leaned forward and peered brightly at my face.

"Wait a minute. There's no Dalziel in the Bible," I protested.

Arundel sat back with a self-satisfied smirk on his pale face. "Your last name is an angel name, Thomas, and I wouldn't be surprised if you had a significant birthmark or pattern of moles as well. That's how it works — one thing verifies the other."

I felt like telling him he was crazy, which needless to say was not an appropriate response. It did clue me in, though, to just how far afield we'd strayed from a traditional client-therapist relationship. I needed to wrestle the conversation back into the therapeutic realm.

"Tell me more about your beliefs," I suggested.

Arundel stared at me. Zig-Zag rolled her eyes as if to say "good luck with that approach, buddy."

"How long have you believed in angels?" I tried.

Even Arundel rolled his eyes at that one.

"Look, exactly what do you want from me?" I finally asked.

"Just be a person," he replied. "Answer me like a person. This doesn't have anything to do with your being a therapist."

'Oh yeah,' I thought. 'I'd really be having this conversation for free.'

"All right," I agreed out loud. "The whole thing is ridiculous. I don't share your point of view and obviously I'm not going to suddenly espouse an alien belief system based on somebody's moles or last name. There are real-world explanations for everything you've mentioned, for one thing. The unconscious is a powerful force. It can create stigmata, moles, illusions of auras — none of that surprises me. Anyway, the only birthmark I have is a totally amorphous blob on my ankle."

"May I see it?" Arundel asked.

I thought about that one. I wasn't under any compulsion to bare my flesh to clients, but humoring him for a few seconds might end up convincing him of his folly. On the other hand, most delusional systems as complex and entrenched as Arundel's have a catch-22 in place to prevent such a contradiction. I decided that I'd need to encounter his particular catch-22 at some point anyway, so I rolled down my brown sock and displayed my dark red birthmark. It really was just a blob; I defied Arundel to make a case for it representing anything at all.

The girl gasped; Arundel smiled.

"What? It's just a splotch." I stared at my ankle to see if the birthmark had changed its configuration when I wasn't looking. Nope.

"My father had one exactly like it," Zig-Zag told me. "It's the shape of his aura. And I know because I've seen it." She turned to Arundel, who was still grinning. "This is too weird, George."

"*Stai calma*," he replied in Italian, and then turned to me. "Do you see now why I've come to you?"

"No."

"It's obvious. You're in that body for a reason, Thomas, and it isn't so you can listen to neurotics whine and complain, any more than Zig-Zag's true calling is to blow-up power stations. The millenium approaches and my job is to find and awaken the key figures involved in this upcoming transition. People like you — people who are more than people. We all have a great deal of work to do if things are going to unfold in the manner they are designed to. Do you understand?"

"I hear the words, Mr. Arundel. But no, I can't say I truly understand. Do you honestly expect me to believe all this?"

"Right now? Of course not. But you will. If I'm right, then events in your life will begin cooperating with this process of awakening. You'll discover who you are because the universe will orchestrate what needs to happen around you. It's not my job to convince you. I'm a catalyst, not a teacher."

"Look at me, Arundel. Have you ever seen a less likely candidate for angelhood?"

"*I* sure haven't," Zig-Zag chimed in. "You're a motherfucking monster."

"Thanks, sweetheart," I growled, forgetting myself momentarily. Sarcasm was one of the first ingrained behaviors I'd had to jettison upon becoming a therapist. "Anyway," I began, trying to save a deteriorating situation, "Angels don't say 'motherfucking' either, now do they?"

"How do you know?" Arundel asked. "You're both in human bodies, with human minds and human tongues. I'll grant you that. But so what? Did Jesus ever swear? Was Buddha overweight? Surely you can see how ridiculous such concerns are?"

It was time to insert some reality into the proceedings. "I'm not going to argue with you," I told Arundel. "You're entitled to your religious beliefs. But I'm concerned that your view of here and now reality is so obviously radically different from the prevailing mainstream's, and yet you seek to bleed it onto Zig-Zag and myself. Idiosyncratic thinking is one thing — it doesn't necessarily harm anyone. But when you begin promoting a self-aggrandizing viewpoint out in the world — this concerns me. Don't you find that all this interferes with your ability to develop satisfying relationships?"

"Let's not digress into psycho-babble," Arundel responded. "I'll see you next week." He stood. "I cede my remaining time to Zig-Zag. Why don't you two get to know each other better?" As soon as he'd finished speaking, he turned on his heel and strode off.

The door closed behind him and I focused on Zig-Zag. I was still feeling off-center but perhaps she could help me understand Arundel better.

"Well," she said, "that's George."

"This is typical behavior?"

"Yup. Well, typical if he thinks you're an angel."

She had softened during the session and her hostility was under cover.

"What's your relationship to him?"

"He's my godfather. He was close to my father. George was the one who took me to the zoo or whatever while my father was in samadhi."

"Samadhi?"

"Like an extended trance. He spent a lot of time doing shit like that."

"Was your mother Indian as well?"

"No. She was from Berkeley. How in the world do you psychoanalyze someone like George?"

"Beats me. Got any ideas?" This departure from professionalism was a calculated risk. It might serve as an invitation for Zig-Zag to meddle in an inappropriate manner, but by matching her vocabulary and tone of voice I was creating an alliance of sorts. It was possible she actually had some interesting ideas about treatment too. It sounded as if she'd known George Arundel for a long time.

"Well," she began thoughtfully, "he's not really crazy. Mostly he's just like all the Krishnanda people."

What a horrifying notion, I thought — dozens, maybe hundreds or thousands of Arundels loose in the world.

"Are you aware of his...other problems?" I asked, treading lightly on the thin ice of confidentiality law.

"You mean the extra personalities thing?"

I nodded, relieved that I'd guessed correctly.

"Well, sure. But I think it works out pretty good for him."

"How's that?"

"He's rich, he's successful, he's as happy as anyone I know — what more do you want?"

"That's plenty. I was just wondering. So what do you make out of this birthmark deal?"

"I'm gonna have to think it over," she told me. "And I've gotta get to work."

We both arose and I handed her my card. I towered over her by a foot and a half.

"Call me if you need to," I told her, unaware of what that simple largesse would lead to.

Zig-Zag tucked the card into the bib pocket of her worn overalls and offered her hand again. "Nice meeting you."

"Likewise," I answered, shaking hands while maintaining eye contact. Her dark brown eyes were really quite beautiful — more liquid than most and very alert.

After she'd departed, I sat and stared at the two empty chairs while my next client fumed in the waiting room.

Chapter 5

George Arundel was not only MPD, but suffered from a delusional disorder — probably schizophrenia. I'm not usually preoccupied by the process of labeling my clients — clinical diagnoses can be very heavy albatrosses to lug around. Once officially identified, a person suffering from a psychosis, for example, becomes 'a psychotic.' Sometimes clients buy into this concept that they *are* their diagnostic category. Worse yet, some feel a need to justify or live up to their labels — expanding their repertoire of aberrant behaviors as needed.

But in Arundel's case the relationship between the two disorders was something I needed to examine carefully. I knew from my reading that the mission-from-God business was not likely to be universal throughout Arundel's personalities. Clearly, the professor character — the one I thought of as my client, actually — was driven by the paradigm, but Jeff, the fourteen-year-old boy I'd met, hadn't even known who I was. Was he privy to the overall plan, but not the details? Or was Arundel more thoroughly compartmentalized? This seemed likelier to me, but there was no way to know.

If I could contact a responsible adult personality that I could ally with in Arundel, perhaps he could help himself to some extent. The idea of organizing an internal revolution and staging a coup d'etat to overthrow the irksome professor... well, needless to say this was a very attractive notion to me. Insofar as the others were aware of his role and his manner, surely they experienced him as a despot.

Traditionally, a therapist helped an MPD client by facilitating an integration of the parts, not by fomenting further conflict. But first things first, I reasoned, and dissipating the delusions seemed to be a precursor to any other work.

Even after all my research, I was still confused about the influence of the unconscious in multiple personalities. Ordinarily, Arundel's denial that my role as a therapist was relevant to his behavior would be a telltale clue. While a client might have a conscious reason to see me that doesn't include my idea of doing therapy, I trust that his unconscious has guided him to me nonetheless, and will participate at some level in the requisite healing. In other words, it might be quite pertinent that the man Arundel seized on as an angel (me) happens to be trained in working with the problems Arundel happens to exhibit (big nutty ones).

I don't believe in coincidence any more. I tried valiantly to hang onto the concept during my tenure at graduate school, and I still maintained a few shreds of belief while an intern. But for years my simple, mechanistic view of the universe, especially people, has become outmoded by my experience. Sometimes I wonder exactly what has replaced it, since the current model is so much more amorphous. I know it has something to do with the way everything is put together. In fact, I'm realizing that it's still mechanistic — just such an incredibly intricate relationship of parts that I know I'll never understand it *as a machine.* The butterfly in China affecting the weather in Iowa — this is the example that springs to mind. I believe that the universe is an infinitely complex clock; we see only the hands of the clock and their relationship to one another, and we think "what a coincidence!"

To reach this perspective I needed to let go of a great deal — my illusion of my faith in science, and even my attachment to outcome. Of course I haven't actually mastered any of this, but I have dragged substantial portions of my interior into congruence with my perceptions of the external world. I once entertained a fantasy of founding a new theoretical orientation — 'Congruence Therapy.' But God knows there's enough of that sort of thing in the world. Besides, such an enterprise would've pulled me back into further incongruence, fostering, as it would, a puffed-up self-image and a great personal stake in outcome.

Thus it was no accident that George Arundel was my client, and that I felt I had a duty to peek at the clockworks on his behalf whenever I could. The more I understood the nature of our relationship, the more I could help.

As usual, at about this point in my reasoning, the penguin metaphor wafted into my mind. I hate penguins. For all my talk of changing and creating theories, that elusive key factor that enabled one to establish useful values — to know which rock is which — well, I was no closer to discovering it. A therapist I saw briefly while in my early thirties postulated that it was the very construct that there was such a thing that was my problem. I could accept that idea intellectually, but how did it help? I still had to bumble through my life since I didn't know what I *felt* I needed to know. The feeling was unaffected by words, or thinking, or *anything* so far.

*　　　　*　　　　*　　　　*　　　　*

The next day I saw Mrs. Volkov, a large, middle-aged woman who was both very depressed and, periodically, extremely anxious. For months, she had been discussing birds, which for a still unknown reason, scared her silly, and I use the term literally. She was not my favorite client, although I was her favorite therapist. Lord knows why.

As usual, she wore a tattered pink housedress and her hair was hidden under a black silk scarf. Not as usual, she began relating a dream she'd had the night before. This was new; according to her, she 'didn't dream.'

"Doctor," she began in her high, squeaky voice, "it was a beautiful dream, but I don't know exactly what it means, so you listen close and tell me."

I nodded agreement, although I wasn't in the habit of explaining dreams.

"I was in a foreign country. I don't know which one but it was very dirty. And hot. I remember thinking that I wish I was in Florida visiting my sister where it's hot too, but it's very clean. She has the nicest place, doctor. Palm trees and everything. And so clean. So I was sitting on the sidewalk in this dirty foreign country, which I would never do, of course. I mean you don't sit on the sidewalk here, even. There could be dog dirt or germs or God knows what. So I don't know what I was thinking, but there I was right on the sidewalk. And it was so hot, Doctor. I thought I'd die."

"Then what happened?" My initial interest was flagging in the face of Mrs. Volkov's narrative style.

"The strangest thing. You know I'm not a religious person, doctor. I mean I try to be a good person and everything, but I don't go to church, and I even change channels when one of those preachers comes on. They are so tacky, those preachers. You know what I mean?"

I nodded.

"So here I am in this dream just sitting there minding my own business when I get this urge to look up. And there she was."

She waited for encouragement again. "Who was that?" I obliged.

"The angel."

"What?"

"There was an angel floating in the air above me. She was so beautiful. I could hardly breathe," Mrs. Volkov reported.

My first thought was that Arundel had bribed her to tell this story, but I knew Mrs. Volkov. She wasn't capable of that sort of pretense. So it must be one of those non-coincidences, I thought. Maybe they both had angels on their minds because of some recent TV show or something.

"Tell me about the angel," I prompted.

"She was all in white, kind of like she had on a wedding dress, and she had these big gold wings. Her hair was black, which surprised me because I always see them with blonde hair on TV and in the movies. And she was smiling this beautiful smile and I felt her love inside me like I'd just had a hot chocolate on a cold day."

Her face was a sweet picture of contentment. It was like seeing a dog fly. I had no idea that she was capable of these feelings. I knew her as a stuck, depressed sack of misery. Or at least I thought I did.

"What are you feeling now?" I asked.

"The love. I'm feeling the love and I never want it to end." She closed her eyes and radiated warmth. I could actually feel it in my gut as if I'd had hot chocolate too.

"Stay with it," I coached. "Stay with the love."

By God, she did. The rest of the session was twenty minutes of watching Mrs. Volkov feel love. It was a wondrous sight — one of the most miraculous events in my experience as a therapist. She was a client I'd been inches away from giving up on more than once. Anti-depressants hadn't helped, anti-anxiety medication gave her hives, and talk therapy usually made *me* feel depressed. I didn't expect one sublime session to change her life, but what the hell did I know? Clearly, I had drastically underestimated my client. Maybe by next week she'd be hosting her own talk show.

*   *   *   *   *

One of my most entertaining clients called himself Bug. After years of life-disrupting involvement in popular conspiracy theories, he had recently shifted his attention to his own idiosyncratic obsessions. I had no idea if this change constituted progress, regression, or just lateral movement. But since Bug needed to talk about his theories and no one else would listen, I was usually more of an audience than a therapist in our sessions.

Before his head injury in a bicycling accident, Bug had been Peter Alexander, an insurance salesman who couldn't have cared less if the Mafia had detested JFK. Sometimes, organic brain damage transformed an individual beyond repair. It could be very frustrating to work with these clients, but as I said, I enjoyed Bug.

I saw him several days after Mrs. Volkov's breakthrough.

"How's it going?" I asked. Our sessions were more conversational than most, since Bug needed a friend.

He was an ordinary-looking fellow in his late thirties, with aviator-style glasses and a sparse mustache. He wore jeans, a tee-shirt advertising an Idaho ski resort, and sandals. In a crowd, Bug would be the last person you'd select as a head injury survivor. He was unrelentingly normal in his behavior until he spoke.

"I'm doing good," he told me. "I think I've discovered the link between all the Perfects."

The 'Perfects' were people like Elvis, Hank Williams, and Marilyn Monroe — flesh and blood archetypes who'd died before their time.

"That's great, Bug. Tell me about it."

"Well you know about some of the ideas I've been kicking around. Were they aliens? Examples of hyper-evolution? A secret government experiment gone awry?"

I nodded.

"I've been awaiting a sign. I just didn't know it before, but now I do. It's really exciting, Tom. I think I may clear up a lot of things for a lot of people."

"Really?"

"Yup. Like is there a God? What happens when you die? And what's the meaning of life? Stuff like that."

"Well, don't keep me in suspense, Bug. What do you think about those questions?"

"I gotta tell you about the sign first. It was a couple of nights ago. I couldn't get to sleep because I was thinking about the Masons again."

"I thought we were through with the Masons."

"Hey, so did I. So I was up real late and then I finally fell asleep and I had this dream."

Two dreams in one week? I was exceeding my quota. When I'd gotten into this field, I'd been expecting dreams galore, but I rarely heard them. I don't know why.

"I was in Egypt," Bug told me. "I knew because there were pyramids all over the place — big ones, little ones, even one covered in blue down comforters."

"Blue down comforters?'

"That's right. And I was sitting on this park bench except there wasn't any park, just a lot of dirt all around. And it was really hot."

I was struck by the similarity of Bug's dream and Mrs. Volkov's; both had transpired in hot, dirty foreign countries. Jung referred to this sort of thing as a synchronicity, attributing it to the collective unconscious.

Bug continued, his eyes closed now. "Suddenly, there she was," he reported.

"An angel?" I interrupted. Shivers ran up and down my spine.

"No. Not an angel. A little dog. She looked like a miniature collie."

I breathed again, embarrassed at myself.

"She could talk and she said 'follow me' so I did and we went to a rug shop where this girl handed me a note and the note said 'The Perfects were sent to advance mankind's spiritual progress.' What do you think about that, Tom?"

I didn't answer and I guess my face reflected my confusion.

"Are you okay, Tom? What's the matter? Are you sad it was a dog instead of an angel? I'm not. She was a beautiful little dog."

"I'm okay," I managed to say. "Can I ask you a few things about your dream?"

"Sure. Go ahead."

"What did the girl look like?"

"She wasn't anyone I know, but she was pretty," he answered.

"Do you remember her hair color or what she was wearing — any details at all?"

"Gosh, I don't know why you need to know that, but let me see...."

I was reminded of myself during Arundel's interrogation.

"Sure — here you go," Bug replied. "She had dark, wavy hair and she wore old overalls. And I remember the name of her store. It was 'Ziggurat Rug Shoppe.'"

This was beyond synchronicity. What the hell was Zig-Zag doing in Bug's dream? Did Arundel have some sort of psychic power that enabled him to control dreams? Was he messing with my clients? Hypnotizing them maybe? Was *I* going crazy?"

I was upset — very upset. As Bug told me all about what the dream meant, I tuned him out and continued to desperately generate explanations. Perhaps Arundel had hired Mrs. Volkov and Bug months before in order to set up an elaborate con game. They could be professional actors. On the other hand, I didn't have any money to be bilked out of. Maybe it really was a coincidence. After all, our culture is saturated with New Age advertising and Christian-oriented symbolism. It wouldn't be that strange for three people to be thinking about similar things in a given week.

Or maybe Arundel was clairvoyant. If he knew what I was going to hear in session, he could backtrack and bring it up first. Zig-Zag could be in on it, since she and Arundel were buddies. I only had their word for everything except the two dreams.

There were holes in these theories, but I liked all of them much better than Arundel's grandiose vision. It dripped pathology. How convenient that in his version he was a messiah-like figure entrusted with transforming the world. This is an unbelievably common delusion, a classic abdication of personhood. When the going gets tough, the schizophrenics bail out.

"And so," Bug concluded, "there are probably Perfects among us now, helping to raise our consciousness."

"What do you think they're like?" I asked.

"They're perfect, just like the ones we know about. Everything about them fits as one piece — the way they look, the way they sound. Everyone is drawn to them. I just hope I meet one someday. I know I could help."

Our hour was up. I was tempted not to charge Bug, since I'd been so self-involved for most of the session. But then I'd be divulging my behavior, which wasn't likely to help him and could easily lower his shaky self-esteem. Clearly, some truths are better left unspoken.

Chapter 6

The evening before I was due to see Arundel again began innocently enough. I perused the newspaper while eating a bowl of raspberry cheesecake ice cream at my kitchen table.

The serial murderer had struck again, I saw. Martin DeVilliers had been an assistant produce manager in Capitola, a town five miles east of Santa Cruz. Once again, seven stab wounds established the modus operandi of the killer. It was the only factor so far that linked the victims, furnishing the police investigation with very little evidence. An accompanying article detailed the arrival of the national media in the county now that the number of victims had surpassed the current threshold. Apparently this was four, although a few years ago it had been three, and speculation was rife that victim inflation would push it to five soon.

Other news was more typical. The mayor wanted to declare Santa Cruz 'pesticide-free,' which opponents claimed to be irrelevant since there was virtually no farmland within the city limits. "The issue isn't about relevance," the mayor retorted. "It's about feeling good about ourselves." Three lesbians were petitioning the zoning committee for a variance to build a women's-only carwash. This concept was proving to be a political hot potato, spawning a slew of absurd letters to the editor.

On the last page of the newspaper, there was an advertisement for a local bookstore's upcoming book signing. Audrey Wilson would be in town shortly to pitch *They Walk Among Us: Angels in the Twentieth Century.*

My reaction was purely intellectual this time. If the ad had been running for a while, it could explain a great deal, serving as the unconscious trigger for all the dreaming. Perhaps Arundel had read the book and absorbed Wilson's ideas into his delusional system. Just seeing the concept in print normalized my experiences somewhat too. If an author could manage to get a book like that published, then the notion itself wasn't as crazy as I'd thought. Well, maybe just as crazy, but more culturally crazy than personally crazy. In other words, there seemed to be lots of people with angelmania, which rendered the phenomenon safer and easier to accept. I even considered attending the book signing, just to see what it felt like to consort with that subculture. Was there a perceivable difference between Audrey Wilson and Arundel? Was the difference quantitative or qualitative? Perhaps he was just a few steps beyond the norm. After all, only a fine line separated religious fervor from delusion.

I realized I was thinking too much again, trapping myself up in my head. It was one of the dangers of living alone, I'd discovered. So I grabbed a sweater and embarked on a walk.

In the evening, Santa Cruz's downtown neighborhoods softened and blended. There was no sunlight to etch in the harsh details of the weathered homes, and the darkness erased the property lines that separated the area into discrete chunks. I strode towards the wharf, conscious of my breathing and heartbeat. Since my knees had retired from active duty, walking was one of the only forms of exercise available to me. Simplemindedly, I felt virtuous whenever I marched around town. I guess after all those years of playing basketball, the idea of deteriorating into a sludge pile was still framed as moral turpitude.

After four or five blocks, one of my clients encountered a difficult social situation — me. Clients never seemed to know how to relate to me outside the office. Was I best dealt with as though I were a friend? A stranger? A man from Mars? Invisible? I'd experienced all these and more through the years.

Bob Granger opted for an analogue of acquaintanceship, first asking me how I was ('Fine' — I was always fine to my clients), and then telling me briefly about his day. His sister was moving to town and he'd been scurrying around scouting housing for her. Bob was twenty-nine, looked like a young Ben Franklin, and was subject to premature ejaculation. This was the sort of thing, of course, that a real acquaintance wouldn't know, and that I wished I hadn't remembered. But I always do. Bob could have been a giant, spurting penis and I wouldn't have been any more conscious of his problem as we stood under a eucalyptus tree on Center Street.

"So I think I found a really nice apartment for Angela," he told me.

"I'll bet she's from Los Angeles too, isn't she?" I asked.

"Yes, but she hates it down there — bad air, traffic, and really scary crime in her area too."

We exchanged platitudes for another minute or two, and then I was in motion again. This angel business was beginning to annoy me. It wasn't okay with me that my free time was being invaded by a client's fantasies. From my perspective, 'Angela' and all the rest comprised a leakage of Arundel pollutants into the sea of my life. It happened to be angels instead of raw petroleum or sewage, but it was just as unwanted.

I was aware that my anger was not a particularly mature or compassionate response to an unusual set of circumstances. But I also knew that such judgments, superimposed by my mind onto my emotional self, were powerless in the face of such a strong feeling. I didn't like George Arundel and I didn't like whatever was going on that he'd catalyzed. At that moment, I didn't care if the ultimate source of the phenomenon was God, an overactive imagination, or poor toilet training.

As I walked, my anger subsided and I became aware of waves of self-righteousness and self-pity. This was a typical progression for me. Next, I'd feel disgusted with myself, impatient for the feelings to dissipate, and then hungry. Knowing all this, I turned left towards Pacific Avenue to put myself on course towards my favorite coffeehouse. All those years of professional training allowed me to feel everything I always feel but now I could get my lemon almond tart five minutes sooner.

As I nibbled on my third dessert of the evening in the pseudo-warehouse atmosphere of Café Beatrice, I listened to the college radio station on the array of high-tech speakers and watched an assortment of students reading, studying, and covertly scrutinizing each other. UCSC students tended to wear costumes rather than clothes; I enjoyed the spectacle.

Before I finished my tart, though, the KZSC deejay began playing 'Earth Angel.' I left.

That night I dreamt I was flying over a football game, wearing overalls and spitting on all the bald-headed spectators.

*   *   *   *   *

George Arundel arrived on time and the professor greeted me in his stilted formal manner. They were wearing — I mean, *he* was wearing — khaki cotton pants and a hideous Hawaiian shirt. This orange and purple monstrosity dominated the room. I wasn't sure if it represented virulent passive-aggressive behavior or was just a testament to monumentally poor taste.

"I need to ask some questions and I'm not going to be satisfied with your usual evasions. Is that clear?" I began.

"It's started, hasn't it?" he replied. "How exciting."

"Have you been tampering with my clients?"

"Of course not."

"Are you aware of everything the other alters do?"

"No. I don't need to be."

"I think you do." I glared at him; his arrogance was aggravating.

"I have much more experience with this type of thing," Arundel responded. "So let me assure you that there's no plot against you, you're not crazy, and whatever else you're wondering about probably isn't the case either. This is simply how these things work."

"What things?" I wanted answers, not vague assurances.

"That which I have previously discussed with you — your angelic legacy. How else could the universe tell you who you are?"

"A letter?"

"Would you believe it?'

"No, but I don't believe this either, do I?"

"Not yet. And that's sensible. For every legitimate spiritual event, there are ten thousand fraudulent ones. I could be a confidence artist or simply deluded. You must proceed carefully. I agree."

"Somehow, your agreeing with me fails to console. My God — now you've got me talking like you."

Arundel smiled. "Look at it this way, Thomas. Something very interesting has happened. That's all you can accept for now. And if what I'm saying turns out to be true, is that really so bad? An angel? With a mission to help transform the world? There are worse fates, my friend."

"That's beside the point."

"Aren't you even open to the *possibility* that I know what I'm talking about?"

"No," I replied. "I'm not. And I'll tell you why. To consider that I might be an angel would be a form of psychic suicide, given my orientation in life. I can't be the me I know and do that. It's like telling one of Mother Theresa's nuns to go hold up a Seven-Eleven. You don't know what you're asking."

"Yes, I do. I'm very much aware of what is entailed. You will need to reorganize almost everything about yourself to accept who you truly are. But it can be done."

"That's easy for you to say."

"Hardly. Do you think I was born with this capacity? I've been in your shoes. I know how difficult it is to undergo a spiritual emergence. But ultimately you're going to choose between going crazy and your destiny. That's what it will come down to. It always does. And I feel confident of your adaptability. Remember, I questioned you carefully before embarking on this."

"My favorite color? House pets?"

Arundel nodded amiably.

"I'm supposed to risk my sanity on the basis of that? Wait a minute. We're way off-topic here. I need some questions answered and you've got us in some hypothetical time-warp." I bent my head and kneaded my brow while I regrouped. "Can you control dreams?" I finally asked.

"No. I don't possess the skills to do that."

"But it can be done? Is that what you're saying?"

"Certainly. Krishnanda did that."

"Could he be involved in this?" I asked.

"I'm sure he is, but he's been dead for nine years, so that's probably difficult for you to accept."

"But you're saying he's creating the dreams?" I asked.

"No. You asked if he is involved. That's the question I answered."

"Well now I'm asking if he's messing around with my dreams."

"I'm not a confidante of the subtle realm's personnel department, Thomas. Why does it matter who or what is orchestrating your coming-out party? The fact that you're receiving signs — this is what matters."

"There are all kinds of signs and they don't prove facts in any case. At best they corroborate things, and nothing's happened that can't be explained much more easily by ordinary means."

"Then why are we having this conversation? If you're so secure in your understanding, why ask me anything? Is this your idea of a therapeutic intervention?"

He was right; this wasn't therapy; I was scratching an itch.

"I'm sorry," I told him. "This isn't my idea of therapy, either, so I won't be charging you today. And I *am* shook-up over what's happening. I can't deny it. It's downright weird and it makes me angry."

"Understandable. There are stages in this process much as there are in grieving — denial, anger, and so forth."

"You make it sound so inevitable. Aren't you open to the possibility that *you're* wrong?"

"Of course, but nothing's happened to support that hypothesis," Arundel asserted. "And this is what I do. If a client came in with a classic array of symptoms for some familiar disorder, wouldn't you feel confident that you understood him? Your training and experience would serve you, just as mine do."

This arguing was getting us nowhere. We were trying to settle an issue of faith, not logic; he had it, I didn't. It was as simple as that.

"How do you know," I asked, "that your alters aren't running all over town producing so-called coincidences to dazzle me with?"

"I know."

"But how?"

"I can't explain," he answered.

"Can't or won't?"

"Can't. You haven't developed the appropriate receptor sites for the information, so there would be no place for it to attach."

"We're not molecules. Try me," I suggested.

"It's akin to speaking in another language. It wouldn't make sense to you."

"Try me," I repeated more firmly.

"I'm sorry, Thomas."

I paused and wondered what to do next. Arundel seemed to consider himself my mentor, which obligated him to answer some questions and not answer others. It also kept him in control of the conversation, as usual. Perhaps if I mustered something unpredictable or insightful, another more forthcoming personality would emerge.

"What about Zig-Zag?" I asked. "She doesn't believe she's an angel either. Haven't the signs failed with her?"

"The young can be stubborn and foolish, and she is somewhat inured to the extraordinary. But I have no doubt she'll see the light."

"See the light? There's a phrase with more than one meaning."

"Yes."

It wasn't much of an insight, I had to admit. "Part of your mission is to help me, right?" I tried.

"Yes."

"Well, you're not helping."

"Yes I am. You just don't like it. Perhaps a phrase devised by Krishnanda would be appropriate to share here. 'Yield gracefully to what is.' If I were you, I'd write that on my bathroom mirror."

"If you were me, you'd do exactly what I'm doing, since you'd be me," I said. "Anyway, we're out of time. Are you interested in continuing therapy?"

"No. Call me when you're ready."

"Ready? Ready for what? To save the world?"

Arundel smiled tolerantly and marched out. I had survived another hour with the king of non-cooperation.

Chapter 7

The eerie synchronicities continued, averaging about three per day. Part of me grew accustomed to them, another deeper part was shoved further and further off-center as the tally accrued. It was like being a defendant in a trial in which the prosecutor presented a myriad of circumstantial evidence. Eventually, inferential or not, the overall mass of the presentation might sway the jury into proclaiming a guilty verdict.

I really didn't want to be an angel. Oh, on some level it would feel good to be special — more than special, really — a legendary creature. But then I wouldn't still be Tom Dalziel, and as miserable as I often was, it was what I knew. This was very similar to the conundrum faced by my clients in therapy. They showed up with certain attitudes and behaviors in tow, swearing that they were sick to death of all the problems these evoked. Then they fought me tooth and nail to hang onto their sense of themselves and *not* change. A great deal of psychic energy is reserved for maintenance of the status quo.

Another issue was responsibility. I didn't need the burden of some holy mission to transform the world. Maybe that sounds selfish but I definitely preferred that somebody else save anything bigger than individual people. My job was hard enough as it was.

Of course, all of this was beside the point, anyway. The whole idea was crazy, and any other processing represented nothing more than my susceptibility to this particular form of craziness. My attraction to amnesia, my desire to start over fresh, my depression — all of these tempted me to imagine that I'd been presented with a choice. I hadn't. I was who I was, regardless of Arundel and all the non-coincidences.

If God told me himself...well, then I'd think about it. Short of that, I was protecting my sanity any way I could.

*   *   *   *   *

The phone rang at three a.m. and I debated for several rings whether to answer it or not. I had two sets of business cards. One listed my answering service only, the other included the line that was ringing. I gave these latter cards out sparingly, which meant that only people I was willing to talk to in the middle of the night could disturb me. Nonetheless, I usually equivocated before answering.

"Hello," I rasped.

"Hello? Is this Mr. Dalziel?" It was an unfamiliar young woman's voice.

"Yes it is."

"This is Zig-Zag. You know — George Arundel's friend?"

"Sure. What can I do for you?" I was about three-quarters awake at this point.

"It's an emergency. A friend of mine is freaking out and I don't know what to do." Her tone of voice was congruent with her words.

"What do you mean by 'freaking out'?" I asked. I've found that clients employ the idiom to describe a wide variety of behaviors, from simple crying to actually running amok.

"It's like she's paralyzed, only she can talk some. It's really scary. Can you help?"

"Where are you?"

"On Brommer Street near Seventh."

"Okay. I'll be there in fifteen minutes."

"Thanks. I really appreciate this. I'll be standing by the side of the road."

"Right. See you soon."

I don't know why I agreed so readily to rush off in the middle of the night to meet a stranger in crisis. Perhaps it was because the last time a client of mine had become inert, her housemates had called the cops, who ended up chasing her down with a police dog, handcuffing her, and hauling her in for a seventy-two hour observation period. Since her breakdown had been spawned by paternal mistreatment —

being locked in her room for days on end, among other things — the episode was far from therapeutic.

My Volvo was a reluctant participant in the housecall. First it balked at starting, then it only grudgingly consented to engage its first gear. Hindsight suggests that my boxy Swedish compadre might've demonstrated more common sense than I.

Zig-Zag was, in fact, waiting by the side of the road, clad in overalls again underneath an unzipped navy blue sweatshirt. When she opened the passenger side door and hopped in, I was confused. Wasn't I supposed to get out instead of her getting in? Also, her face was blackened. What did that mean? The only possibility my three-in-the-morning mind could conceive of was a minstrel show. In Santa Cruz? A minstrel show?

"I'll show you where to park. Take a right in that dirt driveway," she directed, pointing with a slim, elegant finger.

The driveway ran along the perimeter of a vacant lot, next to a church parking lot. Overgrown weeds brushed against the car's undercarriage as I negotiated a series of potholes on the road. A few hundred feet in from Brommer Street, several elderly cars huddled beside a tall cyclone fence.

"Anywhere around here is good," Zig-Zag assured me.

I parked. "Why is your face black?" I asked as I switched off the ignition.

"It's dark out," she answered, scrambling out of the car before I could ask anything else.

I trailed her to the fence, my eyes gradually becoming accustomed to the dim light. Three Blacks loitered by an open steel gate — or were they more white people with blackened faces? I suddenly realized what was going on.

"This is some illegal protest thing, isn't it?" I asked Zig-Zag as we encountered the others.

"Hell no," she barked. "We don't protest. We wreak havoc."

"Havoc?"

"Sure. Right, guys?"

"Right," a short man in army fatigues answered.

"Havoc's where it's at," an overweight teenage girl added.

"Cripple the machine!" Zig-Zag exhorted.

"Eat the rich!" the third figure called, her tone of voice suggesting, thank God, facetiousness.

I stared at this last speaker. She appeared to be a tall, slim woman who was actually black under her blackface.

"Kill their heads off!" she added, grinning. Even in the dark I could see that she was extraordinarily beautiful. Her smile was both lively and sweet, despite the mock militancy of her words. From what I could see of her face, it was strong, with high cheekbones, a long wide nose, and an exemplary pair of dog eyes. By this I mean those large brown eyes that you see on mature dogs that somehow embody alertness, loyalty, and unconditional love all at once.

Suddenly I was conscious of my ugliness. Real dog's eyes didn't care what I looked like, but this woman's probably did. And so I did too.

"Listen," I finally replied, "I share your concern for our world, but I'm not willing to get involved in something illegal."

"It's Sarah," the especially black woman told me. "She's halfway up the tower and she can't move."

Gesturing, she drew my attention to the superstructure dwarfing the power company's transformer site. About forty feet in the air, two dark figures were clinging to the metal cross-bracing.

"Phil's up there with her," Zig-Zag reported. "But he's not getting anywhere."

"So you want me to do therapy in the dark on a tower with someone I don't know who's too scared to even move?"

"Exactly," the black woman answered.

"And I'll be trespassing?"

"Of course."

"And you'll probably expect me to work for free since your cause is so darn just?"

"Naturally," she responded.

"What's your name?" I asked.

"Desiree, but my friends call me Dizzy."

"If I save Sarah, I'll probably get to call you Dizzy, right?" I couldn't believe my ears. I was flirting. In the midst of this absurd situation, in front of three virtual strangers, I was actually flirting.

"That's right," she answered, smiling again.

"Pardon my curiosity, but aren't you black anyway?" I asked. "I mean under the shoe polish or whatever."

"So?"

"Never mind." I paused and thought a moment. "What are your other alternatives?"

The wind kicked up right then; I buttoned my wool jacket and turned up the collar.

"We can't leave her," the man said.

"And we're not about to call 911," Dizzy added.

"Jail isn't an alternative," Zig-Zag agreed. "Sarah's wanted as it is. She'd probably get two or three years."

"Why? Did she blow something up?" Two or three years seemed rather extreme for criminal trespass.

Everyone looked at everyone else.

"Maybe," the large girl replied.

"Great. Is there a bomb up on the tower?"

"No," the man answered. "We had other plans but they've been scuttled."

"So will you do it?" Dizzy asked.

It was obvious that the sane choice was to drive home immediately and go back to sleep. But I found that I didn't want to do that. What I wanted to do was concoct convincing reasons to myself that I should stay and help. I tried for a while but I couldn't think of any. So I just said "yes."

"Follow me," Dizzy directed, striding forward toward the tower, flashlight in hand. She moved like a dancer, pushing each leg ahead as she walked, while maintaining a stable center of gravity in her hips.

Watching her enabled me to maneuver from the gate to the base of the tower without the interference of sensible second thoughts. A metal ladder with tubular rungs and handholds was welded onto the structure and Dizzy hesitated only a second before pulling herself up and beginning the climb. I paused longer, common sense compelling me to reconsider. I glanced up to assess the danger of the mission and the vision of Dizzy's tightly jeaned posterior lured me up onto the first rung. I was being seduced by my own projections onto this woman. I certainly didn't know her — she could be married with two children, for example. But my hormones were overriding reality and my size thirteen feet continued to seek out ever higher rungs.

As I climbed, two problems surfaced. One was my tendency to enjoy the dimly lit view above me at the expense of concentrating on the task at hand. After slipping off the ladder twice, clinging to the tower with only my arms, I was scared into a more immediate focus. Worse yet was a truly painful, once-a-rung collision between the ladder and my raging erection.

Living a celibate lifestyle created certain drawbacks, among them an inconvenient ease of arousal. I've been burdened with erections from hugging elderly women, glancing at lingerie advertisements, and even sitting near lesbians. Am I unconsciously excited by what they do with one another? And what about the old crones? The underwear thing is more reasonable to me, but clearly my endocrine system is completely incapable of distinguishing between such basic dualities as vulgar and aesthetic, realistic and impossible, or even too young and old enough. I detest it when my hormones respond to some unattractive kid in a revealing outfit.

I've heard other men describe their type — tall, slim redheads or whatever. I don't have a type; my arousal is completely unpredictable. Once again, whatever criterion that the rest of the world uses is a mystery to me. Did everyone else come with an owner's manual?

On the tower, en route to the acrophobic girl, at least it was dark and my juvenile response to Dizzy would remain hidden. Also, I was consoled by the fact that my conscious self agreed that the stimulus in this instance was truly exciting. It was an erection on merit. Dizzy would be proud, or at least my projections onto her would be.

When we finally neared the stricken climber, I could see that Sarah was a pale ascetic-looking woman in her late twenties. She wore a black karate gi, fastened by a piece of yellow nylon rope. Her very short, dark hair framed her small-featured face in an old-fashioned manner.

Sarah's distress was obvious. Her eyes were squeezed shut and her tense body was pressed against a cross-strut adjacent to the ladder. Apparently, she'd been maneuvering laterally to reach something I couldn't quite see on the other side of the tower. She hadn't gotten far, though, before an urge to meld herself into the metal had asserted itself. Immobilized, her overall posture was reminiscent of a desperate kindergartner clinging to her mother's leg on the first day of school.

Just above her, squatting on a small platform, a slim, handsome man in his forties spoke soothingly in an effort to convince Sarah to join him. There was no evidence that she even heard him.

The sort of anxiety attack that Sarah was weathering entailed very real physical symptoms. She was probably dizzy, sweaty, short of breath, and suffering heart palpitations. This latter feature could be extremely disturbing, convincing the person that they were experiencing a heart attack, or even dying. No intervention conducted in the panic-producing context was likely to be effective, thus my first task was to devise a way to get her down on terra firma.

I'm often amazed at how little attention is paid to corporeal concerns in my profession. People can't transform themselves when they're hungry, tired, abused, or terrified. I firmly believe that a high percentage of people who describe themselves as depressed, for example, are simply in a state of perpetual fatigue due to poor diet and/or lack of sleep.

As I formed my initial impressions of the situation on the tower and my erection subsided, Dizzy scrambled up next to the man who she introduced as Phil.

"And this is Sarah," she continued as she settled into a full lotus position on the small platform. "Sarah, this is Tom. He's here to help."

The panic-stricken woman blinked her eyes open for half a second, focused on my face, and then hurriedly withdrew back inside herself. I felt as if a human camera had just taken a snapshot of me.

"Do you think you can hold onto me?" I asked.

She struggled to respond, finally forcing the air out in gulps.

"What... do... you... mean?"

I could barely distinguish the words, but that she was talking at all was a good sign. Some part of her was present and interested in a solution to her dilemma.

"On my back," I told her gently. "Do you think you can lock your hands around my neck?"

"I...can't...move."

"Oh I'll do all the moving," I assured her. "All you have to do is transfer your grip from the tower to me. I'll do the rest. I'm sort of like a tower anyway — you probably won't even notice the difference. Dizzy and Phil can hang onto you while you switch over."

"Who...are...you?"

"I'm a friend of Zig-Zag's."

"How... do I know... I can trust you?"

She was speaking in bunches of words now; our conversation was distracting her from her fear.

"Well, Dizzy likes me," I told her.

"The man flirts good," the black woman added.

"Why can't Phil carry me down?"

Not only did Sarah articulate an entire sentence, but the words were much more comprehensible now. Her breathing was noticeably calmer, too. I was encouraged.

I glanced at Phil, who shrugged. He probably weighed about a hundred and fifty pounds and his arms resembled fettucine.

"I'm really big and strong," I informed Sarah. "I do this kind of thing all the time."

"Really?" She opened her eyes and scanned my face.

"Sure. Why do you think they called me?" I smiled and projected sincerity, not one of my most convincing emotions, but apparently good enough for Sarah.

"Well...okay." She closed her eyes. "Let me know when it's time. I don't want to watch."

What a remarkable recovery, I thought. "Sure," I agreed.

It was much more easily said than done, but eventually, after several false starts, I found myself clambering down the ladder while my human backpack choked the living daylights out of me.

The two other activists followed us, taking turns telling Sarah terrible jokes, which she ignored. Her terror had repossessed her as soon as we'd begun moving; I could feel her heart beating frantically against my back. I experienced difficulty remaining calm myself. All sorts of things could go wrong, after all. Sarah might successfully throttle me, in which case we'd plummet to our deaths, or at least to a pile of broken limbs. Alternately, she could relinquish her grip suddenly and fall on her own. If Dizzy or Phil slipped, they'd clobber us and set in motion yet another airborne scenario.

I listened to the jokes, though, and as humorless as they were, I could center myself around them. That is, they provided an anchor for the part of me that wanted to sail off to fear.

Anyway, none of the tragic events I was concerned with came to pass. Instead, Sarah initially refused to abandon her perch once we reached the ground, which was inconvenient. And a squad of sheriff's deputies were waiting for us, handcuffs in hand, which was several magnitudes of adversity worse than any of my fears.

"Oops," Dizzy commented.

Chapter 8

The deputies were utterly uninterested in who was an environmental crusader and who was a therapist. Furthermore, my size intimidated them; they cuffed me much more forcefully than the others. I had to lie face down in the dirt while two of them twisted my arms behind me and a third man planted his knee in the small of my back. It was very hard to fully cooperate with this procedure, since no one announced where any of my body parts were supposed to be next. It also hurt — on more than one level.

I felt humiliated in a very primal sense of the word. Subjugated, really. I was now a captive — a slave — and this metamorphosis from a successful professional to the lowest of the low was fully sanctioned by society at large. This shame-based overreaction created a muddy filter through which I experienced subsequent events. It was like suddenly becoming one of those overwrought protagonists in a Dostoevsky novel.

I did notice that the policemen were gentle with Sarah, whose anxiety level was still marked. Also it was apparent that Zig-Zag, Dizzy, Phil, and the others were completely familiar with the getting arrested drill. In fact, Dizzy addressed one of the deputies by name and another policeman told Phil that he wished "you guys would give us all a break and cut this crap out." It was as if they were sports rivals or opposing lawyers meeting in a bar after a trial. I was the only one deeply affected by the arrest as far as I could tell. Of course, preoccupied with my self-indulgent pathos, I could've missed something.

We were split up and farmed out to the backseats of several police cars. I shared my black vinyl pew with the short man I hadn't been introduced to. He told me his name was Emory and that he was sorry I'd been dragged into this mess.

"No sorrier than I am," I told him. "This could play hell with my professional reputation."

"You know," he responded, "it's not that bad. These kinds of crimes aren't self-serving — they're based on principle — and people are pretty understanding about that. I'm a professional and it hasn't hurt my business at all."

"You've been arrested before?"

"Three times. Nothing serious."

"What do you do for a living?" I asked.

"Chiropractic."

Now that he mentioned it, I noticed his chiropractor demeanor — long, unblinking eye contact that wasn't corroborated by the rest of his face. It was spooky, the sort of false intimacy that a successful gigolo developed. Did they teach a course on it at chiropractor college — 'The Look' 101? I guess you had to do *something* unusual to convince people to let you play with their bones.

"Do you think that sitting on the front edge of a bench seat with your hands cuffed behind you, your legs wedged against the seat in front, and your head pressed against the ceiling is a healthy posture?" I asked.

"I'll give you my card later," Emory replied. "Stop by my office for a free adjustment. It's the least I can do."

"You don't seem very upset for a guy who's just been arrested," I pointed out.

"Like I said, it's really not that bad. If you think of it in a sociological way, the jail is a pretty interesting place, in fact."

In other words, I thought, if you dissociate thoroughly enough to abdicate the realm of feelings, then you can skate through the experience and pay the psychic price later.

"Personally, I'm scared," I told him.

"Of what?"

"The kind of people I'm likely to be meeting soon."

"Are you kidding?" Emory replied. "I hope you don't take this the wrong way, but they're all going to be terrified of *you.*"

"Hey, maybe you're right."

"Of course I am. No offense."

It was a fifteen minute ride to the county jail. No one spoke for the remainder of the trip, although the police radio squawked periodically, triggering my startle reflex each time. As

I lurched forward, the handcuffs dug into my wrists and reminded me not to react to the next burst of noise. Who knows? Maybe after a few thousand of these stimulus-response training episodes, I'd calm down. We arrived at the county jail before I had a chance to find out.

The complex sat across the San Lorenzo River from downtown, and except for the high iron fence and the dearth of windows, it could've been a mid-priced motel. The outside walls were some sort of brown masonry — not cinder block or brick — and the one-story, flat-roofed design sprawled across a well-kept landscape.

Once inside, the differences between the jail and a tourist accommodation became much more evident. Despite the size of the booking area, its ambiance was distinctly claustrophobic, as though traces of apprehension lingered from previous guests. It also smelled like a cross between a hospital and a bar, and it was cold.

We were booked as a group and once again no one was interested in my status as a good Samaritan. I was promised though, that I could tell my story at a hearing later in the morning.

Next, we were sorted by gender, unmanacled, finger-printed, photographed, searched, and our valuables were confiscated. The county personnel were polite but very impersonal; they were hiding themselves in their roles. Finally, Phil, Emory, and myself were led to a large holding cell in which five aromatic men were lying on orange plastic benches. As Emory had predicted, they wanted no part of me, sidling to the far corner of the room to resume sleeping off their various states of drunkenness.

My own fatigue overwhelmed me shortly after reclining on the uncomfortable, too-short bench nearest the cell door. I dreamt that I was lying on an orange plastic bench in a holding cell. In the dream I drifted in and out of sleep, dreaming (in the dream) that I was a gorilla looking for food who fell off a cliff and hit his head and then hallucinated that he was a goldfish trapped in a small muddy puddle.

It was probably the strangest dream I've ever had. I couldn't tell who I really was, which scenario, if any, was real, and what any of it meant. I was hopelessly confused, or at least my subconscious was. It was nothing like the bliss of total amnesia. I hadn't realized that there were different versions of identity loss and that some of them were such miserable experiences.

Much too soon, we were awakened by a loud cheerful voice.

"Rise and shine, campers. Up and at 'em!" the guard called.

"Shut up!" one of the drunks shouted back.

"Now, now. Let's not be a grumpy Gus," the guard admonished.

I sat up to get a look at this character. He was almost as big as me and although he couldn't have been over forty, his short hair was pure white. His teeth, on the other hand, revealed in a broad smile, were quite yellow.

"Why not?" the drunk rasped.

"Nobody likes grumpiness. It just doesn't say 'Hey, I want to be your friend.'"

"Fuck you."

"And we all need friends."

"Fuck your mother."

"Much as I'm enjoying our repartee, I need to make a general announcement. Listen up, gentlemen. You've got ten minutes to primp for your hearings. If you're back in here afterwards, we'll feed you. Any questions?"

"Fuck you."

"You'll need to reorganize your thought into the form of a question."

"Fuck you?"

"That's better. Have a nice day," he added as he turned and departed.

"What's this primp shit?" one of the other drunks asked.

"Beats me," his buddy answered. "Just some wise-ass shit, I guess."

He had a point. There was no mirror or sink in the room — just a lidless toilet. I stumbled over to it and peed. So much for primping.

We were herded down the well-lit hall by two new guards, who were armed with batons and fierce scowls. I missed the sarcastic guy already.

The hearings themselves were boring, list-reading affairs. When my turn came, I simply explained the circumstances, admitted I'd broken the law, and asked for mercy. I was told that if I paid a two-hundred dollar fine, I was free to go. I could call someone to bring the money, or wait until another unspecified official decided if I could be released on my own recognizance. My cohorts were all charged with more serious crimes and their bail was set at five thousand dollars each. Sarah was very upset by this outcome, but the others took it in stride. Dizzy turned out her pockets in a mock search for hundred dollar bills, accusing Zig-Zag of taking them while she'd slept. Phil made a speech likening their cause to anti-war demonstrations in the 1960s, until the elderly judge told him that he was even more annoying than Vietnam-era defendants had been, especially when he was giving speeches.

I decided to wait and see if they'd let me go without my needing to prepay the fine. But before I could find out, the merry guard informed me that my fine had been paid by a "kind gentleman" and I was free to "depart this vale of tears some call home."

Chapter 9

In the lobby, George Arundel and Zig-Zag were waiting by the door.

"Brunch is on me," Arundel declared.

While it wasn't entirely kosher to hobnob with a client, it was certainly rude to turn my back on a benefactor, so off we went to a nearby pancake house where a diminuitive waiter supplied us all with blueberry waffles. June's Breakfast Place was a relic of whatever era mistakenly believed that Americana decor was the epitome of dining ambiance. The booths still wore patterned ruffled skirts and the light fixtures were wagon wheels with lantern-like globes. Every detail in the restaurant manifested the theme, including the salt and pepper shakers (wooden piglets), the menu (nicknames for every dish), and the wall decor (patchwork quilts that I actually liked). Whenever I ate at June's I felt the presence of foreboding grandparents ready to swoop down and catch me using poor table manners.

"Thanks for bailing me out," Zig-Zag told Arundel when we'd finished eating.

"It isn't the first time," he reminded her.

"Maybe it'll be the last," she replied.

"You're willing to give up this foolishness?"

"Nope. I'm willing to not get caught again, though."

"There's no guarantee of that. The only sure way to stay out of prison is by opening up to your angelic nature."

She rolled her eyes. "Here we go again." As Arundel continued to speak, she marched a piglet around the circumference of her plate.

"I'm surprised you haven't begun receiving information about your mission. When that happens, even you won't be able to resist."

"Wanna bet?"

"What do you mean?" he asked.

"I've been having visions for days now."

"Really?" I asked. I wondered if this would happen to me too.

"Yup. I'm supposed to go to a certain bookstore and look at this book. Page fifty-three, second paragraph."

"What did it say?" I asked.

"I'm not going. Who cares what it says?"

"I do," I admitted. "Aren't you even a little curious?"

"Well, a little. Sure. Who wouldn't be?"

"You must go," Arundel told her.

"No way."

"Suppose I go?" I suggested. "You can tell me about it and I'll check it out. It might be very interesting."

Arundel chimed in. "It's a reasonable compromise, Zee. Let Tom do it."

"All right. But I don't necessarily want to hear about it. And George? You have to stay off my back about all this. Is that a deal?"

"Agreed."

"And I'm not going to tell Tom about it in front of you," she added.

"I'm hurt, Zee."

"No you're not."

"Just a bit. I really am," he protested.

"Tough shit."

George smiled uneasily. "There's no need for that type of language."

"I think there is." She glared fiercely at her godfather. "I'm not up for your games today, George. I spent the night in jail and I'm tired. Okay?"

"I understand. Perhaps I'll take my leave and let you two get on with things."

I stood and expressed my appreciation for his financial help at the county lock-up. We shook hands.

"It's the least I could do," Arundel told me. "And I have yet to thank you for your efforts in our therapy sessions."

He seemed to be serious.

"I can only recall one moment that could be termed therapy. If I didn't know you better, I'd think you were joking."

"Sometimes a single insight can be transformative," Arundel replied.

I raised my eyebrows.

"Of course," he continued, "that wasn't the case here."

"I thought not."

He smiled one of his creepier smiles as he strode away with the check.

"George is George," Zig-Zag sing-songed.

"He certainly is. Listen. Are you sure you won't go to the bookstore with me?"

"Oh, maybe I will. As long as George doesn't know about it."

"I won't tell."

"Okay. Let's go. It's that antique bookstore downtown. You know, the one near the library?"

"Sure. We can walk over to the impound lot, get my car, and drive there. How's that sound?"

"Let's go."

On the way, Zig-Zag filled me in on her unusual life. She'd been born on an ashram in India and her mother had suffered some sort of permanent nerve damage during labor. I told her that I'd never heard of that happening and she responded with a one-word explanation — "India" — and then shrugged.

According to my companion, everything was different there — the air, the sky, the colors, the people. I expressed skepticism and she tried to describe what she meant.

"It's like the colors are brighter — no, more intense. They're not really brighter. And everything is more three-dimensional and it's like the air is charged — full of potential for the next thing to happen. Do you know what I mean?"

"No. Could it be because you were younger when you were there?"

"Oh no. I was older then. I've only gotten young since I came to the States."

"Now I'm really confused," I admitted.

"You get a different perspective growing up around someone like Krishnanda. Hell, George was one of the most normal people there, according to Western standards, if that gives you any idea. My father could do miracles. I mean when I was a baby and I was cutting new teeth or something, he'd do a miracle or two to distract me from crying. I still remember the time he levitated to get my kite out of a tree. He didn't let other people see that kind of shit, but to me it was just part of the deal. So I *know* that anything's possible. It's not a theory to me, it's something I know."

Crassly, I fantasized about what a great book a case study of Zig-Zag would be. I struggled to stay in contact.

"So are you saying that because you know there are more possibilities than other people think there are, you can notice things about India that sound odd to someone like me?"

"More or less. Most of what we perceive we filter out, right?"

"Yes."

"So suppose your filter was a more open-minded kind, one that recognized the subjectivity of all experience."

"I didn't realize you were interested in metaphysics," I told her. "I feel like I'm in first grade."

"That's okay. Americans don't know anything about what really matters. And I had to be interested in metaphysics in order to survive — or at least in order to make sense out of what I saw and heard as a kid. So do you see what I'm saying? Suppose you grew up thinking it was okay to sense differences in the air. I don't mean smog or temperature or anything like that. Then you'd see what there is to see. It's simple really. Even regular American tourists know something's up when they get out of their airplanes. They use words like 'vibrant' or 'an assault on the senses,' but it's the same thing. Matter vibrates. Well, there isn't any matter, really. Energy vibrates so it looks like matter. This is in physics books, too. And in India all the vibrations are more intense."

"What does this have to do with nerve damage in labor?"

"Everything. Or nothing if you prefer."

"Thanks a lot."

"If you can't accommodate paradox, you can't get any of this," she informed me.

It was an odd experience being lectured in metaphysics by a young woman who had never previously revealed any personal depth. It occurred to me that my sense of her lightweight status might be due to her spiritual background. I'd heard that really advanced souls presented as light or casual beings. After all, a lot of what we call depth is probably better described as 'complexity' or even 'concerns.'

I was surprised that Zig-Zag's assertions had brought this up for me. I also was very curious to hear more about her life.

"So the rules are different in India?" I tried.

"Let's say the parameters. There aren't any rules."

"Okay. So it's possible for something to happen in India that can't happen here?"

"Not 'can't,' just 'doesn't' or 'hasn't happened yet.'"

"I think I understand. With all this in mind, I'd love to hear more about your childhood."

"Sure. Some of the Krishnanda people wanted me to be my father's successor and they started working on that when I was only six. They made this special little robe and I used to bless people by touching them on the head with this peacock feather. It was really fun for a while but then I got bored with it and I wouldn't do it anymore."

"Was George one of the people encouraging you?"

"No. He and Krishnanda thought it was hilarious."

"Really?"

"Sure. My father found most of what his followers did totally amusing. He laughed at them all the time."

"That doesn't sound very compassionate."

"Well, they *were* pretty silly. Anyway, after that I hung out more with the Indian kids and I got some exotic form of encephalitis. My temperature got up to a hundred and seven Fahrenheit which usually kills you but my father did something so I didn't die. I did have hallucinations for a week, though."

"What was that like?"

"Scary. I was only eight or nine and they were really intense." She paused and looked up. "You know, I just remembered something. In one of the fever dreams, I was walking down the street with this big man with a scarred face."

"You're kidding."

"No. And at the end we both flew away." She glanced at the dismay on my face. "Look, I don't like this any more than you do."

"Yeah?"

"I've got plans. Angels can't even have sex. I've got a lot of living to do. After fifteen years in an ashram, what do you think? I'm ready to sign up to give my life away?"

"Is that what this is?"

"Of course. Don't you even know that?"

"I guess I do."

"And there's no way to tell what's really going on either."

"What do you mean?"

"Well, it could be some weird guru doing all this or it could be my father or maybe one of us is accidentally doing it or I don't know what else. There's no way to tell."

"Suppose George is right. Then who would be doing it?"

"Everybody. God. The other angels."

"Does that appeal to you more than the other alternatives?"

"Well, yes and no. If it's bogus, then I'm right to resist. But if it's really the universe itself, then we'll have to do it sooner or later and I don't want to."

"I see what you mean, but have you considered how unlikely it is that this is for real? There are thousands of people in institutions all over the country that spout this apocryphal nonsense. Historically, there have always been plenty of grandiose religious delusions. It's dirt common. Maybe even Krishnanda was unbalanced. I mean if I could do miracles, I'd probably get a little confused about who I was."

"You don't believe he did miracles, do you?"

"I'm trying to, but no, I guess not."

"That's okay. I don't mind. I just hope there's nothing too great in this book we're going to get."

"Amen, sister."

*   *   *   *   *

At the bookstore, we were greeted by a well-groomed border collie, who acted as if we were all old friends. After this excited boy-it's-good-to-see-you-two-again routine, the little black-and-white dog padded a few steps up a narrow, crowded aisle between ceiling-high shelves of dusty books before stopping and turning her shaggy head to glance back at us.

"I think she wants us to follow her," I told Zig-Zag.

"I can see that but I think I'd prefer some human help. Hello?" she called. "Anybody here?"

There was no reply; the dog watched us assiduously, her eyes shining. When we still didn't move, she barked, took another step, and coquettishly cocked her head again.

"I'm coming," I told her. "I can't disappoint an old friend."

Zig-Zag moved forward with me and together we negotiated a maze of poorly lit aisles by following our canine guide. It was an eerie experience following this strange dog in an empty antique bookstore on a spiritual mission based on someone else's vision. If at any time in my life prior to this, I'd been informed that this episode was going to be part of my future, I'd have laughed myself silly.

We found ourselves in a back corner of the store in the fiction section, according to the faded notecard affixed to nearby shelves. The dog barked again to get our attention and then reared-up to put her paws on a small black volume near the bottom of the stacks.

"That's the one, huh?" I asked, reaching down to pat her head.

She evaded my hand and barked again. It was an alto bark, not too deep and not too yippy.

"Get the book," Zig-Zag said. "I want to see what it is."

As if she understood, the little dog returned her front paws to the green linoleum floor and watched me lean forward and snare the slim volume.

The book was bound in soft black leather and yielded easily to my grasp. There was no title or any other writing on the cover so I opened the book, flipped past several blank pages, and found the name of the work.

An Account of Bat-Ool, the First Prophet in the Time Before History was the title. It was written by Captain M. Larris in 1886.

I read all this aloud to Zig-Zag, who began swearing softly.

"What?"

"It's the one from my vision. God damn it." She pronounced the blasphemy carefully, enunciating each letter.

"Really?"

"Of course. That probably wasn't even a dog."

I looked around for our furry salesclerk; she'd disappeared.

"I didn't see her go either," Zig-Zag told me. "Let's get this thing over with. Page fifty-three, the second paragraph."

"Right."

The printing was crude and not all the pages were numbered but I found the passage.

"And so Bat-Ool let it be known that although life was hard for the people of the big river, there would come a time when everything would change and the plants would grow taller and stronger and the diseases would be gone from the land. When the people asked their prophet how this great change would be affected [sic], he told the people in a fine strong voice that men and women with wings would fly down from the heavens and defeat the spirits who made the life of the people hard. 'When will this happen?' the people of the big river asked and once again their striking prophet spoke. 'You will know when the time of change is nigh,' he told the people, 'as everything will be doubly reversed from that which you know and death and killing will be as eating and sleeping and there will number among the people too many to live in peace.'"

"Well," I began after we'd both read it, "at least it was in the fiction section."

"What do you think 'doubly reversed' means?" Zig-Zag asked.

"Very backwards, maybe — in the sense of perversity."

She nodded. "Let's get out of here."

"Wait. I want to buy this book and read the rest."

"Go ask the dog how much it is." Zig-Zag was quite angry. "There's no one else here. That damn dog or whatever it is can probably work the cash register too."

"Hello?" I called out. As we wandered back to the front of the store, I tried a few more times, but there was no sign of the dog now, let alone her owner.

I left the book on the store's counter with a note saying I'd be back the next day to buy it.

"I've got to get to my office and see some people," I told Zig-Zag outside the store. "Can I give you a ride somewhere?"

"No thanks."

"Let's talk on the phone about this soon."

"Good idea."

For some reason, I wasn't very shook up. Maybe I just couldn't assimilate any more weirdness. I don't know.

Chapter 10

The next day I stopped by the bookstore on my way to see my first client. A slim young man with a shaved head was perched on a high stool behind the front counter. He wore a royal blue velvet sports coat with wide lapels over a white silk shirt, which created a Dickensian effect. He might have been the eldest son of some early English industrialist or perhaps a young dandy whose entire fortune had been spent on a class-climbing wardrobe.

The expression on his face hinted at low-grade boredom, which was consistent with the I'm-only-working-here-as-a-favor-to-a-rich-relative impression I'd formed. His smile, when it finally arrived, was reasonably sincere, though.

"Good morning," he chirped.

"Hi. I'm here to buy that book I left on the counter," I told him.

"What book is that?"

"It's by a guy named Larris and it's a novel about a prehistoric prophet."

"Hmm. Let's see."

Without moving from his stool, he began typing on a desktop computer. After a while he glanced up at me from across the wooden counter.

"Was it supposed to be the *Account of Bat-Ool?*"

"Yes. That's it."

"I'm sorry, but I've never had one of those. I can't afford it, frankly. There are only eight of them according to my information service," he told me, tapping the computer screen with a slender index finger. "The last one auctioned was in 1984 and it sold for forty-four thousand dollars."

"Wait a minute. I was just in here yesterday and I held it in my hand. It had a black leather cover. Why don't you look and see if it's under the counter somewhere?"

"I don't keep anything under the counter and the store was closed yesterday."

"No it wasn't."

"I assure you it was since I was attending my cousin's memorial service." He was losing his patience and his tone of voice reflected that.

"Could I speak to the owner?"

"You're looking at him."

"I'm sorry. I just assumed it would be someone older. You know — antique books — the whole eccentric old man thing?"

"I understand."

"Do you have a dog?"

The man looked alarmed.

"I'm not crazy," I told him. "In fact, I'm a psychotherapist. It's just that yesterday the door was open and there was a small black and white dog in here. It was about noon, I guess."

"I have no explanation. I don't have a dog. Who waited on you?"

"Well, the dog sort of did." I noticed his expression again. "Look, I know how this sounds. I just want to buy a particular book, that's all. I can show you where it was in the stacks."

"My assistant isn't here and I can't leave my stool."

"Just for a minute? Surely no one's going to rush in and steal anything for just a minute. This is very important to me."

"I'm sorry. I really can't leave my stool."

"Can't we even discuss this?"

"You don't understand. I'm dying. I literally can't leave my stool. I can't stand or walk anymore."

"Oh God. I'm sorry. I've put my foot in my mouth again."

"It doesn't matter — it's the least of my troubles. That's one thing you can say about dying. It gives you perspective on the little stuff."

"I know what you mean. It's kind of like that after a big quake. Getting cut off in traffic or something just doesn't measure up on the Richter scale for a while."

"Yeah. So I can't help you, and anyway as I said there's no way you saw that book here. It's rare, it's expensive, and there aren't even any on the West Coast, let alone in Santa Cruz."

"Okay. Fine. Let's just say I'm confused. But can I go look in the stacks anyway?"

"Sure. Help yourself."

Needless to say, the book wasn't back on its shelf. There wasn't even a gap where it had been. I was very glad Zig-Zag had shared the experience so I didn't have to immediately diagnose myself.

Later that day, after work, I tried to sort through my thoughts. Either I was enmeshed in some sort of group delusion, a very elaborate hoax was in progress, or the world was not what I had always assumed it to be. The notion that I was experiencing psychosis was the easiest to dismiss. I was trained, after all, to differentiate this condition from other possibilities, and trying to cram all my experiences into that box just wasn't feasible. The created illusion theory was still viable, but the incident at the bookstore spoke of the enormous resources needed to generate my experiences thus far. Either someone had access to a forty-four thousand dollar book or the means to create a convincing simulacrum. Further, they would need to gain access to a locked store, train a dog to perform a complex series of tasks, and hire all sorts of talented actors to play various roles the last few weeks. As events continued to unfold, the scope of the potential hoax became harder to accommodate. But was the third alternative any easier to swallow?

Zig-Zag had outlined some of the possible scenarios in this realm. Her dead father could be the mastermind? Give me a break. Some other person with mystical powers was doing it? Who? And why? We had no clues, unless George was more than he seemed to be. This idea intrigued me. Why couldn't a hitherto buried alter be psychic or whatever he needed to be to generate everything? There didn't seem to be any limit to how many or what types of alters an MPD could have. It wasn't mentioned in any of the literature, at any rate.

I found myself grasping onto this idea with vise-like intensity. Sure, I told myself, it makes the most sense. I'd need to discard the smallest bundle of hard-learned life experiences to accept this guru-alter concept, and all the responsibility for events would be limited to the current cast of characters. In science, they say that the simplest solution is both the most elegant and the most likely. Why not accept this non-supernatural and non-paranoid solution?

So George was the hub of the phenomenology, and since I already knew that his perspective as one alter was substantially skewed from consensus reality, I was under no obligation to give credence to what another alter might produce.

I was very relieved to figure all this out. As a working hypothesis, it enabled me to move on and take care of business, and God knows my clients needed my full attention.

*   *   *   *   *

A few days later, my new four o'clock client, D.L. Farr, turned out to be Dizzy, or more properly, as I discovered later, Desiree Lucille Farr.

"D.L.?" I asked as she sashayed into my office in denim shorts and a black tee shirt.

"I didn't know if you worked with acquaintances," she explained as she slid into the client's chair.

"I don't."

She didn't seem disappointed but I knew I was no whiz at reading her. With her brow furrowed and her lips pursed, I imagined that she was concocting arguments to further her agenda. When her features relaxed and her tongue wet her lips prior to speaking, I guessed that she'd successfully mustered something convincing.

"Oh. Well in this case it's a matter of life and death so you'll probably want to waive your usual policy."

"Really? Life and death?" I wasn't convinced.

"Well, I'm not sure. Either it really is or I'm paranoid and I'd rather be paranoid so I'm here so you can tell me I'm paranoid which will mean that nobody's trying to kill me."

I leaned back in my chair. "Tell me about it." I was hooked.

"Some guy is stalking me only I'm the only one who seems to notice and that counts the police who say there's no one, it's all in my head. God, I hope they're right. And then yesterday as I was walking home from work — I'm a limousine driver — I got this totally creepy feeling so I started running and I think that serial murderer was chasing me but since I made it home and he didn't kill me I've got no proof and the police said I should 'seek counseling' so here I am. I'm really scared, Tom. Suppose I'm right. Suppose he's after me. Maybe the victims weren't random. Maybe he picked them all out ahead of time and I'm next."

She huddled on the chair, her knees pulled up to her chin. Even in her misery she was beautiful.

"Have you ever had these feelings before?" I asked.

"Yes. And nothing happened."

"So you think it's nothing this time?"

"No. I think somebody's trying to kill me, but I *hope* it's nothing."

"Let's get clear about why you're here," I suggested. "You want me to decide if this threat is real or not. Is that it?"

"Yes."

"How do you imagine I can do that?"

"I don't know. Can't you recognize paranoia when you see it? Don't they teach you that at school?"

"I must've been sick that day. And I'm afraid I don't have any business seeing someone I've been arrested with. It's not ethical to have a dual relationship and there are good reasons for that."

"So what are you saying? You can't help me?"

"Not exactly. I'm not going to take your money and I'm not going to be your therapist, but I'm still a human being and as such I can do whatever the hell I want, can't I? As a human being, I care about what happens to you and I'll help in any way I can. Do you know what I did for a living before this?"

"No, but let me guess. Pro football?"

I shook my head.

"Fireman?"

"No, but that's a good guess. It would explain the burn scars."

"I give up. Just don't tell me you were a serial murderer, okay?"

"I was a private investigator."

"You're kidding."

"Nope. And I still have a gun and a permit to carry it."

"So what are you saying? You're gonna shoot everybody suspicious-looking?"

"Dizzy, you're looking at your new bodyguard."

"Really?"

"If you want me."

"You'll be wasting your time if this is all in my head," she warned.

"No, I won't." I smiled winningly.

She smiled back. "There's that flirty guy I used to climb towers with."

"It's a big gun too," I told her.

"Oh boy."

"The murderer's only got a knife."

"Yippee."

"Of course I'll have to accompany you all the time."

"Of course."

"Into the ladies room, on dates...."

"In your dreams, shrink."

"Well, I do have other obligations too, like all these pesky therapy clients."

"Who pay you, right?"

"You'll be a hobby, Dizzy. A lovely temporary hobby. They're going to catch this guy soon. He's not that careful."

"I hope you're right. I can't live like this. If you couldn't help me I was going to go stay with my aunt up in Oregon."

"Let's keep that in mind as plan B."

"Sure, but tell me more about plan A," Dizzy requested. "Are you serious about protecting me? Do you really have the time?"

"I'll make the time. I'm perfectly serious. Even if it's unlikely that you're in danger — and I'm not saying that it is — then we'll probably have fun hanging out and getting to know one another. If you're right — if there is someone stalking you — we'll be saving your life and maybe taking a killer out of circulation. I don't see how we lose either way."

"What if he kills us?"

"Well, that would qualify as a sub-optimal outcome, wouldn't it?"

"Sub-optimal? I guess so. But you think you can prevent that?"

"Yes. Just being there is probably enough. All the victims have been alone. But I know how to use a gun and I'm big and strong as well. Would you attack us?"

"Hell no, but I'm not crazy," she pointed out.

"I don't think this guy is either — not in the way you mean it. His actions aren't senseless or arbitrary, anyway — just hard to understand. In his way of being, what he's doing is internally consistent, even if it doesn't share the same roots in reality that ours does."

"Maybe they could catch him if somebody like you told them all this."

"They have forensic psychologists who are much better at this than I am. The F.B.I. has a whole branch that works with local authorities on serial killings. But even then they need a lucky break. The usual methodology — looking at motive and so on — doesn't help much."

"Well anyway, I'd sure appreciate your help. Thanks. I feel like I ought to pay you for today too. You could've had a real client instead of me."

"Don't worry about it. You could've had a real therapist too, right? So we're even."

We worked out a schedule of when Dizzy needed bodyguarding and when I was available and the two coincided nicely. Her shifts at work were, for the most part, congruent with my own. When we had finished arranging to meet at her apartment later that day, Dizzy blessed me with a wonderful hug before leaving. I had that hot-chocolate-in-the-tummy feeling again and I liked it a lot.

*   *   *   *   *

I stopped off at my place to pick up my pistol, holster, and the voluminous cardigan sweater I customarily wore when I was carrying. As usual, close examination suggested that a large gun-shaped tumor was sprouting beneath my armpit. But I wasn't someone who invited detailed scrutiny; my stature and scarred face tended to dominate the viewer's attention.

Dizzy lived in a part of town called Beach Hill, which lay between downtown and the boardwalk. At one time, it had been the high ground that the wealthy had staked out, and it was easy to understand why. A sea breeze, a spectacular three-hundred-and-sixty degree view of ocean and mountains, and a feeling of isolation from the troubled world that lay at its feet all made Beach Hill desirable still.

Now, the neighborhood consisted of elderly Edwardian and Victorian homes and relatively upscale condominium complexes. Dizzy's apartment was on the ground floor of a purple fairy-tale monstrosity on a side street that was usually clogged by tourists in tourist season. Santa Cruz's maze of streets confused visitors in patterned ways, disgorging them onto certain streets while leaving others pristine for local use.

Dizzy's doorbell announced me with a loud insect-like buzz that was one of the more obnoxious sounds I'd heard lately.

"Just a minute," she called. "I haven't got the hang of these new locks yet."

After finally swinging the door open, Dizzy retreated to the middle of the room. There was an overwhelming smell of paint and the large studio apartment was very brightly lit. Every square inch of the walls was covered by canvases and every canvas was a portrait of one subject — a black female angel.

"Do you like her?" she asked.

I was too stunned to answer at first. I'd thought I was inured to the synchronicities by now, but I guess I'd developed unconscious expectations in some arenas and not in others. For whatever reason, I was shocked to discover that Dizzy resided in the angel world.

"It's from a vision," she told me. "The only one I've ever had."

"She's beautiful," I responded, moving forward to stare at the largest of the paintings.

The angel was a creature of great age, with lines of knowing and wisdom etched onto her jet-black face. Her body, though, retained a litheness, a supple grace that was explicit in Dizzy's depiction. As a painter, her technique was, for the most part, equal to the task of realistic portrayal. Even the black feathery wings invited the viewer to reach out and palpably feel that which Dizzy had seen. The black angel was naked but completely asexual. The background was a Greek temple, and the grain of the white marble was clearly delineated, as well as a bit of graffiti that resembled the outline of a dolphin. Each canvas was slightly different, yet each contained all these essential details.

"Why so many?" I finally asked.

"I'm trying to get it right. I'm close but I haven't gotten it yet."

"How many are there?"

"I don't know. Forty or fifty so far."

"What does it mean?"

"I told you. I'm trying to get it right."

"No, I mean the vision."

"Oh. I don't know. Zee says it doesn't mean anything, but that's like saying disregard the biggest thing that's ever happened to you and I'm not about to do that."

"Did the angel say anything?'

"No. But I knew what she was thinking. She was thinking that the world was so sad and yet so beautiful — like they were the same thing — and then I knew that she totally loved me, more than I've ever felt from anyone. It was wonderful. I started sobbing and it didn't stop for hours. I think every ounce of fluid and mucus came out."

"Yuck."

"You're missing the point."

"I know, but it's easier to respond to the mucus part."

"Yeah, I understand. I haven't told too many people."

I considered whether or not to share my angel experiences. It would be nice to reciprocate and repay her trust, but on the other hand my information might be unsettling or even traumatic. The fact that she was several dozen paintings into a series based on her vision bespoke her ability to overreact.

"I appreciate your telling me," I decided to reply. "I feel honored."

"Well, hell, if I'm going to trust you with my life...."

"Good point. Want to see my gun?"

"No."

"Want to see anything else?"

She smiled. "Not right now. It's time to get going to my women's group."

"Is that what I'm taking you to?"

"Yup. And I thought it would be fun if you came in and guarded me there."

"You're kidding, right?"

She shook her head.

"Isn't it run on a confidential basis?"

"Nope. It's not a therapy group. Mostly we moan and bitch about men."

"Gee, that sounds like oodles of fun."

"Great. Let's go."

"Don't you recognize sarcasm when you hear it?"

"No," she answered, grabbing my hand and pulling me towards the door.

Chapter 11

So I attended my first women's group. There were nine of us — well, eight of them and one of me. Dizzy sat me next to her and introduced me as her bodyguard.

"Are you really her bodyguard?" an older woman with a New York City accent asked.

I nodded. It didn't seem right to inject a male voice into the proceedings.

"I'm not comfortable with him here," another woman complained.

"Tell me about it," Dizzy responded.

"He scares me. I can't open up with him here. It's not safe."

"It's not safe for me if he leaves. I think somebody's trying to kill me," Dizzy told her.

"Oh my God!" another woman exclaimed. Upon closer examination, she turned out to be the sister of a former client. According to my client, this woman, whom I had observed once through my office window, was constantly campaigning to engage in incestuous sex with her sister and her sister's live-in girlfriend. I wished Santa Cruz was bigger as I surveyed the other group members.

There was no obvious common denominator in the assortment of women. They ranged from early twenties to at least seventy, from black to lily white, from expensively dressed to bundled in rags. It was as if someone had done their best to assemble a completely disparate group, plucking members from ordinarily mutually exclusive subcultures. Fortunately the room itself provided some stability. It must have been the home of one of the participants, but the interior decor was distinctly Holiday Innish, replete with large, bland paintings and a bible on an end table.

"Does he talk?" a skinny woman asked in an abrasive smoker's voice.

"Sometimes," Dizzy answered for me.

"How are we supposed to talk trash about men with that brute in here?" she complained.

"He *is* an intimidating fellow," an elderly matron agreed.

I smiled disarmingly.

"That's the idea," Dizzy told them. "Bodyguards are supposed to be scary."

"That's true, and he does have a disarming smile," the matron admitted.

I smiled more.

"It makes me want to smack him," the ex-New Yorker shared.

"I wouldn't advise it," Dizzy warned. "He's trained in eleven different martial arts, including how to maim and kill with just one finger."

Although this was news to me, I brandished my right index finger and wiggled it menacingly while I scowled at my foe.

"I didn't mean I'd really do it," the woman explained hastily. "I was talking about my *feelings*."

"Smacking isn't a feeling, Ruth," a woman in a blue business suit commented.

"I didn't say it was. I *felt* like smacking him — that was the feeling. You never listen to me, Brenda. We've been over this before."

"You don't speak clearly. *That's* the problem."

"Fuck you too."

There was an awkward pause while everyone decided to ignore her remark.

I decided to smile again.

"He thrives on our conflict," the incestuous sister proclaimed, pointing at me with a stubby index finger of her own, one that looked much more capable of mayhem than mine.

"Maybe he's just friendly."

"I think he's retarded or something."

"Anyway," Dizzy interrupted, "I know we're all anxious about the serial killer, but I am truly terrified. I've seen him stalking me."

"Jesus!"

"Holy shit!"

"No wonder you're spooked!"

Dizzy glared at this last speaker.

"No offense," the woman added. "I mean it in the sense of ghosts."

Dizzy nodded her acknowledgment.

"Have you been to the police?" someone asked.

"Yes, and I couldn't believe it. It was just like in the media where they treat traumatized women like they're hysterical over some fantasy. I mean they never even asked for a description of the guy, not that I got a good look at him. There was just this sense that they weren't going to take me seriously no matter what I did. That was the worst."

"Haven't you done this before?" New York asked.

"So?"

"So it's like the boy who cried wolf."

"Say what?"

"You don't know that story?"

"No."

"Really?"

"I'm black. That's probably some white story. Why don't you tell me so I won't be culturally deprived any more."

"Okay."

So we heard a long, boring rendition of the tale, replete with detailed descriptions of everyone's clothes and even the weather.

"Fuck that," was Dizzy's response.

"I support you," someone else told her.

"Me too."

"You poor thing."

Eventually the group moved on to other topics, including domestic violence, menopause, and rude bus drivers. Procedurally, the women continued to engage in a free-for-all, occasionally confronting each other scatologically. Everyone forgot about me, it seemed, until the end of the two-hour session, when someone reported that they got more out of the group with a male witness present. Several others agreed, although they didn't understand the phenomenon. The group decided to discuss the possibility of a permanent male witness at their next meeting.

It wasn't going to be me. Observation of Dizzy and the others made it clear that these weren't people I was eager to consort with. As usual, my projections onto an attractive woman had proved to be completely incongruent with her actual personality. In this case, Dizzy was younger, more superficial, strident, and impatient than I had assumed. As usual, I'd convinced myself of something I'd wanted to believe and now the discrepancy between desire-driven pseudo-reality and the way things actually were was making me feel like an idiot — an old, ugly idiot who should know better.

I was quiet in the car as I steered us back to Dizzy's apartment.

"It's a zoo of a group, isn't it?" she offered.

"It certainly is," I answered dully.

"Are you bummed? What's going on?"

"It was hard being there. I realized some things about myself that I don't like."

"Like what?"

"Oh, it's nothing new. How I con myself and play games with reality."

"Well, hell, we all do that, right?"

"I suppose so."

"Sure. I've got this whole fantasy about you, for instance. I mean I hardly know you but I've convinced myself that you're really wise and powerful, not to mention funny and sexy. So I came to you for help when I normally would never get near a male therapist. Is this the kind of thing you mean?"

"Actually, that's exactly what I mean. I wasn't able to hang onto my fantasy of you tonight. You're you and there's nothing wrong with that, but compared to my projections... well, it's a process of disillusionment, and ultimately I'm most disillusioned with myself for not having graduated out of this crap yet."

"I know what you mean, but really we should celebrate moving further into reality. That's what happened. You got more authentic, right? That's a good thing."

"It's the contrast. When I suddenly see how things really are, I feel like a moron for how I've been up until then."

"I understand, but I think it's a common deal — nothing to beat yourself up about. Everybody does it. You may be a therapist but you're still an everybody, too."

"You know, you're right."

"Sure. Lighten up."

"Of course your saying all this is fodder for a new fantasy."

"Naturally. I don't mind. Mine's changed too. I love that vulnerable thing of yours but it kind of ruins the all-knowing deal. You know?"

"Yes. It's hard to hang onto something like that even when in this case, of course, I'm actually God-like in so many ways."

"Yeah, right."

"Don't forget about my finger of death. Show some respect, mortal."

She flashed her finger of obscenity, which I began to understand had more to do with her sense of humor than her depth as a person.

There was no one lurking in Dizzy's building or immediate neighborhood, so I hugged her goodnight and drove off. As I pulled up to the stop sign on the corner, a glint of something caught my eye off to the left. I shifted to reverse and backed-up to investigate. Just then another car turned down the street in the opposite direction, its headlights sweeping across the front lawns near me.

A figure hiding behind a slim tree took off running, a large knife in his or her hand. I slammed on my brake and jumped out of the car. As the figure darted down a dark driveway, I began to lumber in pursuit. Whoever it was certainly wasn't an athlete, but my knees were already killing me after a few steps. I concentrated on my footing as the hard asphalt yielded to a recently watered backyard, but before I'd gained any ground, I encountered a sprinkler head, wrenched my left knee, and went down hard. For just a second, I considered using my gun to fire a warning shot, realized that would be inappropriate, and then watched helplessly as the figure blended into the darkness of the garden next door.

I could barely limp back to Dizzy's apartment. I'd be serving time in my Rube Goldberg knee brace for quite a while. When I called the police and got hold of a sergeant I knew reasonably well, he dispatched cars to scour the area. My credibility, unlike Dizzy's, was still intact. I guess the news of my arrest hadn't been fully disseminated yet. Within minutes two detectives had joined us in Black Angelville and were taking copious notes as I detailed my experience.

Both men looked to be in their mid-forties and shared several attributes that seemed unusual for cops. For one thing they sported blond beards. Also, their voices were high-pitched and their eyes were dark blue. They weren't brothers — they had different last names — but these likenesses initially overrode the obvious variations in their features and size. When I studied the taller of the two, for example, it was clear that his nose was twice the size of the smaller man's. And his skin was much rougher; he was pocked even on his forehead from bouts of acne. At any rate, they were polite and methodical, which was what I'd come to expect from Santa Cruz cops.

Dizzy was questioned extensively as well since she represented a live victim who could help determine what, if anything, the targets had in common. Strangely, neither guy asked her about the canvasses surrounding us. It wasn't until I was hobbling to my car that the shorter detective asked me if she was crazy.

"Why do you say that?"

"The paintings seem to be evidence of an obsession, wouldn't you say? And one of the people killed was a therapist — like you. Maybe that's the connection."

"She's not crazy, or maybe I should say no more than me. And I doubt if you're going to get anywhere with the therapy angle. But let me know. What else are you going to do?"

"We're assigning a car to watch her," the other policeman told me.

A third cop called to us. He was over by the tree down the block.

"I've found something," he shouted.

"Don't touch it!" the detective yelled. "We'll be right there."

'We' didn't mean me, so I asked them to give me a call the next day to let me know the status of the case.

"Yeah, yeah," they both intoned in their high-pitched voices as they hurried away.

In the morning I discovered that the suspect had left a mostly-intact footprint of an extra-wide size ten running shoe. The extra-wide part was a promising clue, the detective told me.

"Probably he ordered them through the mail or bought them at a specialty shop."

"That makes sense," I replied.

"Also, he eats bagels."

"Maybe that's how his feet got so wide."

"I beg your pardon?"

"Never mind. Did you find crumbs on the ground?" I asked.

"Better. A half-eaten cinnamon-raisin bagel with at least three toothmarks."

"That's great. You've finally got something to work with."

"Exactly. And please keep all this under your hat, okay?"

"Of course. That's what I do — I'm a therapist."

"Well, Sergeant Marner says that you used to be a private investigator and I can trust you. In fact, he said you might even have some ideas that could help us."

"Not right now, but I'll stay in touch."

"Fine. Take care."

"Bye."

Next I called Dizzy.

"You're my hero," she told me.

"Aw shucks, ma'am."

"Now don't be modest. You saved my life. How's your knee?"

"It's been better."

"You poor thing. I feel I owe you big-time and I want to pay you back."

"Do you usually pay off with perverse sexual favors?"

"You wish. I had dinner in mind. At the restaurant of your choice?"

"That sounds good too," I admitted.

"Tomorrow night? Around seven?"

"Sure. Do you need to talk about last night?"

"At dinner, you mean?"

"No, now."

"Oh. I guess so. I still feel pretty shook-up. The main thing is the whole 'you could be dead any second no matter how much you forget or pretend the world's some other way' thing. That's what gets me. It's like the universe showed me this big black hole that might suddenly appear under my next step when I thought I could count on solid ground."

"That's a normal reaction."

"So?"

"I mean it's an appropriate response."

"What are you — God? I don't care if you think it's 'normal' or not. Is this what you do with your clients? Judge their responses and announce how close to mainstream they are? Jesus."

Every time I began to feel comfortable with Dizzy, she did or said something that confused me as to who she was. This latest example was typical. I had no idea how to reply to her.

"So what do you have to say for yourself?" she finally asked.

"I'm sorry, I guess."

"You guess?"

"Yes. I guess. I'm not sure."

"Well, in that case I *guess* I accept your apology. Anyway, I don't think we should talk about this any more. We're obviously on different wavelengths and things are tough enough right now."

"You're right. I'll see you tomorrow at your place at seven."

"What about between now and then? Aren't you going to keep protecting me?"

"The police assigned someone to you. Didn't they tell you?"

"Yeah, I guess they did. But I'll bet he's not as big and scary as you."

"And I'll bet he runs faster, has better access to reinforcements, doesn't have to see clients, and has more training in surveillance and disarming people."

"Sometimes you're annoyingly logical, Tom."

"It's my job. I'm a guy."

"You certainly are. Take care."

She hung up and I was left alone with my unappreciated masculinity.

Chapter 12

Later that day, I was seated at a small wooden table nibbling on a brownie at Cafe Neo when a malodorous bag lady sprawled onto the wooden chair across from me. She was old for a Santa Cruz street person, perhaps in her early sixties. Her face displayed extensive wrinkles and sun damage, but the way she moved indicated that the aging was premature. Unlike the other senior street people I'd observed downtown, her clothes were tie-dyed in bright rainbow patterns.

"Can I help you?" I asked. Sometimes it seemed that needy souls have radar for spotting caregivers.

"No, I can help *you*," she told me in a surprisingly clear, strong voice.

"How's that?"

"I heard you were confused. Is that right?"

"Most people are."

"No, I mean especially confused. You are, aren't you?"

"I guess so."

"Very good. Now buy me some coffee."

"No. Is that what this is about?"

"No. I'll tell you anyway. I just felt like some coffee."

"I've got to be somewhere soon."

"Fine. Are you ready?"

"Yes."

"This planet," she explained, "is like a spiritual penal colony in which every inmate is serving a life sentence."

"'No matter how I struggle and strive, I'll never get out of this world alive,'" I responded.

She stared at me, her brow furrowed.

"Hank Williams," I explained.

She nodded, although it was clear that the name meant nothing to her.

"Haven't you ever wondered," she began again, "why everyone is so screwed-up here — so far short of any spiritual ideal?"

"I *know* why. I don't have to wonder." I began ticking off reasons on my fingers. "Dysfunctional families, cultural expectations, the educational system, stress..."

She interrupted me. "That's like saying we have brains because it helps us hunt and gather food."

"Exactly."

"This is superficial reasoning. Perhaps another example will illuminate you. Why is there gravity?"

"You want me to try and answer that?"

"Yes."

"Well, things are attracted to each other and gravity reflects that."

"Why?"

"Well, if there weren't any gravity, the universe wouldn't have the same basic structure. Everything would be completely different."

"So what can you conclude from this?"

"Gravity needs to be the way it is so everything else can be the way *it* is?"

"Very good."

"What does this have to do with penal colonies?" I asked.

"You have to look deeper than the specific mechanisms that generate a circumstance. The underlying meaning or pattern is far more significant."

"So you want to talk about why life is less than ideal — why people have problems — but I don't see that as knowable. Everyone needs to develop their own set of beliefs or philosophy to guide them."

"All things are knowable; there are no limits. And reality is a particular thing, not a subjective concept. Therefore some of these beliefs are more accurate than others. Are cargo cults just as legitimate an interpretation of metaphysics as Buddhism?"

"To the people in the cult — yes. It serves the same purpose."

"That's not meaning, it's purpose-serving or whatever you want to call it. Perhaps another example would be helpful."

"I doubt it," I confessed.

"Suppose you read a poem and believed it to be about the literal words. In other words, the symbolism or greater meaning went over your head. How do you think a literature professor would grade an essay based on such a reading?"

"I don't know. Tell me."

"Very harshly. The poet had a specific meaning he or she was trying to evoke in the reader and the reader failed to do his job properly. His understanding was superficial."

"Are you saying there's a God behaving like a poet, so our job is to strive for deeper meaning when examining the world?"

"No. But you're getting closer — less literal. Suppose the world-poem wrote itself and the naked eye could only see part of the poem. That's as close as we're going to get, I think. For now. Do you understand?"

"I don't necessarily buy into it, but yes, I understand your point," I replied.

"All right then. Back to the Earth as a spiritual prison. Souls that utterly fail at life elsewhere reincarnate here. And they keep reincarnating here until they work off their karmic debt and learn enough to resume lives on civilized worlds."

"Did you think this up yourself?" I asked.

"Why do you ask?"

"I've never heard it before."

"So if it's original it can't be true?"

"I didn't say that. Forget it. I've got to go."

"Not yet."

I was rooted in my chair; I tried to stand up and my legs wouldn't respond.

"What are you doing?" I asked. "Whatever it is, please stop. I'm getting really scared."

She smiled, her tongue poking out from the corner of her mouth. "Maybe your legs fell asleep."

"Please," I pleaded, my eyes doing most of the work.

"Just listen. Then you'll be fine. Sometimes prisons need to be refurbished or even torn down and rebuilt. They can be out-of-date for the kind of crimes and inmates that populate them. Are you listening?"

I nodded. I was terrified, virtually shaking with fear.

"It's a lot of work but sometimes it's necessary." She stood up, clutching a soiled grocery bag. "I hope you really listened. Once I leave, you'll be fine, you know. Don't worry."

She ambled off and sure enough, as soon as she had disappeared through the back door, my legs were back under my command. I didn't use them to pursue her; that was the last thing I felt inclined to do.

Instead I sat and once again tried to make sense out of nonsense. My fear lingered, interfering with the process, and the more I pondered, the more sadness seeped in as well.

The Earth-as-a-prison metaphor was a truly depressing notion, even though I could shrug off the literal version I'd heard. It certainly did seem sometimes that a structural or definitional aspect of our world prevented life from ever becoming fully okay. The moral of the metaphor, then, is why try to make it right when it can't ever be right? What's the use?

The business with my legs had been horrible. Was she a master hypnotist? I do happen to be a very malleable subject. Or could she have sprayed something under the table that temporarily paralyzed me? It seemed possible. I'm sure she wanted me to believe it was magic or something, but as my fear began to lessen, I realized how absurd this was. I was simply shocked and momentarily witless — my terror had been no more than this.

*   *   *   *   *

There is always a threshold beyond which a psyche can't hold all the experiences that have accumulated without disrupting the integrity of the container itself. I was dangerously close to discovering where my threshold was, I realized. The encounter with the homeless woman was one more bizarre hot potato I was constrained to juggle instead of file away neatly. It wasn't one too many, but what if the next one was?

I needed help but I was dubious that my own therapist could sort through the mess that I was toting around in my head. Roberta was a very gifted practitioner, but I required a specialist — an expert in the occult. Someone with an explicitly spiritual background could provide a reality check for me.

I knew that a colleague of mine was a follower of Matthew Ferguson, who billed himself as "the guru with a regular name." This local middle-aged man was reputed to be more playful, accessible, and sensible than most folks in his business. In fact, my colleague saw him weekly to sort out the "weirdness" in his life. This wasn't a term I usually identified with, but I was desperate and I knew my acquaintance could set up a meeting on short notice. In fact, I saw Ferguson the same day I made contact with him — just twenty-four hours after my cosmic lecture.

Ferguson had written several books, including *Dying Into Life*, which had sold well nationally. I hadn't read it but I knew it was a quasi-psychological exploration of non-denominational spirituality. Basically, it was the kind of book Santa Cruzans read instead of seeing therapists. When it didn't save them and their desperation mounted, then they came in and together we unlearned whatever they'd read.

Surprisingly, Ferguson preferred to meet in my office and wouldn't accept a fee for his time. It hadn't been necessary to reveal the nature of my concerns to arrange things, so I had no hint of the man's attitude towards angels or legs that wouldn't work.

He was about six-feet tall and big-boned. His initial demeanor was friendly and open. Based on looks, I would never have picked him out of a guru line-up or chosen to bare my soul to him. Other than rather arresting light blue eyes, there was an ordinariness to Ferguson's features. His nose and mouth were pleasant enough, yet not particularly evocative of strength or wisdom. The patterns of wrinkles on his face implied some squinting into the sun, some frowning, some smiling — nothing unusual. I was disappointed. I hadn't realized it ahead of time but I wanted him to look impressive, even majestic. Anything less represented a sub-par set of credentials.

Once we'd exchanged greetings — he possessed a low, mellifluous voice — I sat him in my chair and became a client.

"What can I do for you?" he asked.

"I'm confused. I don't want to be."

"Sometimes confusion is very worthwhile," he told me.

"Maybe. But just listen first. Some very strange things have been happening."

Without referring to anyone by name or hinting that clients were involved, I related my bizarre story to my consultant, who listened carefully, his eyes fixed on mine. I tried to emphasize what had happened outside my office — the supposed corroboration of Arundel's news and my experience with the old woman. These were the parts that disturbed me the most and were also the least confidential.

"Well," he began. "That's fascinating and the first thing I'd say is that you need to be open to all the possibilities. That's the value of true confusion. It opens you up. If you really don't know something, there's room for whatever it is to show you its meaning. You aren't restrained from the truth by your usual filters of logic or experience."

"I'm not sure what you mean."

"There is a continuum of possibilities implied in your narrative. At one end it's all craziness — none of it's real. At the other end it's completely true — you *are* an angel. Then there's everything in between. I'm saying that your best bet is to begin by opening up to the entire continuum."

"Tell me why again?" I felt like an idiot. For some reason I couldn't understand Ferguson's perspective at all.

"The best version of confusion entails perceiving all the possibilities as possible," he replied.

"So I might be an angel?"

"Of course. I might be a spider."

"I doubt it."

"Of course you do."

"What do you mean? Because I'm sane or because I'm close-minded?"

"They're the same. Take your pick."

"I like sane better."

He nodded agreeably. "How do you like my help so far? Pretty nifty stuff, huh?"

I stared at him, unsure how to respond. Finally I asked if he understood our process in the room.

"Certainly."

"Tell me."

"You are resistant to some of the alternatives inherent in your situation. As I suggest you stay open to them, you either don't understand, or express doubts. This is only natural. I'm accustomed to this type of interaction."

"What do you mean by natural?"

"If you become an angel, or even substantially different in some other way, Thomas Dalziel dies. To the ego, enlightenment represents the ultimate threat."

"Who said anything about enlightenment?"

"Gee, I think it was me, but I might be wrong."

"Look, let's back up a little. Why is it best to consider all the possibilities?"

"I'm not telling."

"What?"

"I'm not telling."

"You sound like a fifteen year old."

"Thank you."

I paused. "Will you tell me why you won't tell me?"

"Sure. It doesn't matter and I don't feel like it. There's nothing fun about convincing people. I prefer to offer my point of view. If it resonates, great. If it doesn't, well that's fine too."

"Okay, that's your prerogative. But what about all these synchronicities?"

"Yes. What about them?"

"Did they really happen?"

"You said you were sane, so I presume they did."

"Do they mean anything?" I asked.

"Of course."

"What?"

"Beats me."

"Thanks a lot. Could they be an affirmation of something?"

"Yup."

"Disproof of something else?"

"Yup."

"An indication of what color underwear people in Mali will buy next year?"

"Now you're getting the hang of this. It certainly could."

"Terrific."

I considered what to try next and decided to ask about the old woman's beliefs.

"Is this planet a penal colony for troubled souls?"

"Suppose I said yes. What would that mean to you?"

"I don't know."

"Let's try it and see. Yes."

"Hmm," I hmmed.

"Do you believe it?" he asked.

"Well, no. Not just because two people I don't know said it."

He smiled. "All your questions seem to lead to more questions instead of answers, don't they?"

"I guess so."

"Perhaps this is an indication that our meeting now is not going to prove fruitful."

"Why do you say that?"

"If you ask a question but aren't moved by an answer, why bother asking?"

"Because I'm very uncomfortable not knowing," I told him.

"Listen to me closely. This is the crux of the matter. You are even more uncomfortable knowing what there is to know. This is clear."

"Are you saying the truth is some monstrous thing?"

"I think my comment was focused more on you than on any truths."

"So I'm incapable of dealing with reality? Is that what you're saying?"

"More questions. They're piling up and burying us. Is there any point in describing the color blue to a blind man? Or reading your VCR's operating instructions to your cat?"

"Do you know George Arundel?" I asked.

"No. Why do you ask?"

"Never mind." I gathered myself again. "This is very frustrating. There doesn't seem to be anything I can do to settle things."

"Oh, but there is. Live your life. The future will show up and you'll see what it is."

"Isn't that rather a simplistic notion?"

"Sure. Got a problem with that?"

"I guess I do. I guess I have a problem with all of this."

Ferguson suddenly began singing. He had a beautiful baritone voice.

"Like a moth to a flame, I'm drawn by your will.
Consumed by your fire, but my love can't be killed.
Like a moth to a flame, I know that it's right
That I should transform on this fiery night."

I was deeply moved, much to my surprise. My
frustration disappeared and tears filled my eyes. Then there
was heat in my chest as though someone had rubbed Ben-Gay
directly on my heart. I didn't understand what was happening.
I began sobbing, hunched over, bringing the heat to my lap.
The experience was so intense that I have no idea how long it
continued. My mind was completely shut off and my
experience was rooted in my flaming heart.

When I recovered, or at least became coherent again,
Ferguson was gone.

Had this been some sort of help? What had he done?
Was I still me?

Chapter 13

There didn't seem to be any ill-effects from my music appreciation experience, other than the contrast it provided with everything else. Whatever had happened had been so intense and so sublime that now life in general felt pallid — a charcoal sketch by a fifth-grader. I assumed this impression would fade and my world would return to its usual ninth-grade watercolor status. In the meantime I did my best to ignore the phenomenon.

I was still, of course, accumulating even more concerns than I was capable of ignoring. From a mental health perspective, I knew that stuffing things didn't defuse their energy, it just postponed their release. In fact, when the concerns made themselves known down the line, they would probably explode out of their compressed state with more power than they'd started off with. Nonetheless, I kept signing up for this disastrous process; I guess the alternatives were even less appetizing.

Gradually, over the next few days I began to notice something that was at least as positive as the stuffing was negative. The easiest way to describe it is to say that my heart had been jumpstarted and now I was (temporarily?) aware of it as an active participant in my day-to-day life. I don't mean 'heart' in the sense of rescuing kittens or crying at movies portraying terminal illnesses. Lower case 'heart' was distinct from upper case 'Heart' in a way that I now felt viscerally. The upper case version wasn't an emotional realm. It wasn't connected to events or thoughts either. There was an unconditional quality to the state that transcended what I'd known before, and my ability to describe it accurately. In short, I knew it mostly by what it was not. Perhaps to say that some force had stripped away all the layers of crud that had stood between me and my Heart would be less misleading, although my Heart also participated in its own emancipation. I give up. Something was different and I liked it.

*   *   *   *   *

Dizzy could sense I'd changed. During dinner at Esposito's, "...where you never want to say 'basta' to the pasta," she shared her impressions.

"You're warmer and lighter," she told me. "And your eyes are different — softer and browner."

"Browner?'

"Yup. It's nice. What happened?"

"I had an intense experience where I was in my heart so thoroughly that I didn't know which end was up."

"How wonderful! What's her name?"

"Huh?"

"Weren't you with someone?"

"Oh. It was a man."

"You're gay?"

"No. What are you talking about?"

"When that's happened to me, it's been with a partner. After sex, actually. I just assumed...."

"He was a guru — he sang a song."

"Really? Wow. So you're spiritual and musical, huh? I had no idea."

"I wouldn't describe myself as either of those things. It's very hard to explain."

"Try."

"I'm mixed-up in something I don't understand. In fact, it has to do with angels — much like your concern with your vision."

"I knew it! I knew there was something more than just chemistry between us. What did your angel look like?"

"Ugly. Real ugly."

"How strange."

"Listen, have you ever thought that particular people might be angels?" I asked.

"No. Have you?"

"Lately, yeah. I don't want to, but some experiences seem to be pointing that way."

"Like what?"

I told her about the dog and the book, leaving out Zig-Zag, who, after all, knew Dizzy better than I and would've already mentioned it if she'd wanted her to know. I was surprised at how easily the story unfolded; it was already substantially less unsettling simply by dwelling in my head for a few days.

"So what do you make of it?" she asked when I'd finished.

"There's more to this 'life thing' than meets the eye?"

"Can you be more vague, please?"

"I don't think so."

"Me neither. Do you think it really happened?"

"Oh yes. That's not the issue. What I wonder about is how I need to shift my reality paradigm to accommodate such experiences."

"Reality paradigm? Accommodate such experiences? Who the hell talks like that? If you can't say it simply, it's crap. That's what my grandmother told me and she's right."

"Your grandmother uses the word 'crap'?"

"Not any more. She's dead."

"Sorry."

"For who? She's fine. There's nothing wrong with being dead."

"Fine. I'm beginning to wish we weren't having this conversation. Why do you have to give me such a hard time?"

"You're a man. You're full of shit and you don't even know it. No more than other men, I'll grant you that, but it's enough."

"So what are doing here with me? You're the one that sought me out."

"Like you could care less, huh? Who are you kidding? Some men undress women with their eyes, but you knocked me up with fucking triplets at least. Anyway, I tried to be a lesbian. It didn't work out for me. So you're my first foray back into the straight world. It's hard for me. This is a hard time right now. I mean I'm being stalked, I got arrested again, and it's back to goddamned cock. Sorry I'm not currently meeting your standards," she finished sarcastically.

"Whoa. Calm down. I'm not attacking you. I just wanted to know why it feels like *I'm* under attack. Now I know. Fair enough."

"Circling the wagons, huh? It's too late. The flaming arrows are sticking out all over you."

"I feel like it. Why should I get dumped on because of your generalized anger and frustration at men?"

"Because you're a man. You're not exempt. You're not some special exception. You're part of the problem."

"I don't recycle plastic either and I ran over a snake once," I told her, trying to allude to her environmental interests.

She stared at me.

"Another time when I was six I ate Twinkies and threw the wrapper down a storm drain. If this disqualifies me from deserving considerate treatment by people with problems, please let me know."

"Yeah, it does," she snarled as she walked out on me.

So much for opening up to beautiful women and sharing intimate anecdotes. I reacted to our squabble by retreating back up into my head; I was completely out of touch with my heart again.

*   *   *   *   *

George Arundel made an appointment through my answering service/billing agency and I wondered why. Had he become impatient with me? Had he finally recognized his need for therapeutic intervention? Did he merely miss playing his delightful game of let's-see-how-frustrated-I-can-make-Tom?

He looked the same, although his bald pate was pinker than I remembered. He wore a khaki ensemble straight out of an L.L. Bean catalog, except for new ratty black high-top sneakers that I'd seen offered at the flea market for eight dollars a pair.

"Greetings, Tom," he began, sinking into the client's chair with an air of satisfaction as if he'd been on his feet for days.

"Hello, George. How have you been?"

"Busy. Much too busy. In fact, that's enough small talk. Tell me about your ethics around confidentiality."

"Okay. Everything in a session is completely confidential, except for certain situations which I am mandated by law to report."

"What are those?"

"If you tell me about child, dependent adult, or senior abuse or neglect. If you are intent on harming yourself. If you speak of a plan to seriously harm a specific other person. And then there are special cases such as court-ordered counseling, clients involved in litigation who tell the court they're in therapy, and if a client signs a release of information form."

"So is there anything I've said that you can talk about?"

"No. I'm obliged not to. If I did, I could lose my license and even go to prison."

"Suppose I told you I was the second gunman in the Kennedy assassination?"

"I would keep that fact a secret."

"Really?"

"Absolutely. I take confidentiality very seriously."

"Suppose somebody offered you a million dollars?"

"It wouldn't matter." Clearly, Arundel wanted to tell me something but wouldn't go ahead until he felt satisfied that it was safe.

"Suppose you knew I was going to kill someone else?"

"I could only report it if you said who it was and I was convinced it was a serious threat. So you have something you want to tell me?"

"Perhaps. Are you saying that you'd stick to the rules even if it could cost a life?"

"Well I've never been in that situation, but if clients don't feel they can trust their therapists, we wouldn't be able to help much. So, yes, I'd certainly try to never break the rules."

It's been my experience that the revelations that follow this sort of probing are usually anti-climactic. One man's shameful confession is another man's 'is-that-all?'

"Trying isn't the same as doing something," Arundel pointed out.

"All right. I promise I won't divulge anything you tell me unless the law mandates that I must. Is that satisfactory?"

"Yes. I believe you."

He still appeared hesitant, but in a moment I realized what was actually transpiring. He was changing personalities and he had slipped into neutral for a moment while the gearshift disengaged and then reengaged.

"Let me introduce myself," the alter began in a flat, low-pitched voice that I seemed to hear as much in my gut as my ears. Immediately, it struck me that this time a client's hidden secret might be much more than anti-climactic. This voice was chillingly unemotional; in fact, 'aemotional' would be more accurate. It was the way a sentient robot would sound — an entity without a heart or a soul.

"My name is Credula. I am not human."

"No?"

"No. Can't you tell?"

Involuntarily, I nodded.

"Good. George assures me that I can be straightforward with you, that this meeting is necessary to convince you of certain things."

I nodded again. I couldn't summon speech. Credula was clearly an inhuman, no, non-human personality. All the factors that lent warmth, character, and even personal ego were filtered out by that awful voice. It was the way a sociopath would sound if you stripped away the artificial charm and scraped down to the bone.

I realized that in all my experiences of evil, pathology, or whatever you want to call it, I had only experienced various versions of dilute good. Maybe barely recognizable compassion and tiny pockets of caring passed as bottom of the barrel attributes, but there was a world of difference between what I'd known before and Credula. He embodied no hint of goodness; in fact evil and good seemed to be completely irrelevant concepts as I listened to my new client. Clearly, there was no part of him that operated within the realm in which they existed. I don't know how I knew all this, but I did.

"Thomas?"

"Uh... yes?"

"Do you remember the names of the victims who've been stabbed?"

Oh God. I couldn't make my mind translate the words into sense. There was brief relief in this self-induced brain damage, but then Credula spoke again.

"Thomas?"

"What?"

"The names of the dead."

"Hellman. I knew Denise Hellman."

"Hellman, Horn, Klovin, and DeVilliers. So far."

Oh my God. That 'so far' penetrated deep into me. I was too stunned to register anything else, but I knew something intense and awful was looming.

"They're devil names, Thomas. Devil names."

"Devil names?"

"Yes. It was necessary that they die."

"Necessary?"

Suddenly, meaning flooded me. This was the serial murderer. He'd been hiding inside Arundel and now he was sitting in front of me confessing and explaining the insanity that motivated him. And I was supposed to keep his secret? I realized I could be the next victim if I played my cards wrong.

"How do you know it was necessary?" I asked. My voice was surprisingly normal. The rest of me wasn't.

"You're an angel. There are devils too — well, demons, technically. It's almost time for the ultimate battle. The more we can identify and neutralize the opposition, the better chance mankind has to survive and flourish."

"I knew Denise. She was a lovely person."

"A cunning impersonation of a lovely person. I saw the demon leave the body. I know what I know."

"What about Dizzy? Why kill her?"

"I know no Dizzy."

"Desiree Farr — Zig-Zag's friend."

"I have no interest in her. Look at the name. Think."

"Someone does. I thought it was the same person who killed the others."

"You are mistaken."

"Why are you telling me this?"

"We need your cooperation. It has been determined that you are an archangel. Congratulations." The dead voice conveyed no emotion.

A reply popped into my head. "Does that mean I outrank you?"

"You will. Your role is pivotal."

I tried to think. Surely anything this crazy must incorporate some degree of inconsistent logic. I wanted a debate — a chance to refute Credula. Better yet, I wanted to push a button and make the whole thing go away.

"Why does telling me this make me more cooperative? That doesn't follow."

"We are changed by what we know, Thomas."

"I'm not changed — except for the additions of horror and disgust."

"You will be."

"So you know the future?" This tactic showed clients their magical thinking; a lot of irrational thought lay behind problem attitudes.

"Yes," Credula asserted.

So much for *that* antidote.

"How does that work? Do you read tea leaves? Does God tell you?"

He didn't reply. I tried something else.

"Why is all this happening here in Santa Cruz? Four devils, two angels that I know of — this isn't exactly a metropolis, is it?"

"The energy here is pure and strong. This is where it starts."

Performing the role of stooge for a string of Credula's oracular pronouncements wasn't helping. I remembered I was a therapist.

"Tell me more," I said.

"No."

"What are you feeling?"

No reply.

Even I knew that had been a stupid question. Obviously he — it — wasn't feeling anything and never would.

"So you're going to kill again?"

"I wish I could. Unfortunately, I am merely banishing demons from this plane, and yes, there are more to deal with."

"What do you really want from me? Right now, I mean."

"Nothing. Do you recall the various phenomena that followed George's announcement that you were an angel?"

"Yes."

"You will experience the new proof you seek in much the same manner."

"I'm not seeking anything."

"That isn't important. The work has been accomplished on the energetic level. It will manifest shortly on the physical."

"What do you mean 'on the energetic level'?"

"Our work here is more than words. Our energies have merged and danced and that which was in me has guided that which was in you."

"How did you do that?"

"You misunderstand. It is an impersonal process, different only in magnitude from what happens when any two people sit and talk."

"So in this sense, you're like a person."

"No. It is the very absence of a body and a personality that allows such intense energy to reside in me."

"What's that sitting in my chair, then? It looks like a body to me."

"It is George's. His lungs move the air, his tongue forms my words. We are a symbiosis, made possible by George's rare ability to step aside and allow others to be in him."

"It's a disorder, not a glorious achievement, for Christ's sake."

Credula didn't trouble himself to respond.

"And speaking of Christ," I continued, "where does he fit in? You seem to be working from a Christian paradigm, yet no one's mentioned Christ or even God so far."

"Christ? God? What do you mean?" George was back.

"George?"

"Yes?"

"What do you know about Credula?"

He smiled his creepy smile and was silent.

I remembered something he'd told me in one of our first sessions. "You said you were the number two man in an organization, right?"

He nodded. "You have a good memory."

"Is Credula number one?"

"Very good."

"Is the entire organization contained within you?"

"That's enough. I need to be somewhere else."

"This is craziness, George. Lethal craziness."

He stood and extended a hand. "Good luck."

We shook hands and then I called to him as he departed, but in a moment I was alone with my thoughts.

What a mess. My client was a homicidal maniac — no, make that a homicidal psychotic — and I was shackled by the law and my ethics. But how could I stand by as the body count mounted? Was my honor more important than human lives? If I was really working with Arundel — engaging in effective therapy of some kind — that would be different. In that case, I might be able to stop him by helping him to understand the wrongness of his actions — or Credula's actions, actually. But as it was, only a breach of confidence would protect the innocent.

I could make an anonymous phone call to the police. What was wrong with that idea? Well, if they didn't nab him, he'd probably know I ratted on him, and I wasn't sure that my archangel status would protect me.

I'd never heard of an actual criminal with multiple personality disorder, although I'd seen one on a lawyer show on television once. Certainly, killers like Son of Sam had obeyed voices, as paranoid schizophrenics tend to do, but kowtowing to an alter was somewhat different. The legal ramifications were unknown to me. Would they lock Arundel up in prison, execute him, or send him to an institution? My best guess was life in prison, but I realized that these concerns weren't a significant factor in my deliberations, which in turn led me to understand that I was engaged in decision-making.

The bottom line was that I could do something or not do something. What the something might be was another issue entirely. Postponing a decision was the same as doing nothing, although I was more drawn to this pseudo-solution than any other option.

There was a knock on my door at this point. Startled, I remembered that I was scheduled to see another client immediately following George Arundel. Vincent Perone had recently shaved off a sixteen-year-old beard and was having trouble adjusting to his new face. I experienced an adjustment of my own as I tried to focus on the remainder of my clients that afternoon.

Chapter 14

A friend suggested that if I was experiencing problems with a given client around a confidentiality issue, why not discuss it in session with my own therapist? After all, she was obliged to keep it confidential too, and I would be discussing myself, not the client per se. Didn't I have that prerogative?

I called the legal advisor for my professional association and asked about this possibility in the most general of terms. As long as I wasn't consulting, being supervised, or otherwise meeting my therapist as a fellow therapist, it was okay. In fact, he recommended I do it, both to cover my ass and to work through whatever I needed to in order to best help my client.

Roberta Chan wasn't Chinese, or even Asian. She was a slender sixty-six year old who had married Bob Chan, who was also a therapist. This therapist to therapist liaison was common in Santa Cruz. I reasoned that only another trained professional could withstand prolonged exposure to someone as screwed-up as a therapist, but a male colleague of mine, when drunk, would always proclaim that "only highly qualified individuals deserve the bliss of being with a wise partner." After a few more drinks he'd shout that "once you've had a therapist, you can never go back."

Roberta's office was in Aptos, an unincorporated town eight miles east of Santa Cruz. She was situated above a small, upscale restaurant, whose cook was a former client. I always felt surreptitious when I parked in the rear lot and climbed the back stairs, as though my ex-client would "catch" me needing therapy myself. It was irrational, especially since our paths had actually crossed once and all that had transpired was a friendly wave.

The interior of her office reflected her interest in folk art, especially pre-Columbian stone work from Latin America. Museum-quality sculpture crowded her shelves. Sometimes I wondered if it served less as a decorating scheme and more as a warehouse for the pieces that wouldn't fit in her house.

Her furniture was Danish modern, with blond woods and smooth black fabrics. Surprisingly, the two styles complemented each other, perhaps contrasting so drastically that the basic qualities of each were highlighted.

Roberta was an outstanding therapist, elevating her livelihood into an art form. She worked with a great deal of intuition, derived from a vast wealth of experience, having begun as a twenty-three year old back when the licensing requirements were nil.

"Hi Tom," she greeted. Her gray hair was piled elegantly in a loose bun on top of her head, exposing her long, thin ballerina's neck.

"Hello Roberta. Thanks for fitting me in."

"No problem. Have a seat."

When I was comfortable on her couch, I closed my eyes a moment to connect with myself. It was a ritual that aided me in the transition from therapist to client. Usually, after thirty seconds of this, all thoughts of technique, diagnosis, and self-consciousness disappeared.

"I'm confused," I began. "I'm seeing an MPD who's involved in wacky spiritual stuff and some very serious crimes and my ethics and morals are clashing."

"You mean you don't know how you want to respond?"

"Exactly. Ethically — legally — I promised and I'm bound by law to respect his confidentiality. Morally, I feel there's a higher priority to prevent further...uh... damage to the world. Am I being clear?"

"I think so. Because of the particulars, you think perhaps you should break confidentiality in this case. Is that it?"

"Yes. And the particulars are very compelling."

"How do you feel right now?"

"Scared. Nervous. Weak."

"Where are they?" She meant where was I feeling them in my body.

"The fear is a tightness in my chest, under my sternum. I'm nervous in my gut. It's tingling and feels strange. And I feel weak all over, especially in my arms."

"Your arms?"

"Yes. It's like if you told me to lift something, I don't think I could do it — even something light."

"Is what you have to lift light?"

"God, no. It's incredibly heavy." I didn't even know exactly what we were talking about but I knew it was heavy.

"So you can't lift it?"

"No, I can't." I felt tears welling up. "But I want to."

Roberta was silent.

"I feel I need to," I added.

"But you can't."

"No."

"Is it too big?"

"No, just too heavy. I could never budge it."

"And this is sad?"

"Yes. It hurts."

"Where?"

"In my head."

"Suppose you hired someone to lift it for you?" she asked.

"It wouldn't work. I have to do it myself."

"But you can't."

"Don't you think I know that?"

"You don't know anything," she declared.

"Yes I do!"

"No you don't. You don't know anything and you can't do anything."

"Yes I can. I know what to do."

"You don't."

"I do. I can tell the police!"

"I thought that was too heavy."

"What? Too heavy?"

"Yes."

"No, it's not too heavy. I can do it."

"Are you sure?"

"Yes."

I flipped into my therapist self, although I'd never done that before in a session with Roberta. I saw that she had been using my awareness of my body sensations to allow my unconscious to express itself, then she'd helped me intensify my feelings around that, and finally she'd successfully employed paradoxical intervention to let me defeat my own weakness. It was a seamless sequence that she'd probably never conceptualized in these terms, if at all.

"Where are you now?" she asked, noticing the shift.

"Up in my head. I'm dissecting your work."

"That sounds painful."

"Painful? No, I don't think so. For who?"

"For you. I've always thought that in dissection, the greater violence isn't to the corpse or the animal or whatever. It's to the dissector."

"I'm not sure I understand."

"That's all right."

"But I want to understand."

"Yes. You do."

"But you won't tell me?"

"No. What do you feel?"

"Frustrated. Annoyed."

"Are you still up in your head?"

I smiled. "No, you little sneak."

Roberta smiled back. "Are you going to tell the police?"

"Yes. I need to."

"Why?"

"Uh...I don't know. I just need to."

"Good. Good work. We're done."

"There's still a lot of time, actually."

"We're done."

She rose and opened the door for me.

"Okay, we're done," I conceded.

She nodded crisply.

I left.

Problem solved.

Maybe.

*   *   *   *   *

I made an anonymous call to the authorities from a pay phone at the bus station. Maybe I was being paranoid, but I planned to complete it in less than a minute to thwart them from tracing the call. On television, cops don't capture kidnappers if the phone conversation is sufficiently brief.

"Santa Cruz Police Department," the woman's voice answered.

"Listen closely. I know who the serial killer is. His name is George Arundel and he lives at 298 Branciforte Drive in town. That's A-R-U-N-D-E-L. Be careful. He's crazy."

"What is your name, sir?"

"Never mind."

"How do you know this?"

"He told me," I replied, and hung up.

*   *   *   *   *

I felt a great deal of relief following the disclosure. I had expected to pay a high psychic price for my behavior, perhaps feeling treacherous or unclean. But I didn't. I just felt lighter. I also experienced an urge to spend a few days in a nice motel somewhere far away, perhaps under an assumed name. However, my sense of responsibility to my clients restrained me.

I wondered how the police would proceed. They couldn't very well search his house based on one anonymous call. They would check to see if he had a criminal record and maybe follow him. Perhaps they'd just knock on his door and interview him. And how would Arundel respond to that? Would he switch to a disarmingly innocent personality? Even a trained detective would be deflected by that. Would he cease the killing when he knew he was under suspicion? That didn't sound like him. He'd probably try and convince me to do it.

Since I had no pending appointments with Arundel, my best source of feedback was Zig-Zag, although this was just as unethical as tipping off the police had been. The second step on the road to therapist Hell, however, proved to be much easier to take than the first.

I called her the following morning during a break between Mr. I-want-custody Jacobs and Ms. I-can't-face-turning-forty Carlyle.

"Hello," a woman's voice answered.

"I'd like to speak to Zig-Zag. I'm afraid I don't know her real name."

"That *is* my real name, Tom. My mom named me Zig-Zag Love Cassiel. 'Zig-zag love' was some idea of her's about lightning and love and God. I've never understood it."

"Have you ever thought of changing your name?"

"When I was a kid I went by Jennifer for a while and then I tried Zelda, but they didn't stick."

"I actually like Zig-Zag, but I know it's hard to have an unusual name."

"You're not kidding. So what can I do for you?"

"I was just wondering how you and George are doing. Have they set a trial date yet? Is he still bugging you about being an angel?"

"No and yes. Dizzy's lawyer asked for a continuance because she's going to be out of the country for a while."

"Dizzy?"

"No. Her lawyer. We can't go anywhere. We're out on bail — remember?"

"That's right. Speaking of unusual names, how is our friend Desiree?"

"She doesn't use that name — just Dizzy or her middle name. She's pretty upset right now to tell you the truth. She might have to serve some time."

"God, I hope not. What about you?"

"No chance. This is only the second time I've gotten caught. I haven't been doing this as long as some of the others."

"How about George?"

"Hell, I doubt he's ever even gotten a speeding ticket."

"I mean how's he doing?"

"Oh, I see. Well, I haven't seen him for a few days. He's probably fine, though. He isn't a real up and down kind of guy."

"No, I guess not." My phone call had just been rendered moot. Damn.

"How about you?" she asked. "What happened when you went back to the bookstore?"

"The book wasn't there any more and the owner said he never had it and the store was supposed to be closed the day we were there."

"It figures. I'll bet the dog was my dad."

"Really?"

"Oh, I don't know. Maybe. What do you think?"

"I don't know what to think any more," I told her. "I guess I still attribute most everything to George somehow. I'm very disturbed by the whole thing. That much I know."

"It must seem kinda creepy to you, huh?"

"Yes, it does. I can't integrate any of this into the rest of me. Do you know what I mean?"

"Yup. How about the mess I got you into with the police? How're you doing with that?"

"Not too bad, really. I'm glad they didn't mention me in that newspaper article, though. That could've been a real problem for me."

"Why? Don't you think crazy people care about the planet?"

"Of course they do, but they also care about a safe space with someone they trust. Some people don't trust lawbreakers. All things being equal, would you want to work with a big scary guy who's also just been arrested?"

"I getcha. You've got a point there. I wondered about you being so big before."

"I thought I was a 'motherfucking monster.' What's this 'big' thing?"

"Aw, come on. That was just a weird situation. I thought I was going to help George with some problem he was having and the next thing I know you're bringing up all that angel shit. I was kind of pissed-off."

"Speaking of which, are you still having more phenomena happen around the angel business?"

"Oh sure. Just yesterday I had a good one. But that kinda stuff happens all the time, right?"

"Not to me."

"You get used to it."

"I hope not. I hope it just stops."

"Well, anyway, thanks for calling."

"Oh sure. Take care."

It was a thoroughly dissatisfying conversation in which I'd learned nothing.

Over the next several days, though, I received three phone calls that were much richer sources of information.

The next day, Matthew Ferguson told my answering service that he'd be available that evening if I wished to speak with him. I'd tried phoning him after our meeting, but he had consistently failed to return my calls. After dinner, I sprawled in my oversized armchair and punched in the new number I'd been given.

"Hello?"

I recognized his voice immediately.

"This is Tom Dalziel."

"Hi Tom. Thanks for calling. I felt an urge to check in with you."

"I appreciate that. Whatever happened when you sang was a very profound experience that I don't really understand."

"Good. Trying to understand it would be a mistake," he told me.

"Why is that?"

"You would need to reduce it — to throw out the un-understandable parts. Some experiences aren't meant to be filtered through the mind."

"I do have that tendency."

"Don't we all. I also wanted to ask you about your invasion of angels. Has it continued?"

"Yes. If anything, it's worse. And I've found out it's mixed in with some alarming criminal activity."

"How peculiar."

"I've taken steps to resolve the problem, though."

"Good for you. So you no longer need my help?"

"I wouldn't say that. I still feel lost — in unfamiliar territory without a map or a guidebook."

"That's exactly it. You *are* operating in a realm where there are no maps. The trick is to get used to it so your anxiety doesn't interfere with noticing the rather subtle directional cues that are always there in the moment. Perhaps they're in the periphery, or maybe you know them by seeing parts of their shadows."

"Parts of their shadows? Isn't that a little too tenuous a relationship to use as a guideline?"

"What else have you got? Anything better?"

"No, not so far."

"We established last time that my telling you things wouldn't work. Books don't work. Your own sensory input has become suspect — am I right?"

"Yes."

"So forget about the obvious and pay attention to the subtle. That's the level of help I can offer. It doesn't challenge your general orientation or bludgeon you with my alien point of view. After all, this is your life and you're the one who's supposed to live it. It's like getting a friend to take a test at school for you. You really do cheat yourself — it's more than a cliché. You miss out on an opportunity to learn. At school the effects are usually minimal, but in your life you can't afford to sidestep your lessons. They're what life's all about, really."

"I understand your reasoning, but I *am* a therapist. I believe that people need help sometimes."

"Absolutely," Ferguson agreed. "But you don't."

"How do you know that?"

He didn't answer.

"Why should I believe you?"

Again there was silence on the line.

"Are you going to say anything?" I asked.

"Yes. Be open. That's it. I'm done."

"Well, okay. Thanks for calling."

"You're welcome. I'd say 'good luck' but I don't subscribe to the concept. Good-bye, Tom."

"Bye."

I hung up and headed back to the refrigerator for more dessert.

Chapter 15

Dizzy called the next morning. I had just finished trimming the gratuitous hair that had recently begun infesting my ears. It probably wasn't true but I felt as if I could hear more clearly as she launched into an elaborate apology.

"I was a real bitch the other day and it doesn't feel good at all now. I really appreciate what you've done for me — saving my life among other things. And I'm grateful. I really am. I always hate it when other women use this excuse, but the truth is it was PMS. My hormones were raging and I couldn't handle it and you paid the price. So I'm sorry and I hope you can forgive me."

"Well it's not like I hate you but to tell you the truth I'm affected by that kind of behavior. The bottom line is that it's hard for me to trust someone once they've attacked me without provocation. So on one level I feel forgiving, but I can't make the incident just disappear. If you said 'Let's go camping this weekend,' for example, I'd say 'No thanks.' Based on my experiences with you it would represent too big a risk. I might be trapped for two days in a tent with... well, I can't think of the right word but it might not be a laugh a minute. On the other hand if you said 'Why don't we go for a walk and see where we stand?' I'd say 'sure.'"

"Why don't we go for a walk and see where we stand?" she asked.

"Sure."

"You're a man of your word, Mr. Dalziel. Did you have somewhere in mind?"

"Me? You're the one that brought it up. I was only speaking hypothetically."

"Well hypothetically, then, where might you want to walk?"

"I have to admit that if any beautiful woman suggested Fall Creek Park, I'd probably be very agreeable to the idea. Hypothetically."

"Are you free next Saturday?" she asked.

"I am. Ten o'clock? I'll pick you up?"

"Great. I hope my cop likes the woods. So far the poor guy has had to frisk the pizza delivery boy and a squad of Mormons. Then last night I got him to drive me to the grocery store. I don't think he's been around black people much."

"Why do you say that?"

"He's really nervous around me."

"Maybe he's just shy."

"Maybe."

"Anyway, they may catch the killer by Saturday."

"Do you think so? Have you heard something?"

"They've got some new clues. I think they'll wrap it up soon."

"Great. So I'll see you at ten in the morning on Saturday?"

"Yes. Enjoy your day."

"You too."

*   *   *   *   *

The third phone call was from Credula. Its voice was even less human-sounding on the phone.

"Thomas," the voice declared impassively.

"Yes."

"Do you know who this is?"

"Yes."

"Don't use my name."

"Why not?"

"The police have taken an interest in a mutual friend of ours. Don't say his name."

"I understand." The hair on the back of my neck was standing up and my whole body was rigid with tension.

"We need to meet," Credula said.

"No."

"We need to meet," it repeated.

"No."

"You must be activated. The archangel within you is needed now."

"No."

"If you aren't activated properly, the forces of darkness will be able to use you for their own purposes."

"No."

"This world depends on you."

I decided not to answer. The 'no's' weren't getting the job done.

"You must not shirk your responsibilities. A world of darkness cannot be tolerated."

I hung up.

*   *   *   *   *

That night I dreamt that Dizzy was a black angel and George and Ferguson were white angels and I was a small gray dog trying to run away from all of them but they could fly so I couldn't get away no matter what I did. As a dog, I could only think simple thoughts and I was very conscious of smells. Dizzy smelled like a dentist's office and the others smelled like bread. I woke up panting.

I decided to see my therapist again and luckily she'd had a cancellation for the next evening.

Roberta looked tired; it was the first time I'd seen her this way.

"Hello, Tom," she greeted.

"Hi. Thanks for seeing me on such short notice again."

"I need the money. What's up?"

"Craziness. Two friends and myself are all having visions, synchronicities, and just plain unexplained events about angels. A client says I really am an angel — no, an archangel — and he's trying to get me involved in his delusions. Someone's trying to kill one of us but it doesn't seem to be the serial murderer — who I also know. I can't concentrate on my other clients. And I'm not sure about anything any more. What's real? What's crazy? What's spiritual? I don't know. I just don't know."

"That's quite a bundle. What do you want to work on first?"

"I don't know. Can't you be in charge?"

"No. You know it doesn't work that way."

"I guess the synchronicities, then. They're all over the place. I'm seeing connections between things that can't possibly be connected and other people verify they're really happening too. This has all the signs of an early psychosis but I'm not alone and I can provide real world evidence to support it all."

"So you've ruled out a psychotic break?"

"No. That's the problem. I haven't been able to rule out anything. I know how compelling an inner delusional world can be. And I know I have a tendency towards dissociation. So I can't just assume that my perceptions or my so-called evidence is real."

"So you think you're crazy?"

"No. I don't. I think it's the least likely alternative, actually. But obviously it's the scariest."

"Is it? With murderers in your life?"

"Yeah. It is. You know my history. I'm not saying the rest isn't hard too, but if I know what's what, I can deal."

"I'll level with you, Tom. I'm concerned. Have you thought of getting a diagnosis from someone more accustomed to working with this kind of thing?"

"A psychiatrist? No. And if you can't handle this, what kind of message is that? That I'm too screwed-up for a regular therapist? That isn't what I need to hear."

"I'm dying, Tom."

"What?!"

"I'm dying. I found out last week. I don't know if I'll have the time and energy to see this through."

"Jesus. Oh Jesus. What is it?"

"Bone cancer. I don't mind dying, but I'm scared to death of the pain. It'll be bad near the end."

"Roberta. What can I say?"

"Say you'll make an appointment with Jim Orsac. He's good, Tom. He can sort this out for you."

"Is this some kind of emotional extortion?"

"Yes."

"Really? You should be ashamed of yourself."

"I should, huh? Just do it. Make a dying old lady happy."

"All right. But only if you invite me to your funeral."

"You're a ghoul, Tom, but if I have to invite every Tom, Dick, and Harry in town, I guess I will. Is that it? Are you sure you don't want me to will you some artwork?"

"That'd be nice too. And I must say you have a lot of pep for a 'dying old lady.'"

"Aren't we breaking the frame enough without your vile accusations? Next you'll be telling me you want to go out on a date." She smiled as if to entice me.

"With a terminally ill grouch? Not likely."

"So shall we keep this banter going and avoid facing what's up for us?"

"Gee, when you say it like that it doesn't sound quite as fun any more."

"I'm just making explicit that which was implicit. It's what I do."

"Yeah, yeah. So where do we start? Don't bother answering; I already know. With my feelings. Let's see... I'm upset."

"Stomach gas? Indigestion?"

"You're so mean to me. All right...." I paused and contacted my root feeling. "I'm angry. You can't be there for me and I count on you — I've been counting on you for six years on and off and now you're abandoning me. I'm sorry but that's how I feel. I'm mad."

We worked on this for the rest of the session and concluded with a gentle hug.

Later that evening I cried myself to sleep. Roberta was precious to me; I would miss her terribly. Why was everyone dying all of a sudden?

*   *   *   *   *

I took the risk of calling one of the detectives working on the serial killings to see what I could find out about George.

"Any luck?" I asked.

"Maybe. We've got a suspect under surveillance and it may not be a coincidence that we've had no more murders for a while."

"You think it's him?"

"I don't know. He's an odd one but he hasn't got a record. We'll see."

"How'd you get onto him? The footprints?"

"No. In fact, his feet are wrong for it. We got an anonymous tip that we're still trying to track."

"What do you mean?"

"We've got the voice on tape. If we can find the guy, we'll know more."

I coughed and excused myself. How could I have forgotten to disguise my voice? Was that enough for them to find me? No. I knew it wasn't. But while they were monitoring George, would he contact me again, tying me into the case? With the recording, they could eventually prove I had been the caller. This was a career-ending possibility, but there was nothing I could do about it now so I ate ice cream.

I was beginning to understand more of my clients' behaviors as I found myself doing them. Got a problem? Eat. Facing a series of confounding experiences? Go into denial. I had always been familiar with depression, stuffing feelings, self-pity, and lots of other popular favorites. Lately, though, I'd begun filling in the blanks on my maladaptation resumé. Would it make me a better person? A better therapist? Crazy? Dead? God knew.

*   *   *   *   *

Jim Orsac returned my call the next evening. I had met him once or twice years before but he didn't remember me.

There are several schools of thought on how to conduct oneself during the first contact with a prospective client. Personally, since I wasn't interested in screening anyone out, I left the whole business to my phone service. At the opposite end of the spectrum, some therapists held extensive interrogations, even charging for their time.

Orsac fit somewhere in the middle. He wasn't concerned with the details of my problem, yet he obviously wanted to get a feel for who I was before he agreed to see me. Our conversation lasted about ten minutes and ranged from who'd referred me to what was my earliest memory as a child (falling off a stack of lumber and landing on my chin).

We made an appointment for a week from Friday, which was his first available slot, proving that Orsac had built a better practice than I had.

*   *   *   *   *

On the way to Dizzy's apartment on Saturday morning, I realized that I had no idea why I was getting together with her. True, she was beautiful, but if she invited me to sleep with her, I was fairly sure I'd turn her down. I didn't need the grief that accompanied the short-term pleasure. The angel paintings did hint of some sort of mystical connection, but once again what difference did they make in the real world? Was I still feeling protective of her? Not with her own personal cop following her everywhere. Did her environmental activities pique my interest? No. Was I just bored with my life and seeking distraction? Not even close. I finally decided that our interaction was unpredictable, and therefore intriguing. There was a certain tension to being with Dizzy. Would she be civil? Contentious? Appreciative? Funny? I had no idea what to expect. I'd experienced all of these traits at one time or another, but I had rarely understood why.

Anyway, for better or for worse, I found myself on Dizzy's doorstep with a small vague smile on my face. I was surprised that my inner process manifested itself in such a simple expression, but I guess the relationship between inner and outer was as reductionist as Ferguson had suggested.

Dizzy was beautiful, as usual, and the sight of her in worn jeans and a purple turtleneck sweater banished my musing.

"Hi big guy. Friends again?"

She reached out for a hug and I stepped forward into her arms. I wasn't prepared for the intense wave of lust that enveloped us both. It was all I could do to remain standing and my erection threatened to pierce the intervening layers of clothing. I was also dizzy, nauseated, and sweaty — all in about five seconds. In short, another novel experience had arrived to help trash my way of being. I broke away before I discovered what came next.

"Whew!" she exclaimed. "That was incredible. What happened?"

"I don't know. I've never felt anything like that. Well, maybe *like* that, but not *that*. Oh hell. You know what I mean."

"I sure do. Talk about chemistry. They could mix our energies together and make a new kind of bomb."

"Is that what it's about — energy mixing together?" I asked. That sounded a lot like what Credula had asserted, which scared me.

"Sure. Because of our karma or whatever, we each have a certain energy configuration and I guess when you get ours too close to one another, all hell breaks loose."

I found myself able to dismiss this simplistic New Age version of lust.

"Well," I replied. "We'd better get going."

"Okay. I'm ready. Let's roll."

So we did. Her cop followed us dutifully in what must have been his own car — a Honda station wagon.

Our route to the park traversed an assortment of small-scale ecosystems including a pine forest, dry scrubby meadows, stands of redwoods, and a narrow valley with a swift-running creek. Each encompassed a completely different combination of light, temperature, vegetation, topography, and wildlife. The stretches alongside the creek were my favorite. The sunlight was filtered down through the multitude of conifers that thrived on the steep hills bordering the creek. Everything was partially in the light and partially in the shadows. This lent a common context to the disparate elements of the setting that allowed the eye to capture directly the unity that was ordinarily available only as an intuition or a mental construct. As the creek itself raced through all this, its waters were always alongside us, yet always arriving and departing too. There were no boundaries between the creek's past, present, and future. Its length was seamless — all of a piece, all now.

In lieu of conversation, I was content to watch the various panoramas that presented themselves. As I guided the Volvo on the winding road, Dizzy was also silent. Eventually we reached the town of Felton and the entrance.

The dirt parking lot at the trailhead was composed of a strange sort of dirt. Most of the time it could best be described as dust, but in the rainy season it was transformed into deep gooey mud that sucked at car tires, shoes, or whatever else was handy, threatening to pull everything down into some messy underworld.

Today was a dust day so we waited for the dirty clouds to settle before leaving the car. It was warm at the trailhead but I knew that once we'd descended to Fall Creek itself I'd need a sweater, so I slung mine under my arm. At one time I'd experimented with the sweater-draped-over-my-shoulders look which in my case hinted of some terrible mutation experiment that had gone awry over in Italy. I'd also tried the sweater-tied-around-the-waist method but I always seemed to forget it was there until I sat down on something filthy.

The first part of the trail was downhill, which was actually harder on my knees than uphill. With each step, I had to catch all my weight, which made something in the joint pull and send pain up into my quadriceps muscles. Even with the aid of my cumbersome brace, I had to work hard to keep up with Dizzy, who hiked as though she could maintain her brisk pace indefinitely.

"I need to go slower," I finally told her.

"Oh I'm sorry. I forgot about your hurt knee. How's it doing?"

"I'll be fine if we go slow and maybe only as far as the lime kilns."

"Sure. We can rest there and talk a while. That sounds good."

Chapter 16

The lime kilns are old brick structures that were used to cook limestone to extract lime, which was widely used as an ingredient in mortar at the turn of the century. The three kilns are arranged linearly, sharing side walls and sporting small arched doorways. From the front, then, they resemble row-houses in some fairyland city peopled by gnomes. A path leads to the top of the brick walls, which no longer support roofs, and there are numerous perches up there. On the walls, I've always had the feeling I was visiting Mayan ruins.

After twenty minutes of walking, interspersed with pauses to observe banana slugs and birds, we reached our destination. By then, I was more than ready to shed my knee brace and reclaim my leg.

"It's great up here," Dizzy proclaimed once we'd settled in atop the wall.

"I love this spot," I agreed. "You know my favorite thing here?"

"What?"

"It's when a leaf falls and you watch it all the way down. I love the way it defines the space — makes you aware of the in between places in the woods."

"That's nice. I like that. It's kind of Zen, isn't it?"

"I don't know. Is it?"

"Sure. Everything's kind of Zen. If you're ever at a party and you don't know what to say, just say 'It's kind of Zen, isn't it?' and see what happens."

"Maybe I'll try it sometime."

"Another good one is 'Isn't this boring?' I think everything is at least partly Zen and partly boring. Anyway, even if it isn't either one, people tend to respond to that kind of thing."

I didn't have much interest in this subject but I managed a grunt while I watched a squirrel stare back at me.

"So what do you really think about angels, Tom?" Dizzy asked.

Her face was turned in profile but as I studied it she swiveled her head and caught my gaze full on. I was aware that she was suddenly very present, perhaps more than she wanted to be. Involuntarily my awareness blossomed into the moment and I experienced an intensity of sensory input and emotion that was almost too much to handle. My chest tightened for a moment before something in me adapted and I found myself breathing freely and deeply. An extraordinary calm asserted itself and despite the continued barrage of sensory information, my peace of mind was unassailable now. I felt as if I were Buddha.

"What's going on?" Dizzy asked. "What's happening?"

"No words," I replied. "New thing." I could hear that I was answering her in Tarzan language but I didn't care.

"Well, I'm here if you need me," she asserted, grabbing one of my meaty hands and pulling it over to rest on her thigh.

I peered out of my body at the intricate puzzle of the world before me. One thing was clear immediately. Everything out there fit together perfectly and we were a part of it too. I didn't know how it worked or how I knew but somehow I was aware that it was all working just the right way, including Arundel, the murders, and everything else. There was no sense of wrongness, problems, or worries. Nothing needed fixing or even demanded my attention.

And it was all so incredibly beautiful. Each square inch was a universe. Each plant, each rock, each cloud was an amazing creation which both stood on its own and fit sublimely into the whole. I felt that if I just sat and looked long enough I would become what I saw. It's hard to explain now but it was as if the delineations between things — where I left off and the rest of the world began, for example — were revealed as arbitrary constructs that could be transcended simply by understanding the oneness in which we all played our parts.

At the time, of course, I wasn't thinking about my state or what words could best describe it. I just was. That's really the most faithful description of that wonderful twenty minutes. I was.

My return to ordinary consciousness was abrupt. One moment I was one with the world, the next I was Tom with a sore knee sitting on a hard rock. Fortunately, the experience remained with me as a strong memory, softening the otherwise harsh contrast presented by my return to a normal state.

"I'm back," I announced.

"Wherever you were, it looked fun," Dizzy told me. "Your hand got really hot too."

"Hmm."

"Can you tell me about it?"

"No. I'm not ready to talk about it."

"Did you see an angel?" she asked.

I shook my head and shifted myself on the rock wall; my butt was killing me.

Then my ordinary consciousness began nibbling at my experience. As usual, it started with a plethora of questions. Was what happened related to my Heart experience with Ferguson? Was it just a coincidence that it happened with Dizzy? How was it connected to Arundel and all that? Did it validate the philosophy of naturalists such as Emerson? Was it less a statement about nature and more about me?

As I played with these questions, I was once again off in my own world and this time Dizzy was less patient.

"Hey!" she called as she poked me in the ribs. "Snap out of it, would you? We're supposed to be getting to know each other."

"Sorry." I returned my attention to Dizzy and our setting and was struck by how odd it felt to be sitting next to her on the kilns. For one thing I hadn't spent this much time with anyone black since my basketball days. There just weren't many African Americans in Santa Cruz and these few were generally so different than the guys I'd played with in college that they barely seemed black to me. Dizzy would've fit right in with the urban refugees that constantly out-jumped and out-mouthed me back when I was number seventeen.

Also, of course, sitting in the woods with a single woman was a rare event for a hermit such as myself. The fact that Dizzy was breathtakingly beautiful added to the surreal tenor of the context. I decided to share my general impression as a way to re-establish contact.

"Of course it's strange," she agreed. "You've been in Never-Neverland since we got here and now you're back."

"I'm sorry again, Dizzy. I was having some sort of transcendent experience that's never happened to me before."

"You've been hanging around with Zig-Zag too much," she told me. "That girl is the spaciest thing around. I wouldn't be surprised if she had something to do with the vision I had."

"She's told you who her dad was, right?"

"No. She never talks about her family or her childhood. Who was her dad — Billy Graham? The Pope?"

"Krishnanda."

"I've never heard of him. Was he an Indian?"

"Yes. A guru. She says she grew up with miracles happening all around her."

"That explains a lot. I wonder why she'd tell you but not me. I'm kind of hurt."

"I'm a therapist. She's not my client but people tend to tell me things. I guess they know they can trust me."

This, of course, was not exactly why Zig-Zag and I had spoken about her past.

"You mean they trust you not to tell other people? If that's it, you just blew it, didn't you?"

"I guess you're right. Oh well. That reminds me. I called the newspapers and the TV stations about your vision. I hope you don't mind."

"Hey, don't even joke about that. I feel crazy enough as it is. A friend of mine keeps telling me it's better to just forget it even happened since it could be the beginning of a breakdown. What do you think about that? Could I just be losing my grip?"

"It's possible. Lately, I've wondered that about myself too. But I wouldn't worry about it if I were you. It's not visions or religious beliefs that get people into trouble. It's how they react to them — do they think they're God or get too scared or anxious to function? That's the key thing and your life doesn't seem like it's been too disrupted."

"Yeah. You're right. It's not like I'm really freaking out. I'm just painting and that's how I always spend my free time anyway."

"You're really talented. Have you had any shows?"

This question triggered a long recitation of her history as an artist. I half-listened and half-watched the forest around us.

As a result, I spotted Arundel as he surreptitiously worked his way towards us, using redwood trees for cover. He wore camouflage raingear which must've been designed for a completely different kind of forest. Something about the particular combination of green and brown clashed horribly with the flora of the hillside below us. There was no sign of either of the cops — Dizzy's or Arundel's.

For a moment I froze, unable to think, then my adrenaline kicked in. We were in trouble. I wasn't armed and a serial killer was stalking us. Presumably he was after Dizzy but it was possible I was the target, based on my role as a stool pigeon. At any rate, Credula wasn't likely to leave witnesses hanging around, so what did it matter?

I spoke to Dizzy in a whisper. "There's a guy following us who might be the one that's after you. We need to get out of here."

She whispered back. "Where's my cop? Can't he deal with this guy?"

"I think he's out of the picture. Follow me."

I stood and walked quickly along the wall towards the back of the kilns, leaving my brace propped against a rock. Arundel was in a position to cut off our access to both trails that led to the parking lot, but as Dizzy hurried to follow me I discovered a narrow path winding back into the hills. We darted onto it, now that we were out of sight.

At first I was confident that our head start and our good luck finding the trail would save us. Then my knee gave out. A few minutes later, limping painfully as I maneuvered along the now rocky path, I discovered that we weren't exactly navigating through the hills either. We were in an old limestone quarry; it was probably the only dead-end topographical feature in the entire park and I'd found it on the first try.

"Shit," Dizzy commented as she realized why I'd stopped.

"We can go back or try to climb it," I said. "I don't suppose you're an experienced rock-climber by any chance."

"Actually I am, although I've never done any free-climbing. But you can't climb anything with that knee."

I gave it a try anyway but only ascended a few painful footholds before slipping and falling back onto the rocky ground.

At that point, I experienced an odd sensation as if someone had flipped down the on-off switch that controlled me, and then thrown it back up before I'd fully shut down. Later, I'd remember this as a key event in the sequence that followed.

"You're right," I answered. "You scoot up there and get some help. I'll play hide and seek and stall this guy."

"Maybe we could get by him if we double back off the trail."

"I don't think so." We turned and surveyed the scene behind us. "Look at how narrow the opening is. If it weren't for all these damn trees, we'd have noticed before."

"I guess you're right."

I slapped her on the back. "Get going. Hurry."

"All right." She gave me a kiss on the neck — as high as she could reach — and lithely scurried ahead.

I stumbled off the trail to find a hiding place. If I could confound my five-year-old nephew in a three-bedroom house, surely I could hold out for quite a while on the forested floor of this abandoned quarry. And if Arundel missed me on his way up the trail, I could try to limp back before he noticed his mistake.

All of this reasoning became moot. Arundel simply tracked me, following the obvious carnage a huge limping man created in an otherwise pristine environment. Within five minutes he stood a few feet from where I'd sequestered myself behind a monstrous redwood stump.

"The woman is gone," I called.

"I realize that," Credula intoned.

I shivered. That dead voice was worse than I remembered.

It continued. "I've told you we have no interest in her. I am here to speak to you."

I unfolded myself and rose; Credula moved laterally to stand facing me, perhaps six feet away.

"What do we need to talk about?" I asked. "There's no point in beating a dead horse."

"Unfortunately we are dealing with matters beyond mere death," I was told.

The creature's pronouncement terrified me. Up until this point it had still been a game. With the aid of adrenalin I'd responded to circumstances, trying to win. Now this ungodly entity faced me and I knew there could never be any winning against such a thing. Its eyes were beyond dead; clearly, they had never lived. Would I soon wish I hadn't either? A shiver started at the top of my skull and flashed down my spine.

"It is time," Credula continued. "You must declare yourself."

"As an angel, you mean?"

"Archangel. If you don't transform now, your energy will be used by the dark forces."

"The dark forces? Isn't that a little corny?" I don't know how I mustered the nerve to say this.

He stared into my eyes, ignoring my comment. I suddenly felt even more vulnerable. Basically, this was an ultimatum — you're either with us or you're against us. And I knew how Credula dealt with those he perceived to be against him.

"Okay, you're right," I said. "It *is* time. I hereby declare I'm an archangel. What happens now?"

"You die," he stated flatly. "The words are not enough. You must mean them."

He reached into his jacket pocket and I lurched away, trying to run. After two steps, a throwing knife whistled into the muscle mass behind my left shoulder. I went down hard, breaking my nose on a tree root. I could feel the bone splinter.

In a fog of blood and tears, I scrabbled and pivoted as Credula approached me cautiously, a large kitchen knife held low in his right hand. There was no time to think. Reaching backwards, I yanked the weapon out of my upper back. As Credula realized what I was doing, he lunged forward.

I threw instinctively and he took the knife in the throat, just below the Adam's apple.

His lunge became a fall but the large blade remained on an intercept course with my chest. My follow-through had rendered me completely vulnerable. I was a wide-open target. I wriggled and twisted sideways a millisecond before Credula stabbed me in the upper thigh. The knife shaft stuck — God it hurt — and he fell away, gurgling horribly from the wound in his windpipe. At that point I passed out.

Chapter 17

I awoke the following afternoon in intensive care, my wounds throbbing sharply with each heartbeat. The pain was both localized and diffuse. At the center of each of the two major traumas, a searing, piercing pain pulsed jagged waves through the surrounding tissue, which, in turn, ached as though someone had been pounding them with a sledgehammer. My nose was packed with cotton and bandaged; my face hurt terribly. Even breathing (through my mouth) was a problem. I felt as thoroughly bruised as I felt cut and the combination was overwhelming.

Gradually my eyes focused and I glimpsed the white-coated back of a male nurse across the equipment-filled room.

"Hey," I called weakly. "Hey. I need a pain pill."

He whirled and hurried over. "Welcome back, hero," he greeted. His smile annoyed me.

"I need a pill," I repeated.

"I can do better than that. Now just hold still while I send you something intravenously. That's it. There you go. Now...."

I was gone again, the flood of warmth banishing me back into blackness.

My next foray into consciousness was, unfortunately, more successful. When it became obvious to the young woman on duty that a dose of Demerol wasn't going to shut me up, she summoned my doctor.

The car accident that had scarred my face had also taught me a lot about hospitals. I now subscribed to the squeaky wheel school of receiving oil and I planned to negotiate my own painkiller schedule as well as discover exactly how seriously I was hurt.

Dr. Rodriguez was the most reasonable surgeon I'd ever met. If therapists are crazy, then doctors are arrogant, but Rodriguez displayed little of his profession's core trait.

"Certainly," was his response to my request to self-medicate. His assessment of my physical condition was lengthier but just as cooperative.

"You almost lost too much blood," he told me in a slightly accented soft voice. "It was close. And the smaller knife missed your heart by less than an inch. But actually it was the thigh wound that gave us the most trouble."

I was having trouble concentrating but I asked him to tell me more.

"We had to repair one of your adductor muscles which had been completely severed, as well as reroute a damaged artery, which is not an easy job. But I'm happy to say you're out of trouble."

"You mean I'm going to survive?"

"Exactly. And I think it unlikely that you'll walk with a limp or be permanently disabled in any other way. But we're keeping you here in I.C. for at least another day and you're looking at at least six months of rehab."

"Oh boy."

"I know your medical history, of course. From here on this should be a breeze compared to your post-accident recovery. I'm not even sure how you managed that one."

"Me neither."

"So get some rest. I'll leave instructions with the nursing staff concerning your medication."

"Wait a minute. What about Arundel? Is he dead?"

"I don't know anything about that."

"How can I find out?" I asked.

"The police want to talk to you, of course. But I think tomorrow will be soon enough."

"I can talk now."

"No. Rest. Doctor's orders."

For once I followed orders; I simply couldn't keep my eyes open any more.

*   *   *   *   *

The police chief himself visited me the next day and filled me in on things. He was an unlikely-looking middle-aged character, with curly red hair and black plastic glasses. His nose was squashed flat and his cheeks were concave, but his lips jutted forward as if they were trying to escape this face with which they didn't jibe. The overall effect was very busy, almost distracting. He told me to call him Fred.

"George Arundel is dead," Fred told me. "Ms. Farr and the park ranger — I can't recall his name offhand — rushed back after radioing in but he was deceased when they got there and you were in the process of bleeding to death, I gather."

"So I hear." Cruising on painkillers, I felt very detached from all that.

"The knife in your leg was definitely the murder weapon in the first four serial killings," he continued.

"What do you mean?"

"The knife blade and the wounds match and we found microscope fibers that correspond to some of the clothing the victims wore."

"No, no. What do you mean 'the first four killings'?"

"I'm afraid it hasn't stopped. Since you've been in here, we've had another murder — complete with seven stab wounds, but someone's using a much larger weapon now."

"How could that be?" This news diminished my recent ordeal and even made we wonder if I'd made a heinous error.

"Arundel was guilty," Fred assured me. "There's no question about that. It looks like we've either got a copycat killer or the deceased was working with someone else. We know he belonged to a Hindu cult — it's possible that another member has been ordered to continue the rampage."

'Rampage' struck me as a wildly inappropriate term for Credula's behavior, but I understood how it must appear to a police chief.

"I don't think he was working with anyone," I offered. "At least not outside himself."

"I don't understand."

"He was a multiple — one of his alters did the killing."

"Really? We didn't know that — which reminds me. When we're done talking, I want to send in a couple of detectives to question you. Do you feel up to it?"

"Sure." I suddenly thought of something important. "Who's dead?"

"I beg your pardon?"

"Who's the new victim?"

"Oh. A waiter named Robert Schatan."

"Shit. It's not a copycat. Somebody is carrying on Arundel's mission."

"Arundel's mission?" the chief echoed.

"He murdered people with 'devil names.' Hellman, Klovin, Schatan — I can't remember the other two."

"Devilliers and Horn. I can't believe we missed this. So it's probably some associate of Arundel's — someone in the same cult."

"I don't know about that, but Arundel believed that he'd been called upon to help the New Age begin by activating people with angel names and killing people with devil names."

"Activating?"

"I'm not sure what that means either. He said I was an angel, for example, but he never convinced me. He was still trying right before he went after me."

"Why would he try to kill someone he thought was an angel?"

"I wasn't cooperating. He said I would be used by 'the forces of darkness' if I didn't go ahead and become an angel."

"So he was insane?" the chief asked.

"That's not a term I'm comfortable with. Let's say he was deeply disturbed."

"Fine, fine. Disturbed, then. Let me get my men in here. We need to get on this right away."

"Sure."

It was a long, tedious afternoon, which I probably shouldn't have weathered in the condition I was in, but the idea that another maniac was on the loose restrained me from taking care of myself. Dr. Rodriguez, on the other hand, was firmly focused on my welfare when he arrived at four fifteen. He not only tossed the trio of policemen out of the intensive care unit, he gave them holy hell as well, cursing in English, Spanish, and something I'd never even heard before.

*   *   *   *   *

I felt semi-human the next morning and even better once they moved me into a private room. Not only was the brightly lit room filled with flowers and fruit baskets, but now I was entitled to solid meals and television. Until I could read, and I was still too doped-up to manage that, the remote control would be my best friend, except perhaps for whichever nurse emptied my bedpan.

I was rooting for the one who scooted in around two to tell me that virtually everyone on the planet was downstairs waiting to visit me. She was blue-eyed, blonde, and willowy. Her name was Susan.

"Well, Susan, what should we do?"

"I took the liberty of having them sign-in so you could decide who you wanted to see."

"That's great. Thank you."

It was an interesting list. All the major television networks were represented, as well as the news wires and several tabloids. On the personal side, Dizzy, Ferguson, and several clients who I barely wanted to see when they paid me were cooling their heels too. I told Susan to send Dizzy up and then have Ferguson visit a half-hour later. I further instructed her to thank my clients and tell them I'd be in touch, and to suggest to the media that they piss up a rope.

Susan actually giggled; I liked her even better than Fred.

Dizzy was a proverbial sight for sore eyes. She'd dressed up in a brown silk shirt and black slacks, which she tucked up under herself as she sat next to my bed.

"More scars, huh?" was her first remark.

"You just can't have enough," I told her.

"It's that whole Frankenstein thing. You should get some electrodes glued on your neck."

"Thanks. You really know how to cheer a guy up."

"Actually I do. But I don't know you that well yet and I don't think your door locks."

"That's more like it."

"So how're you feeling? Are you in pain?"

"What do you think? Of course I'm in pain," I replied. "My nose is killing me right now and my leg isn't too great either."

"I'm sorry. They said you almost died."

"I would've if you hadn't gotten back so quickly. Should I thank you or curse the day you were born? That's the question."

"Don't you think it's better to be alive?"

"I'm not sure right now. I guess so," I admitted. "But if I were dead I wouldn't have to wonder about things like this."

"That's true. Say, can I eat your fruit?"

"Sure. Go ahead."

Dizzy began foraging through the various baskets that littered my room.

"Here's one from your Aunt Dora," she informed me as she snared a small, perfectly-formed tangerine.

"Terrific."

"So why'd you think Arundel might be the guy?" she asked as she stood at the foot of the bed and peeled the fruit.

"He was a client of mine. He told me."

"Why didn't you turn him in then? You could've got us both killed."

"Confidentiality."

"Oh give me a break, huh? Like some principle is worth people's lives."

"You've got a point there," I responded. "I should've, I guess. I was covering my ass."

"It's too big to cover," Dizzy told me.

"You're so sweet. Let me tell you about my ass. It's a counterweight — think about it."

"That's disgusting."

"Thank you."

"You don't seem so hurt to me," she said.

"I've got raccoon eyes, a nose as big as the Ritz, multiple stab wounds, and I'm out of it on heavy-duty drugs. That's not good enough?"

"You only have two cuts. That's not multiple."

"Sure it is. More than one is multiple."

"No, more than two."

I just stared at her. I couldn't believe Dizzy was arguing about something so petty.

She finished her tangerine and began to peel a banana as she resumed sitting in the white plastic chair next to me.

"Anyway," she continued, "I still don't understand why Arundel was trying to kill me."

"I don't think he was."

"Wasn't he the one behind the tree that night?"

"Probably not. Say, listen, I forgot about those cops following you two. Arundel didn't kill them, did he?"

"No. He conked them on the head somehow. They're all right."

Just then Matthew Ferguson strode through the doorway, spied Dizzy, and halted.

"I'm sorry. I didn't know you had company," he apologized.

"No, no. Come on in," I replied. "Dizzy, this is the guru with a regular name — Matthew Ferguson."

"Hi," she greeted, standing to shake his hand. "I've heard of you."

"Hi right back at you," Ferguson responded. "I've heard of you too. My TV tells me that you're a 'rock-climbing savior' who might even play herself in an upcoming blockbuster TV movie. Is that right?"

She glanced at me sheepishly as she sat down. "Well, I might. I've been playing myself for years now. I've got the most experience."

Ferguson stood beside the bed watching both of us as she spoke. He was wearing a pleated yellow Mexican shirt, white cotton pants, and thong sandals. He reminded me of a Tijuana pimp for just a moment.

"How's the patient?" he asked me.

"I could be worse."

"That goes without saying. I could poke you in the eye, for example."

Dizzy glared at him. "You better be joking."

He smiled beatifically. "I'm a guru. We never say anything serious — just all this life and death crap."

She wasn't sure how to react, but I was beginning to appreciate the man. He consistently defied my expectations of how a spiritual leader should act, which I found refreshing.

"I hurt a lot," I complained.

"Physically?" Ferguson asked.

"Yes, of course."

"That's terrific. Physical pain is so much easier to bear than the other varieties."

"I guess you're right."

"I don't agree," Dizzy protested. "I think it can be the worst thing that's ever happened to you."

"What *is* pain?" Ferguson replied. "No — don't answer. I will. Pain is resistance — what we feel when we refuse to experience a sensation, a feeling, or whatever else exactly as it is."

"Look," Dizzy began in an aggressive tone of voice, "why don't you keep your philosophy to yourself? Nobody asked you."

"I asked me. Don't you remember?" He responded cheerily.

"That doesn't count."

"Why not?"

"It's obvious."

"Not to me," he told her.

"Hey," I interrupted. "Visit me. This is boring."

"Okay," Ferguson agreed. "So, Tom. How does it feel to have killed someone?"

Dizzy jumped in again. "What kind of a question is that?"

"I think 'incisive' would be an accurate description," he replied.

"I think 'horseshit' fits better," she told him. "Tom's a mess. He doesn't need guilt thrown at him on top of all the rest."

I decided to answer. "I don't feel guilty. It really was him or me. In fact I don't feel much of anything about it. I guess it'll hit me later."

"You just rest," Dizzy suggested, glaring at Ferguson.

"Isn't this hostility interesting?" he confided to me. "I think I know what it's about too."

"What?" I asked.

Dizzy continued her withering stare; if anything, it was even more fractious now.

"I think that a deeper part of her knows we are enemies," he answered.

"Enemies?" I echoed.

"Yes. Perhaps it's time to bring things out into the open. Dizzy?"

"What? What do you want now?"

"What name have you used most of your life — when you were growing up, in school and the like?"

She cocked her head, puzzled. "My middle name — Lucy."

"And what's your last name?"

"Farr. Why do you want to know?"

"Lucy Farr," he mused. As he continued to speak he lifted his yellow shirt and pulled an enormous bowie knife out of a leather scabbard that was strapped to his ribcage. "Say it fast and it sounds just like Lucifer, doesn't it?" He pointed the knife at me and Credula's voice issued from Ferguson's mouth. "Tom knows what this means. He has chosen to side with you and your kind."

I was too shocked and terrified to react. Dizzy stood up but Credula waggled the huge blade in her direction and she froze in place.

"Oh yes," the entity continued. "I still live. Did you think I did all my work through George? That killing him would kill me?"

I nodded dumbly. The back of my mouth was awash in bile; the front was bone dry. I tried to move. I couldn't. My bad leg was a dead weight, anchoring me to the bed.

"I am not alive," Credula continued. "I cannot die. I occupy an office — a role — not a physical space." He kept the weapon trained on Dizzy. "Are you ready to die, Demon?"

At this point, something gave way inside me. I can't explain it and it didn't match anything I'd ever read about, but it was definitely some kind of altered state. For one thing, everything began moving in slow motion — as though Credula and Dizzy were underwater. Also, instead of normal sounds, I only heard a high-pitched tone — sort of like a tuning fork, but less pure. I wasn't focused on all this, it was just the way I witnessed what came next.

As Credula slowly inched forward, holding the outsized blade low and in front of him, Dizzy reached down to her ankle and produced a throwing knife not unlike Arundel's. I was transfixed — a statue watching a film unfold on a screen. I saw Dizzy's mouth move in slow motion, yet I heard nothing but the constant tone. I tried to move and now I couldn't even swallow or blink. I tried to think and nothing happened.

Credula lunged forward and Dizzy danced away. With time slowed down, there was an awful grace to their movements — a defiance of physics that was both gloriously transcendent and horrifically primal.

Once more he stabbed forward and once more the black woman eluded him. This time as she moved she raised her much smaller knife and cocked it for throwing alongside her head.

Credula immediately charged her. Would she have time to throw? Did she even know how to?

There was nothing but time. The scene slowed down even more — was it me? — was it them? — and I watched as Dizzy's arm crept forward. Just before Credula reached her, the bowie knife extended, she released her blade and dove sideways. The knife was airborne for an eternity. As I watched I gradually became aware of a feeling that wasn't an emotion so much as a very visceral intuition. It was a sense of momentousness and profundity that I realized had been residing in me somewhere but was only now making itself known to the whole of me. Whether that knife struck its target or not *Mattered* with a capital 'M'. That I knew.

So I waited. And watched. And waited.

Finally the knife reached its destination, embedding itself in Credula's belly.

Time suddenly resumed its normal pace and what I observed next seemed to happen too fast to truly register.

Credula dropped to his knees and his bowie knife fell with a loud clatter onto the white linoleum floor. Dizzy scrambled and scooped it up, holding the heavy blade in two hands as she knelt in front of the stricken man. With a fast, powerful thrust she sank the ten inches of steel deep into his gut beside the smaller knife. Then she ripped upwards and blood and gore cascaded out of the gaping wound.

I couldn't believe my eyes. What was going on?

As Ferguson crumpled backwards onto the floor, Dizzy maintained her grip on the knife, which slid out of his lifeless torso dripping blood and God knows what. Then she calmly rose, turned, and began to approach me, the knife held high.

"Your turn," she announced.

I tried to shout but no sound came. I tried to move again but I was still.

Suddenly I saw Dizzy for who she really was. Horned, fanged, grossly misshapen, the demon she was reached forward with the blade.

I rose off the bed into the air. My heart was suddenly a pure white light and it carried me up and over the demon. As Dizzy whirled and snarled, I felt energy flood through me and I heard the high-pitched tone again — only ten times louder this time.

I knew now that Arundel had been right about everything and the lightness of my true being was an inexorable force that no entity could withstand. I knew that I had lived only to fight this fight, that Tom Dalziel was no more, that an archangel had claimed his birthright.

"Go," I commanded. "Return to the void from whence thou came." My lilting voice was the same pitch as the ubiquitous tone I'd been hearing.

"Fuck you," the demon growled, kicking Ferguson's body to one side and dragging itself forward.

The creature was a hideous amalgamation of raw tissue and spare parts, oozing pus from multitudinous sores, and blood from every natural orifice.

Since it was my nature, I loved the demon. I *was* Love. Love was both my process and my content. I knew that Love, Beauty, and Truth were all reflections of the same phenomenon — the perfect core reality that comprised everything — even the demon. Its very ugliness was perfect. Just as I was Love, it was itself — exactly the way it should be — hideous. The problem was that the demon was trespassing in a realm in which it had no legitimate business.

Quicker than I could react, the creature flung the huge weapon at me, which passed through the white light I had become and sunk into the wall behind me. I reached back and willed it into my hand. As the demon cowered and backed away, I apologized to Dizzy before destroying what had once been her body. Then I began stabbing.

When the police arrived I was still stabbing. Over and over I stabbed. Over and over and over.

Chapter 18

Why did it happen the way it did? Let's just say that everything happened so that this perfect moment right now could be just the way it is. Do you understand? It doesn't matter why penguins give each other rocks. It doesn't matter who died or that I am where I am now. The realm of cause and effect and logic is only meaningful in terms of how it serves the deeper purposes of the cosmos. And these purposes I cannot reveal. Not yet.

The police and the judicial system, of course, operate within certain parameters and therefore can only produce limited versions of the truth. Not only couldn't they comprehend the basic principles that guided me in my actions, but they also couldn't even assemble the physical evidence accurately.

So I was arrested and tried for both killings at the hospital, as though a man one day out of intensive care could've managed all that. It was ludicrous, really. Some of the so-called evidence insulted the intelligence of everyone concerned. I guess that man's need to generate a false sense of closure is more urgent than his quest for the what-isness of a given situation.

I've been in Napa for about three months now and my wounds have long since healed. I think of this place as a high-security warehouse to store people who have been deemed too dangerous to be allowed anywhere else. True, there are criminally insane inmates here, but I've also met three other angels and a man who can make himself invisible. Obviously, if you're beyond physical law, you threaten the power structure. And I for one know firsthand just what happens to serious threats to the cozy prevailing paradigm. We're locked away where our existence needn't be acknowledged and we're kept doped-up on old-fashioned anti-psychotics to render us more manageable. Zombies need fewer keepers, which makes the whole farce cheaper too. Fortunately I've developed several successful strategies to avoid ingesting my so-called 'medication.' By and large they monitor us by observing our behavior so if I imitate the characteristic thorazine listlessness of the others, it's assumed that I swallowed. No one in an asylum could control themselves, after all. Sometimes the ignorant assumptions of the powers-that-be can be twisted to work for you.

Yesterday afternoon they decided to let me receive my first visitor. With no advance notice, I was informed by a fat orderly that a young lady was waiting for me in another wing of the hospital. My escort waddled behind me, occasionally transmitting directions by tapping me on the shoulder as we navigated our way through a maze of long hallways. I shuffled convincingly and vacuously watched my feet as if they were an award-winning film — perhaps a documentary on why thorazine isn't the optimal drug for our Olympic athletes to cheat with.

Eventually we reached a lovely glassed-in courtyard which was being monitored by two nasty-looking, baton-wielding guards. Looking past them, I spotted my visitor sitting in the sun on a lacquered wooden bench.

Zig-Zag wore her usual overalls and also sported a red baseball cap which gleamed in the bright sunlight as if it were brand new. She was so small I wanted to cry, but then I was struck by her beauty so I smiled.

When I'd maneuvered myself closer to where she waited, she smiled back uncertainly. I lowered myself next to her, leaving the kind of space between us that someone needed when she thought she was sharing a bench with an insane killer.

"How's it going?" Zig-Zag asked, her voice betraying her fear.

"It's very dull here, actually. But I'm fine. I really appreciate your coming." I spoke calmly and soothingly.

"I wasn't sure I wanted to but now that I'm here I'm glad I did." She managed another small, slightly more authentic smile.

"I know it's scary to visit someplace like this. I used to have to do it for my job."

"It's ironic, isn't it?" she offered.

"Yes. But you know, they have a whole ward of ex-therapists," I told her.

"Really?"

"No, not really. That was just what we therapists call an icebreaker."

"We other people call it that too." She folded her hands together and glanced down. She was working herself up to something. "Tom? Can I ask you something?"

"Go ahead." So far I was pleased with my I'm-still-just-regular-old-Tom act.

"Do you understand that you're crazy? That you killed George and Ferguson and Dizzy because you're crazy?"

"First of all, I'm not crazy. I've been through some severe trauma and I'm not the same man you met that day in my office, but I'm not crazy. Secondly, I didn't understand who George really was so I foolishly resisted him, which eventually led to my defending myself when he attacked me. This was wrong and I admit it. But Dizzy killed Ferguson. And when I killed Dizzy, she was already dead."

"That doesn't make sense. Don't you see?" She was very agitated, which attracted the attention of the nearest guard. Surely this mercenary wannabee didn't subdue visitors if they became too rowdy?

"It's just hard to explain," I replied, winking at the guard. He probably thought I was making a pass at him.

Suddenly, deep inside me, something gave way again and I was shunted to the side of myself. I could see and hear but it was as though it were happening at a great distance. I couldn't seem to do or say anything. My initiative had been completely replaced by a radical form of passivity. And I was calm. You would've thought I'd be upset or even panicked, but I wasn't. There was a sense of rightness to the experience — that it was natural and appropriate.

Then my mouth opened and Credula spoke.

"Listen carefully, Zig-Zag. I am the same entity that worked through George. I am not Tom. My name is Credula."

"This is *really* crazy. Can't you hear yourself?"

I could. But Credula continued.

"Tom is now an archangel. He has made the transition from the physical to the subtle which is also required of you. George spoke truly to you. You are an angel and you are needed."

"Stop it, Tom. This is giving me the creeps."

She shuddered and I remembered what it had felt like to first hear that eerie, inhuman voice.

Hearing it now was different. We were members of the same team and I welcomed him — it — in my head or wherever it was.

"You must fulfill your destiny," Credula told her. "You must become who you are."

"I'm getting out of here," she announced, springing to her feet.

Credula was gone then and I resumed control of my body. "Wait," I called as Tom.

The guard glared at me, defying me to chase her and get my ass kicked. I remained seated on the wooden bench and watched her leave. Just before she turned a corner and passed out of sight, I saw golden wings sprout from her back and soar over her small, slim body.

She was going to be a hell of an angel one of these days.

*   *   *   *   *

I haven't seen — felt? — Credula again but it doesn't matter. The important thing is that I don't try to reduce or compress myself in order to fit back into the Tom Dalziel husk that I once inhabited in ignorance.

This is vital. I must be ready when the change time comes. I yearn for the moment when the light will once again carry me airborne. I yearn for the total transformation of our depraved world.

I know who I am.

I know what I know.

I have seen the demon leave the body.

Chapter 19

I woke up at the foot of a wall of limestone, completely bewildered. Where was the institution, the guards? How did I come to be outdoors, somewhere in the woods? Had I blacked-out, escaped — was I dreaming? Even with everything else that had happened — or had seemed to happen? — I felt the most lost, the most thoroughly confused at that moment.

Then Dizzy's voice cut through the internal fog. She was dead, I knew, but from somewhere up above me I distinctly heard her call "Tom! I don't know if you can hear me or not but I'll be back soon with help. Hang on!"

I glanced up, my head throbbing with nauseating pain. The rock cliff that loomed ahead of me was familiar now. I was back in Fall Creek behind the lime kilns and suddenly the true memories flooded in.

We had decided to climb our way out — both of us — and I had fallen. Everything else I thought I'd experienced had been generated by my subliminal mind while I'd been unconscious. I'd read of such phenomena, but the textbook descriptions of the experience in no way captured its amazing verisimilitude — the details, the emotional textures, the sense of tangible reality. Consequently, the process of reawakening evoked a surreal disorientation and a momentous sense of loss even as I knew that Arundel was probably stalking me and might stumble onto me momentarily.

All the feelings, all the sensory input, all the insights and realizations that accompanied my unconscious version of future events — all of this had been instantly transformed, violently yanked from the "it happened" category and tossed into a new "who knows what it means?" circular file. For that matter, if the dream/vision had fooled me so thoroughly, how could I be certain that what I believed to be my current waking reality was authentic? What was actually happening? Was it another convincing dream? Could I trust myself to know — or even find out?

I had to admit that being handed the opportunity to create a new outcome that didn't entail additional murders or a permanent stay in the Napa State Hospital was appealing. On the other hand, I survived the fabricated account. Was I about to die in this one?

"Tom!" Arundel's professional voice bellowed. "Don't be frightened. It's me."

I struggled to my knees, neither of which was functioning properly, and tried to stand. Dizziness and pain pitched me to the rocky ground, where I broke my fall, and possibly my wrist, with a spastic flounce of my left arm.

"I saw you fall," Arundel called from slightly closer. "I only want to help."

Using my good arm, I levered myself onto my back and wriggled towards a grove of acacia trees. If I found a good hiding place, perhaps Dizzy would return with help before he discovered me.

This thought triggered an episode of potent déjà vu and I remembered that hiding hadn't worked last time. Should I try something else? Wait a minute, I told myself, there wasn't any last time. Nonetheless, I transferred my energy into gathering good-sized rocks, filling my pockets with the only available weapons.

"Ah, there you are," Arundel announced, stepping into the small clearing where I lay. "Are you badly hurt?"

"Yes." My voice was hoarse and shaky.

"Is there anything I can do?" he asked as he strode forward in his ridiculous camouflage outfit.

"Go away," I told him. "Go shopping for clothes." Talking made my head pound more and for the first time I was aware of blood dripping down the back of my neck.

"I can't do that, Tom," he replied. "We have something we need to discuss, don't we?"

I managed to sit up, which gave me the capacity to hurl my rocks if I needed to. Arundel squatted down a few feet away and then a ripple spread across his large pink face, beginning at his chin and working its way up. The new demeanor wasn't

Credula's or anyone else's I recognized. Arundel was gone, though. That was clear.

"Hello, Tom," a low smooth voice began. "My name isn't important. What you need to know is that I am the being who acts as the gatekeeper between this world and that which transcends it. As such I hold a meta-perspective in relation to Credula and I have consulted others who have access to these higher levels as well. We've arrived at a compromise."

"A compromise?" It was difficult to assimilate any of this.

"Yes. Although the timing involved here is delicate, we are willing to accommodate a schedule change which will give you more time to accustom yourself to your role. You are simply too important to this operation to squander needlessly."

"What about Credula?"

"I've already spoken with him — or should I say *it?* — and he is cooperative. You must understand that Credula was constructed to perform required tasks — no more and no less. He has no free will. In that sense, he is neither a person nor a personality."

"And that's a good thing? Someone did this on purpose?"

"Oh yes. We could never let a human soul kill on our behalf. The karmic retribution would constitute too great a burden."

"Oh."

"Individuals with multiple personalities are in a holy state. Their alters perform vital spiritual tasks for the good of all, although they are usually not aware of this."

My mind was blank and I simply stared dumbly at Arundel/Whoever. His features implied kindness and warmth, especially his eyes, yet something behind them was unyielding. It was as if he was one sort of being up to a particular threshold and then someone much tougher past it.

"True compassion is utterly ruthless," he told me as if he had read my thoughts. "It's 'tough love' times infinity."

"That's counter-intuitive," I managed to reply.

"Intuition is capable of evolution. If you become mired in the as-is Tom Dalziel mode, nothing beyond your current understanding will ever make sense to you. That would be a tragedy."

"What's so special about me?"

He smiled a gentle smile. "Right now, nothing. I confess I expected more. However, when you transform, all the qualities of an angel will begin to take root in the fertile manure that sits before me."

"Thanks a lot." I paused and remembered how it felt in my reverie to become angelic. As I formed a question, the entity in Arundel anticipated me again.

"It will not be exactly as you have imagined it," he told me. "Now I must go. George's body will be in hiding for a time and you will be on your own. Live your life and do what you are drawn to do. Even in the matter of the life or death of a species, an attachment to outcome is unhealthy. Que sera, sera. Adieu."

"Wait a minute," I tried, but he was gone. He moved with a casual agility that Arundel himself had never demonstrated.

I lay down again and waited to be rescued, which was about as energetic an activity as I was capable of mustering. The recent vision/dream returned to the foreground of my consciousness, shouldering aside the new being's information, as well as my pain.

I was struck again by the lifelike quality of the experience; it had been truly astounding. Except for the intial sensation of being switched off and on, the experience consistently generated the trappings of reality — or whatever I thought was most real, anyway. The images were just as intense, the colors as bright, and the emotions as deep. This compelling montage, in turn, generated impressions and moods in the same manner that waking life did. Once again I had to marvel at the sheer inventiveness of the human psyche, much as I had upon first confronting MPD.

Gradually my thoughts became more stuporific until I couldn't focus on anything beyond my physical pain. By the time Dizzy arrived with a park ranger, I was basically an inert, bloody mess. In a way it was a relief not to be able to think, but by the time the ambulance guys and the police hiked in I was thoroughly ready to be hauled off to anywhere that provided drugs.

They loaded me onto a stretcher while I told the sheriff's deputy about Arundel. One ambulance guy complained that I was so heavy it was as though I had rocks in my pocket, which, of course, I still did. I confessed, and since I was too exhausted to explain more than the essential details, the older of the two men called me a "weisenheimer." The other one said I "didn't need rocks to be a motherfucker of a load." I couldn't argue with either of these assessments.

With every shift or jounce on the trail or in the crowded ambulance, my head hurt like hell. I realized that I could have sustained very serious damage and I remembered reading about someone who'd suddenly dropped dead two days after a seemingly minor skull injury. I may have weathered Arundel for now, but my survival was still in question, and I was scared.

Chapter 20

The hospital was quite different than I had envisioned it in my dream. For one thing, although it was run by a Dominican order, I had secularized the interior, eliminating the numerous crosses and other Catholic motifs. In my vision/dream, too, the lobby was half as spacious as in real life, while the rooms were much more opulent. It was close on the paintings — flowers and landscapes — and dead on regarding the food — totally unappetizing.

Since I didn't pass out again, I was all too present for every bit of the painful examination, wound cleaning, stitching, and bandaging procedures. My doctor was young and his bedside manner needed work. Mostly he discussed his recent trip to Bali with particular emphasis on his dining choices and just how efficiently he was able to digest his food. At one point, a deputy sauntered into the emergency room cubicle to tell me that Arundel had gotten away and the surveillance cops had been drugged but were okay. For these two minutes, at least, I was able to distract myself from the pain.

My wrist wasn't broken — just sprained — but my good knee was no longer good and would probably require surgery eventually. The concussion I'd endured prompted the young gourmand to remand me to an overnight hospital stay for "observation." As far as I could tell, this translated to "for no particular reason."

My semi-private room contained an unpleasant surprise in addition to the usual negatives — fluorescent lighting, sterile decor, antiseptic smell, etc. The unpleasant surprise was named Jack.

Jack was a twenty-eight-year-old patient on a hunger strike for animal rights. He was facing imminent kidney failure and a court had ordered his hospitalization to ensure he received intravenous fluids. Physically, my roommate was a stick insect, with bones protruding where I hadn't known there were bones. His deep-set dark eyes were surrounded by inky black circles and his large nose jutted out defiantly as if to dissociate itself from the deteriorating body to which it was attached. Jack's long brown hair was his only lively feature, although I knew perfectly well that hair was actually inorganic.

Although his voice was weak and soft, Jack seemed to enjoy using it. After a half-hour of complaining about most everything, an hour treatise on his inter-disciplinary major in college — the physics of literature — and a recitation of his favorite poem, he decided to confide in me.

"This isn't really a protest," Jack told me.

"How's that?"

"I know they won't stop what they're doing because of it. The world doesn't work that way."

"Then what are you doing?" I asked.

"This is an elegant suicide — a way of creating meaning out of a meaningless life."

His explanation was obviously rehearsed, yet I sensed that he hadn't previously told anyone. What was it about me? Did these people have radar? Was I wearing a sign or something?

"Why me?" I finally asked.

"Well, we're in the same boat," Jack answered.

"In the hospital, you mean?"

"Dying."

"I'm not dying."

"Sure you are. Denial is a crutch — toss it away."

"I mean I plan on dying eventually and it's okay with me, but it's not likely to happen right this minute."

"Aren't you the head injury?" he asked.

"Yes."

"Well?"

"Well what?" I was becoming quite annoyed.

"Serious head injuries are usually fatal," he told me.

"This isn't that serious."

"Sure it is. You're doomed."

"Jack?"

"Yes."

"Shut up."

"Okay."

And he did, too. For a while. Why he wasn't too depleted to talk was a mystery to me. Like an old man who'd given himself permission to say whatever the hell he pleased, Jack spouted off relentlessly, only curbing himself when I directly ordered him to shut up. At one point I wondered if he wasn't part of the "observation" team — planted as a psychological stressor to test my responses. I decided that doctors lacked the requisite imagination to concoct such elaborate cruelty.

I was allowed visitors but I received none. I was very disappointed. Where were the friends I'd always intended to cultivate? Why hadn't Dizzy or Zig-Zag put in appearances? If I'd ever truly needed support — a boost from people close to me — it was now. I hurt and I stewed and I pondered while Jack droned on and on in the background. If I'd been dying, would I have died alone, staring at a blank white ceiling while strangers wearing nametags scurried around my bed?

*   *   *   *   *

My apartment was no better. After the unpleasant night in the hospital, I expected to receive some sort of emotional nourishment from my return to my own space. At the least I anticipated temporary relief from my bleak mood. A ticker-tape parade would've been fine too. All I encountered was more angst.

Of the five clients I'd stood up during my internment, only one even left a message on my machine to complain. The local newspaper ran a front-page story on me, but of the array of colleagues, friends, and family who surely must've heard or read about the incident by now, only two called — and one of them was a senile aunt who believed I was still eight years old and wanted to know what kind of toy to buy me so I'd feel like her "itty-bitty honey-bunny" again.

There's nothing like high drama to provide a new perspective on the mundane. My mundane was very mundane,

I realized. Without the ongoing invasion of all the craziness, I basically ate, slept, read, walked, and saw clients. What kind of life was that? I chose it, I could see now, to try to guarantee that nothing drastic would disrupt my supposed peace of mind, which I now perceived to be a fear-based sham mentality. Recent events certainly shattered the long-held myth that I could elude the intensity I feared. Why construct a boring life if it can't even keep you safe? All the tumultuousness — my head injury serving as the final straw — had cracked open the "my-life-makes-sense" facade. It didn't; it was that simple. I hardly had a life, let alone something sensible.

So what did I need to do to get one? This was an approach I often employed with confused clients. On a process level, clearly, I needed to summon courage, break my pattern, and attempt something new. In terms of content, I was less sure. Should I actively seek friends, chase Dizzy, join the chess club, ascend to angelhood, or eat out more? This was the spectrum of ideas that surfaced first. Then I conceived of warning or protecting other devil-named people, buying a sports car, placing a personal ad, volunteering at the homeless shelter, and flying to India. My attraction or repulsion to all of these plans seemed to be based solely on how much they scared me. Thus, eating out was my favorite, followed by purchasing a sports car. I was struck at this point by how unsophisticated my internal dialogue had become. Where was the keen psychological analyst who had aided so many poor souls? Would I continue to uphold the rich Dalziel family tradition of living in our heads — identifying ourselves as our thoughts? It wasn't necessarily my favorite piece of early conditioning but the syndrome was a cornerstone to my self-esteem and my career. I pictured myself repeatedly asking clients if they were scared of engaging in ordinary activities. Perhaps it was the Gomer Pyle voice I imagined employing, but the intervention seemed to lack a certain *je ne sais quoi*.

The surreal feeling that had coalesced in me upon awakening from my dream/vision now returned. Once again I wasn't at all certain of what was real, but this time in an internal sense. Was I who I thought I was? My identity now seemed to be an arbitrary scaffold that had been erected in front of god knows what. The possibilities ranged from a substantial building to a vacant lot. My images of potential vacant lots varied a great deal; I imagined virgin grassland, sandlot baseball fields, and bombed-out rubble. The buildings were configured in a melange of styles, and included banks, houses, restaurants, and even public restrooms.

My few insights were like small, random holes in the scaffolding, enabling me to peer through and beyond, yet that uncharted territory was nothing but a foggy blankness upon which I projected my theories. Perhaps that's who I am, I thought — a foggy blank guy. Whoopee.

Chapter 21

I drank myself to sleep that night, the first time in many years, and I woke up feeling as though I'd been beaten with a two by four. The jeans and blue chamois shirt I'd slept in seemed to be bruised and battered as well, and I was hesitant to brave even the anemic spray of my drought-conscious showerhead.

Coffee helped, as did a liberal slathering of Ben Gay on my knees, wrist, shoulder, and ribs. I smelled like a colossal cough drop but the chemical warmth was a blissful substitute for the jangling pain. I wished I could immerse my entire head in a bucket of Ben Gay, but I knew my scalp wound would scream at me if I tried it. I settled for aspirin.

After an hour of daytime television, jabbing the remote channel changer every few seconds in the manner that all my female clients lamented, the phone rang. An unfamiliar voice — growly and uneducated — asked if I was me. I wasn't sure anymore, but I decided to answer yes since I was, at least, probably more me than anyone else was.

"I've got Desdemona and the little one who calls herself Zig-Zag. If you don't do exactly as I say, they're dead meat."

"Dead meat?"

"Fuckin' A."

I couldn't think of anything to say.

"Are you there?" he asked.

"Yes."

"So I'm gonna call back later and you're gonna do what I say — right?"

"Right. Except how do I know you really have them?" My brain was returning to active service.

"Hold on," the voice replied. "I'll go get the one that doesn't kick."

I expected Zig-Zag but I got Dizzy.

"This guy isn't George Arundel," she blurted out before she was cut off.

"Satisfied?" the voice asked.

"It's her," I agreed.

He hung up.

Before I could work out any of the implications of the call or even how I felt, the phone rang again.

"Tom? It's George. The girls are missing." His voice actually conveyed emotion; he was scared.

"They've been kidnapped," I informed him.

"By whom?"

"Not you, apparently."

"Not me?" Arundel was puzzled and a bit defensive.

"That's right. That's all I know. Instead of five billion suspects, there's only four billion, nine hundred and ninety-nine million."

"This is terrible. Was there a ransom demand?" he asked.

"Why would there be? I don't have money."

"I do. Quite a lot. And Zee is like a daughter to me."

"The guy said he'd call again later."

"What guy? The kidnapper called you?"

"Yes."

"Why?"

"I don't know. Maybe he couldn't get hold of you — you're on the lam, right? Anyway, I'd better get off the line and call the cops."

"No cops. We can't risk it." The professional voice was adamant.

"Wait a minute. What's this 'we' business?" I protested.

"We're in this together, Tom."

"No, we're not."

"We can't let a minor disagreement interfere with the welfare of our friends."

"A minor disagreement? Multiple murders? You think that killing people constitutes a 'minor disagreement,' George?"

"Well, I may or may not have actually killed anyone," he answered.

"What do you mean?"

"Exactly what I said. It's open to question."

"And what does *that* mean? I'm not in the mood for your games, Arundel."

"It's not a game, Tom, but I don't think arguing would serve either of us. Why don't we talk later, after you receive your next call from the kidnapper? In the meantime, please don't contact the authorities. You could be risking lives before you have all the facts in hand."

"I'll think about it," I answered, and said good-bye.

So there I was in my friendless apartment, still in a great deal of physical pain, with far more new information than I could readily assimilate. *Would* contacting the police be dangerous? Should I stay home to receive the next call from the kidnapper? What would he want? Money from Arundel? And what was this business about *maybe* not killing people? Was George running another scam to manipulate me? What else could it be? As usual, throughout all the craziness, I was accumulating questions a lot faster than I was able to stumble onto answers.

I decided to eat. Then I decided to urinate. Then I scratched my leg. Then I ate again. As an overall strategy, this attention to the physical didn't accomplish much. Finally I sat on the couch and pondered the situation in greater depth.

Not much of that session was worth reporting, but I did remember that I'd promised the police that if Arundel called, I'd let them know. Also, while at the hospital, I'd vowed to myself that I'd only participate further in the whole scary mess in my capacity as a therapist. So how did I respond to rediscovering these pledges? I threw them out the window and called Matthew Ferguson.

At first it was impossible to relinquish a powerful residual connotation of danger stemming from my memories of Ferguson from my vision. Gradually, though, after some preliminary chit-chat, I felt ready to trust him again, and poured out a detailed update. His feedback seemed to confirm the wisdom of my decision to seek expert help.

"I'm glad I'm not you," he began in his beautiful voice. "But let me ask you this. So you think Arundel is a murderer?"

"Yes."

"Do you think he sincerely cares about the women's well-being?"

"In his way, yes." I shifted my weight uncomfortably. Even sitting hurt.

"Do you have any idea who the kidnapper might be?"

"No. None at all."

"Do you trust the police?" he asked.

"Yes."

"Have you enjoyed your involvement in this affair?"

"Hell no. It's been deeply disturbing, terrifying, and... well, sickening."

"Not your favorite feelings, huh?"

"Hardly."

"Well here's another question," Ferguson announced. "This one might be a little harder to answer. Why are you here?"

"In Santa Cruz?"

"I'm a guru, not a travel agent, Tom. Why are you here on this planet, in that body?"

"Because that's the deal," I answered without a great deal of thought.

"What deal?"

"I mean that's the way it works."

"How do you know?"

"Because that's the way it is."

"How do you know?" he asked again.

"My senses, my brain... books."

"So the world is the way it seems to you?"

"Of course not. I'm not saying I've got everything figured out, but what else have I got to go by?"

"That's a good question, but I'm going to sidestep it for the moment and ask you this. Why are things the way they are? For what purpose?"

"I don't know."

"Guess," he prompted.

"Maybe there isn't a purpose. Maybe God likes suffering. Maybe we're here to learn. Maybe it's all a big joke. I really don't know and to tell you the truth I'm getting tired of being interrogated." Perhaps I would've been more patient if my head and wrist weren't throbbing so much.

"Good," Ferguson responded. "Now pick one of those maybes — the one you believe the most."

"We're here to learn. That matches my life experience the closest, I guess."

"Okay, so what's the curriculum in your situation and how can you best learn it? That becomes the key question here. Will your studies on the planet be best advanced by calling the police, working with Arundel, or what?"

"How can I know that?" I asked.

"Take your best guess again."

"It's complicated. Calling the cops supports what I've learned about boundaries and taking care of myself in the simple sense. But it doesn't break new ground or truly challenge me. Obviously, partnering up with a psychotic murderer represents the biggest challenge, but that doesn't mean it's necessarily the best thing to do. I know from my work that if people are presented with too great a challenge, their ultimate failure just reinforces their old patterns. You don't challenge the heavyweight boxing champion after you've only taken a few lessons. All you learn from that is how much damage punches can do. I don't know. Maybe some new alternative — something I haven't thought of yet — would be the most instructive."

"Okay, go ahead and create something," Ferguson suggested.

"Just like that?"

"Sure."

"Well, the first thing that comes to mind is doing both — contacting the police and working with Arundel. But I don't want to be around the guy. At this point I'm afraid he might turn around and kill me. And I also don't want to jeopardize the women's lives."

"So cross that one off."

"Right. Then there's tackling the case myself. I used to be a private investigator, you know."

"I didn't know. What a coincidence!"

"Was that sarcasm?"

Ferguson laughed. "Were you a gumshoe what was one of the gumshoes?" he asked in a heavy 1930s gangster accent.

"What?" I had absolutely no idea what that meant.

"Were you good at it?"

"Not particularly. I worked for my uncle. But after all my training and experience as a therapist, I've got skills now that should help a lot."

"Okay. You're in business. Get busy," he pronounced.

Chapter 22

When I was a detective, my first stop in a new case usually entailed basic research at the library, local credit bureau, or county registrar. I decided to begin my current investigation with an even safer, easier form of information gathering — the phone book. First I journeyed to the other end of the couch. From there I stretched and reached for the opus that might answer such questions as where did Zig-Zag live? Were there any other Arundels — relatives — in the immediate area? Was there an organization listed under Krishnanda's name?

The only new fact I unearthed was that Zee lived at 207 Cayuga Street, so I hoisted myself up out of the soft cushion, gasped at the pain, and headed over there in my old Volvo sedan. This was the car of choice for Santa Cruz psychotherapists — herds of them assembled outside our professional meetings — but lacked panache for detecting. I did drive rather fast, though, and the wind rushed through my hair quite alluringly.

It was about six-thirty in the evening and the fog was just beginning to drift in. Cayuga was in the heart of the Seabright neighborhood, about a half-mile from a small beach favored by dog lovers. 207 was a large mustard-yellow Victorian that would easily qualify as a handyman's special in a real estate ad. The paint was flaking off in stocking-like runs and the wooden front steps were weak with dry rot. The roof displayed three or four layers of gray composition tiles, providing an historical cross-section that reminded me of an archaeological dig, albeit upside-down.

The landscaping, on the other hand, was meticulous and colorful, with flowering shrubs, young trees, and several beds of ornamentals. Someone loved to garden even more than they hated to paint.

A slim young Latino man answered the paneled front door after some loud knocking.

"Yeah?"

"Is Zig-Zag home?"

"No. I haven't seen her today."

"Do you mind if I come in and wait for her?" I asked. This was a ploy, of course, to gain access to the interior of the building, where I might discover something helpful.

"Who are you? You don't look like any of her friends." He crossed his arms in front of his black tee shirt and glared defiantly. His efforts to appear fierce were lacking depth, but sometimes it was impulsive types that were capable of the most mayhem.

Just then the border collie from the bookstore trotted up from behind the young man and sniffed the cuff of my khaki pants. After a moment she wagged her bushy tail and kind of yodeled at me. I was stunned.

"Oh well. If Sadie knows you...." He stepped aside and the dog and I wandered into the old-fashioned parlor, which was festooned with garlands of bananas.

"We had a party last night," the youth told me. "I've gotta go, but make yourself at home," he added before ambling up creaky stairs.

The strings of bananas were the only evidence of merrymaking. Otherwise the high-ceilinged room was decorated in a decidedly Spartan fashion, with only two posters on the walls — satellite photographs of the Middle East — and a mishmosh of threadbare furniture and even older lamps. Through an archway was a formal dining room in which a card table and three wooden folding chairs huddled. The hallway I'd passed through was completely bare, which directed one's attention to its well-worn fir flooring.

Finally I studied my furry hostess. Sadie sat up on her haunches in front of the overstuffed brown sofa on which I roosted. She was watching me at least as intently as I was her. My thoughts, under control during my visual exploration of the room, were now a maelstrom.

"Are you a conspirator?" I finally asked.

She cocked her black and white head as if she'd gotten most of that, but what was that long word at the end?

I reached out and ruffled the fur on her chest. How could I be angry at such a cute dog?

"They made you do it, didn't they?"

They? I rubbed Sadie's head and considered who 'they' might be. Arundel and Zig-Zag were definitely in on it. Dizzy? Probably. The old woman at the coffeehouse must've been a plant. Perhaps she'd sprayed novocaine or curare on my legs. The bookstore owner might've been hired too, along with the assortment of clients who had so obligingly presented their supposed synchronicities.

Was *any* part of it true? Was Arundel a multiple? Were they only capitalizing on the serial murders or were they truly involved in them? Was anyone actually connected to Krishnanda? Was the kidnapping real? And why me? Better yet, *why*, period? What was the point of the hoax?

The scale was boggling, which suggested big money, but there was no obvious fortune to be made. I didn't see how the so-called kidnapping justified everything else, for example. Was Arundel extorting money from himself for insurance purposes? Then why bother with all the angels and demons?

I began brainstorming possible explanations as I continued to pet Sadie, whose pink tongue lolled out in canine ecstasy. Did they want to use me to establish an insanity defense for the murders? Worse yet, were they planning to frame me somehow? Did some cult leader order all this for his own twisted reasons? Was it a bet or a game between bored rich people? Could my vengeful ex-wife have concocted everything to drive me crazy? Was it all part of a broader conspiracy to discredit Christian dogma or psychotherapy? Maybe the murder victims were faking too — paid off to disappear for a while. Then that meant the cops were in on it too. No, I was going too far, I realized, and I decided to catalogue what I knew for sure.

A slew of people had been stabbed to death. I'd been jerked around by a talented cast of assholes. Sadie the dog enjoyed being rubbed. My head hurt. That was about it. It was a depressingly short list.

Sadie licked my hand and my attention returned to the banana-laden parlor. Her tongue was almost as scratchy as a cat's and her brown eyes gleamed at me in silent connection. I liked her better as a regular dog than a retail clerk/mysterious guide. She was a very sweet creature.

I communed and ruminated for about twenty minutes, approaching my feelings but backing off each time before truly reaching them. Then, just after I'd vowed to plunge in and see how I felt, a clear high-pitched woman's voice called from outside the front door.

"Sarah? Sarah honey, are you home?"

"Come in!" I answered. The detective in me was curious about anyone visiting the house.

"Thanks," the middle-aged woman acknowledged as she sidled through the doorway. "Oops," she added as soon as she spied me.

It was the woman from the coffeehouse, minus the bag lady outfit and gobs of attitude. Now she was wearing a chic emerald green pantsuit and a large straw hat, which she removed and held in front of her midsection as if it were a shield.

"Sit," I commanded, withdrawing my hand from Sadie's neck ruff. The dog, who was sitting already, lay down in an effort to please. The woman plunked down in a blue Goodwill loveseat across from me. Her movements were disciplined as if she had once danced or ice-skated.

"Tell me the truth or I'm heading straight to the police," I said.

She tilted her head up and gazed at the ceiling for a moment. Then, as she began speaking, she snapped her head down and stared me in the eye.

"All right. I have no choice, do I? Here you go. We're all part of an improvisational acting troupe based in Seattle. Even Sadie here has performed in several movies. We were hired by somebody with more bucks than sense, I think, to do all that we've been doing."

"Who?"

"I don't know. Only Tony — I mean 'George' — has contact with him. I don't even know why we're doing it. But the money's good."

"Is Zig-Zag's real name Sarah?" I asked.

"Yes. I'm Jessica, by the way."

"How do you do? You're a good actress."

"Thank you. Once I met you, I was sorry we were doing this."

"It's a little late for that, isn't it?"

"I suppose so," she admitted.

I considered what she was telling me. It struck me that this so-called confession was being surrendered far too easily. I began investigating an hour ago and now I knew everything? I don't think so.

"Why are you telling me all this?" I asked.

"You told me you'd go to the police."

"So? Why should that be a big deal to you? Where's the illegal part? Impersonating a bag lady? Pretending to be a client or a holy man's daughter? Something doesn't make sense here unless you're leaving something out or lying outright."

"Well, I have had second thoughts about my role lately because of the murders."

"How's that?"

"I didn't realize at first that what we're doing might be mixed up with that. For all I know, I might be wanted by the police."

"You might be. Maybe we should go down to the station right now and find out."

"Maybe." Her face gave nothing away. She gazed at me evenly, her pale blue eyes holding steady for several seconds.

It was a classic match-up — an actor versus a therapist. One of us was trained to project fiction while the other was trained to ferret out the underlying truth. I judged the confrontation to be a stand-off thus far.

"How do I know what you're saying now isn't bullshit too?" I tried.

"Why should I lie?"

"Why should you misrepresent yourself at Cafe Neo? Why is anyone doing this? That's what I want to know. Haven't you even wondered?"

"Of course."

"Then give me some guesses. You've had more time to think about it."

"Revenge, greed, guilt — I'm sure there's a primal emotion in this somewhere. Maybe you're due for an inheritance and another relative is trying to drive you crazy. Or it could be a psychological experiment some rich buddy of yours is conducting."

"That's it? You don't have any better ideas than that?"

She shrugged. "I've been busy writing a play."

"I should be very angry," I told her. "I'm not, but I should be. You people have seriously disrupted my life. I could certainly sue you in civil court even if I couldn't press charges."

"Whatever you think you need to do . . ."

Her blank expression was back. She looked like an Easter Island statue in a pantsuit.

"Is George — I mean Tony — really a multiple?"

"No."

"How about Dizzy? Is she for real?"

"An actress."

"I'm not sure I buy it," I responded, shaking my sore head. "How can people be so convincing without even having lines to study? I'm not an idiot, you know. I'm a professional who's studied behavior and personality."

"Maybe you wanted to be convinced," Jessica suggested. "Maybe you needed a little excitement in your life. Were you stuck in a rut? That can affect your judgment."

"I'll ask the questions here," I snapped, although she'd certainly raised a valid point.

"Go ahead. It feels good to get all this off my chest." Her expression was congruent with her words, but what did that mean? I was dealing with very talented people.

"What do you know about this supposed kidnapping?" I asked.

"What supposed kidnapping?"

"Zee and Dizzy — or whatever their names are."

"I don't know anything about it. It wasn't in the plan."

"So you're saying it's real?"

"No. I'm just saying I don't know about it. It's possible I'm out of the loop these days. Like I say, I'm working on a play. But why would anyone kidnap them?"

I shrugged and continued my interrogation, but got no closer to answering that question or any of the other remaining unknowns. Finally, after a frustrating half-hour, I petted Sadie good-bye and strode out. When was I going to find hard answers?

Chapter 23

So what was real and what wasn't? Back at my apartment I pondered the question for longer than was probably healthy for someone who already spent too much time in his head. But what else could I do? There was no book to consult, no 800 number to call.

How could anyone function without a secure foundation of basic knowledge? How did psychotics do it, for example? They invented their own paradigm, I realized — a personal reality that was easier for them to cope with than the consensus version. What were other strategies?

I could give up. I could drive to the airport, fly to Hawaii and lay on a beach until everybody else lost interest. For a moment, I was tempted. Then I remembered what Ferguson had drawn out of me. Where was the lesson in running? Was my current psychological status so insecure that I had to jet to the South Pacific to protect it?

I could also fight fire with fire and launch a counterattack of disinformation or manipulation. This wasn't an appealing notion at all. I knew that you can't beat people playing *their* game with *their* rules. I would be a beginner engaged in a process that disgusted me. No thanks.

Before I'd generated any more stupid ideas, the phone rang. I took the call in my bedroom, lying sideways on my king-size bed. It was Arundel.

"Hi, Tony," I greeted him.

"Who?"

"Tony. You know — your real name." I wasn't at all sure that Jessica had been telling the truth, but an aggressive approach seemed worth trying.

"I don't remember a Tony," Arundel answered. "And anyway, why would one of my names be more real than another?"

"Look, the cat's out of the bag. You can drop the act."

"Any more clichés up your sleeve, Tom? That's quite a barrage."

"Are you denying it, then?"

"Denying what?"

"That you're an actor named Tony."

He laughed. "Wherever did you hear that?"

"From Jessica — the woman at the coffeehouse. I saw her over at Sarah's house."

"Who?"

"Sarah — Zig-Zag."

"Tom, I'm getting worried about you. None of this makes much sense."

Clearly, I was getting nowhere. Either the old woman had fabricated her tale or Arundel was truly an imperturbable stage veteran. In either case, I might as well employ another conversational strategy.

"So what can I do for you?" I asked.

"What do you mean?"

"You called me. What do you want?"

"I'd like to discuss our collaboration vis-à-vis the kidnapping," he answered.

"Forget it. I'm not even sure there *was* a kidnapping."

"Why? Did you receive another phone call?"

"No. I just think it's possible that the whole thing's a hoax."

"We can't take that chance," Arundel admonished.

"There's that 'we' again." I was becoming very annoyed. Whether he was acting or not, the man was a relentless farthead. Why didn't he just go hide somewhere like a normal fugitive?

"I have business," he told me. "I'll call again." Then he hung up.

I was truly aggravated now. Before I knew what I was doing, I'd thrown the telephone across the room, where it knocked over a table lamp. On my way to pick it up, I stubbed my toe against the leg of my oak dresser. Naturally I upended it, scattering books, socks, and pistachio nuts across the blue

Mexican throw rug. Next I kicked the nearest object, a philodendron in a green plastic bucket. It tipped over, spilling black potting soil everywhere and damaging numerous leaves that were dry and stiff from weeks of neglect.

My mood shifted and I regretted the damage I'd wreaked on the hapless plant. Apparently inanimate objects had it coming, though, because a moment later in the living room, I'd picked up a book of waterfall photographs and hurled it at a wall poster.

Therapists don't do things like this. We handle our emotions maturely, I told myself right before battering the armchair to the floor. Then I lay down on my stomach in the hallway, my face buried in the itchy acrylic carpet fibers. As uncomfortable as I was, I wished I never had to get up. I wanted to merge with the carpet — become inanimate — stop thinking and feeling. Nobody lied to carpets. Nobody expected carpets to help them. Carpets had it easy.

*   *   *   *   *

When I woke up the next morning, I knew something I hadn't known the day before. The old woman was lying about the acting troupe business. In a dream I'd been reading a novel that had been popular locally a couple of years ago. In *The Santa Cruz Guru Murders,* the main character is tricked into accepting a host of weird spiritual phenomena including his own vaunted status, and is then framed for several murders by a guru. In my gut, I knew that the woman had plagiarized this plot in her effort to neutralize my unexpected confrontation. Looking for a quick explanation? How about actors perpetrating a hoax? It's a cheesy, facile plot device. I wished I'd been more lucid the day before. I could've pursued quite a few more lines of inquiry if I hadn't become sidetracked by the implications of Jessica's story.

For a moment I was reminded of my ex-wife, who had been fond of these types of mind games. For years, Susan's adept manipulations had kept me guessing, nearly breaking me down before I'd finally become healthy enough to divorce her.

A shower and a huge breakfast helped rejuvenate me and I found that I was actually looking forward to resuming my sessions with clients later that day. Then the phone rang again. I was becoming conditioned in Pavlovian fashion to hate hearing that sound. The damned thing always seemed to know just when I'd mustered a healthy attitude worth demolishing.

"Hello?" I said.

"This is the guy that said he'd call back. You know who I am?"

"Yeah. We have mutual friends, right."

"That's right. Although I'm worried about them."

"What do you want?" I was tired of verbal jousting.

"I want you to take back all that bullshit you told the police. That client of yours didn't kill anyone. I want him out of the goddamn spotlight."

"You want me to lie to the cops?"

"It ain't lying. The guy had nothing to do with the murders."

"He said he did."

"Shut up. Just shut up, asshole. So you want to see your friends again?"

"Of course."

"Then quit giving me a hard time. Just call the cops and tell 'em you were wrong — or confused, maybe, 'cuz of the bump on the head. I don't care. That part's up to you. But make it convincing.

"How do you know Arundel didn't do it?" I asked.

"'Cuz I did it."

"Oh."

"Be a good boy, Dalziel. Do what's right."

"You got it. As soon as you hang up on me, I'm back on the line to the cops."

So he hung up, but this time it didn't faze me at all.

Captain Fred, my important policeman buddy, decided to handle my call personally. My name was becoming a passport to the stars, I guess.

"How are you feeling?" he asked.

"Shitty. Listen, I think I got a call from the killer."

"Arundel?"

Here's where I needed to start fudging. I *had* talked to George, of course, but that wasn't what I meant. Also, I'd decided not to divulge the kidnapping angle since that might endanger the victims, if there really were any.

"No. Someone else," I replied. "He said Arundel didn't do it — *he* did — and I think it's quite possible. Arundel may have had other reasons to claim responsibility."

"Like what?" The captain's voice was skeptical and for the first time I heard a slight speech impediment too.

"I'm not sure, but I just want to go on record as saying that I no longer feel that my client is your man."

"Is Arundel there? Is he holding a gun on you? I can have a car there in five minutes."

"No, no. I'm fine. I've just been thinking things over."

"And that's why we should change the focus of our investigation? You've got to give me more, Tom. A crank phone call and a little thinking aren't very compelling evidence, are they?"

"Suppose you're right and I'm wrong. Isn't it still a good idea to put out the word that Arundel isn't a suspect now — that he's just wanted for questioning or something? Then he might come in and help you nail this thing down — whether it's him or the other guy."

"That's your sense of Arundel? That he'd respond that way?"

"Yes. Tell the newspapers you have a new suspect. What have you got to lose?"

He sighed heavily. "My job. The credibility of the Santa Cruz police force. The murderer. More victims. Do I need to go on? You're talking about the kind of stunt you see on a TV show. This is the real world."

"Look. You'd be letting the other guy know you're onto him and maybe you'd hook Arundel. It would be killing two birds with one stone," I argued.

"That's if you're right — if there *is* another guy." He was quiet for a moment and I didn't interrupt his thoughts. Finally he spoke again, his speech impediment more pronounced now. He had trouble with k's and t's. "How do you feel about me getting the FBI to put a tap on your phone?"

"That's not an option. I'm a therapist. It would break confidentiality with the clients I talk to."

"You think that's more important than a serial murder investigation?" Fred was irritated.

"I don't get to make that choice. I simply have to follow the laws that pertain to me."

He sighed again. "You're right. Okay, here's how I want to deal with this. I'm gonna put a detective on and he'll question you about the phone call from the new guy. When he's done, I'll review what he's got and make a decision."

"Great. That's all I can ask," I told him.

"Actually, that's a lot more than you've got the right to ask. But we're pretty desperate and you seem like a fairly reliable type."

"Thanks."

"I'll be in touch. Stay on the line for Detective Pellegrino."

"Right."

The remainder of the call was a guided, methodical, redundant reporting of the facts, which I dressed up slightly to influence the captain to cooperate with the kidnapper's demand. I enjoyed hanging up first when we were through.

Chapter 24

I'd never realized that listening to my clients' problems could be so soothing. Everything was completely straightforward — eating disorders, depression, anxiety. I knew all about these small inconveniences and not only that, they weren't *mine*. Lost in the lives of others, I idled away the afternoon and early evening. Why had I ever thought my line of work was stressful?

On the way home, still limping slightly as I traversed downtown, my temporary peace of mind was rudely shoved aside. I was abreast of the new movie theater, maneuvering between the two ticket lines, when I heard a loud flapping of wings immediately behind me. I ducked and whirled, startling a young family nearby, but I couldn't find the source. A few tentative steps further, I heard it again, this time combined with a strange tingling in my shoulders and upper back. With a sense of dread, I twisted my neck and beheld — there was no other word for it — I *beheld* magnificent ghostly-white wings. They shimmered in the fading sunlight — of this world and some other, not quite opaque and not quite translucent. As I watched, the wings flapped several times and I felt myself lifted up onto my toes and then returned to earth as the wings settled down onto the length of my back.

I was truly freaked. I stumbled to a nearby wooden bench and my face fell into my hands.

Either my unconscious had opted for the self-generated reality of psychosis or Arundel was right about my angelic destiny. Both of these options remained unacceptable to me. There was a moment of sensing the proximity of darkness — an abyss — and then I began sobbing. I just couldn't handle it. My body began heaving and shaking as I pulled myself into a smaller and smaller ball. Within the cocoon of my meaty fingers, my mouth grimaced to its limits with each racking sob. My nostrils streamed snot. My gut was a vortex of nausea.

I have no idea how long I suffered on the slatted bench before I felt an insistent tapping on my shoulder, just above my left wing.

"Go away," I mewed.

"Some are called," a woman's silken voice told me.

My head snapped up; I'm sure I was a terrifying sight — tears and mucus liberally smeared over my nasty burn scars. The beautiful woman in the white dress didn't flinch or hesitate.

"May I sit with you?" she asked.

I nodded raggedly before feeling overwhelmed and once again hiding my face in my lap.

"You're not going crazy. You're in the midst of a spiritual emergence."

"What?" I grunted.

"Everything's going to be all right. I have experience with this and I can see that you are undergoing transformation, not an emotional breakdown."

"Angel?" I croaked.

She laughed. "I'm not an angel. I'm a transpersonal therapist."

"No. Me — am I turning into an angel? I saw wings."

"Don't worry about that. You're not an angel, but when someone makes a great shift in their spiritual being, there's usually some sort of symbolic representation. Have angels been important in your life lately?"

I nodded and she continued.

"You're moving beyond the literal world. Don't let your old small mind limit your perceptions."

I sat up and examined this woman. She wasn't actually beautiful in the ordinary sense of the word. Her face was too round and her eyes were too big. She must have been in her late forties and she looked all of it. Not only was her skin quite wrinkled, it was leathery and sun-damaged as well. Her smile was sweet but also slightly tentative — she wasn't completely confident she was doing the right thing. She wore a white Mexican dress and purple sandals.

Compassion was etched into her face, as well as a lightness — a very casual air — that I rarely saw in an intelligent adult. Obviously she cared, but my plight certainly hadn't ruined her day either.

"How can you tell all this about me?" I finally asked.

"I can see your aura. It's very beautiful." She smiled thoroughly and I felt some of my despair slide off me. In its place was a freshness — a hint of a powerful new sense of seeing, hearing, and smelling. Seconds later, fear kicked in and I began to shake again.

"It's okay to be afraid. There's a great deal to grow accustomed to. For a while, the intensity of your experience will be harrowing. Hang in there."

I straightened my posture, although I was still quivering, and wiped my face on my shirt sleeve.

"Do you have a business card?" I asked. "I don't want to take up any more of your time out on the street."

She handed me a teal-colored card that introduced her as Aileen Van Der Voot. It seemed to be the most beautiful object I'd ever seen. I reached into my back pocket and gave her one of my plain-Jane cards.

"Tom Dalziel," she read. "I've heard of you. You take on the tough ones, don't you? Should we have our cards shake each other's hands or would you rather we did it ourselves?"

I stuck out my big mitt and we shook. Her touch was electrifying — but somehow didn't sting you.

"Thank you," I told her.

"I do have to go now," she announced.

"Okay. Bye."

"Good-bye, Tom. Remember what I said."

"Right," I answered woodenly.

After she left I staggered home and immediately fell asleep. Trauma was tiring.

Chapter 25

I dreamt that I was a hunting dog, totally immersed in the moment, revelling in my senses. I woke up to a knock on the door.

"Who is it?" I called from the bedroom doorway, rubbing my knee.

"Paper girl!"

The fellow that delivered my newspaper was in his seventies.

"Try again," I suggested.

"Pizza girl!"

"For breakfast?"

"Egg girl! Get your eggs here!"

I opened the door and Dizzy beamed at me from my small front porch.

"My hero!" she proclaimed, offering me a bouquet of mixed flowers. "If it hadn't been for you, I guess we'd still be kidnapped."

My eyes were flooding me with information as though my sensory amperage had gained juice since the night before. It reminded me of the momentary glimpse of freshness I'd experienced downtown on the bench. The intensity of direct sensory input was more pronounced, but it seemed to be the same general phenomenon. I accepted the bundle of blue, red, yellow, and purple and smells and a tiny insect or two, and I invited in the beautiful creature who stood behind them. She hugged the daylights out of me before skipping past. If you ever want to experience an intensely pleasurable few seconds, wait until you've made a big shift spiritually and then get hugged by an enthusiastic, shapely woman. I was momentarily speechless.

"Nice place," she said. "Is this where you store the recyclables?"

There were numerous empty bottles and newspapers strewn around.

"This is the living room," I told her. "The rest of the house isn't up to these strict standards."

As I limped stiffly into the kitchen with the flowers, Dizzy plopped onto my sofa and hugged herself.

"I don't recommend being kidnapped, by the way. It's not much fun at all."

"I'll keep that in mind," I told her, returning to the room, which I must admit could've benefitted from extensive tidying.

"Is Zee okay too?" I asked after I'd settled carefully into the armchair.

"She's fine. She's home sleeping."

"With Sadie?" I watched her reaction closely.

"Probably. You can't keep that dog off the bed — I've seen Zee try."

Zip. No hesitancy, no sign of distress, no nothing. That was interesting.

Dizzy was wearing black jeans and an orange tee shirt. Her hair was a bird's nest and she obviously hadn't showered since her ordeal. Her body odor was a combination of sheer rankness and something else that mildly aroused me.

"Tell me more about the kidnapping," I prompted. I didn't need to be thinking with my hormones.

She wrinkled her nose and pursed her lips for a moment. "We were somewhere near the ocean. Sometimes I could hear it. And twice a day a train went by — maybe a quarter of a mile away."

I nodded. That would be the Lone Star cement plant freight that ran along the southern part of town. Combined with the coastal clue, that limited a search to about a six-mile corridor of beach houses and condominiums.

Dizzy continued. "The kidnapper had the worst breath I've ever smelled — we never saw his face — and he fed us hot dogs." She screwed up her features into a truly hideous grimace. "Ugh. Hot dogs! Can you imagine?"

I shook my head. "The cruelty of my fellow humans never fails to amaze me. Was there mustard?"

"Go ahead — laugh. The hot dogs were the worst part. Well, after the fear — I was terrified the whole time. Zee even wet her pants, but don't tell her I told you."

"How'd he grab you?"

"We were walking on the sidewalk over near my house — kind of by the motel next to the taco bar? — and he jumped out of a junky old car wearing a ski mask, waving this huge gun. So we got in the car. From that point on he kept us blindfolded."

"You're right. That doesn't sound fun at all."

"Uh-uh. I knew you'd think it was Arundel, by the way. That's why I said what I did over the phone."

"That was helpful." I leaned forward and smiled. "I'm glad you're safe."

"Me too. How have you been?"

"Confused, lousy, and in pain. But then last night I had a vision and a good cry and a therapist told me I'd be okay and now I am."

"Good deal."

I noticed at this point that when I was engaged in conversation, the sensory overload was greatly diminished.

"Have you been to the police?" I asked.

"First thing. The creep dumped us off at Lighthouse Field and we walked downtown. I didn't tell them about the guy calling you, though, in case that would get you in trouble."

"Thanks."

"They'll probably call you anyway. They remembered we knew each other from the Fall Creek mess. Listen, I've gotta run."

I stood. "Okay. Thanks for stopping by."

Another monster hug and a peck on the cheek and I was alone again. Alone and hungry.

This time my craving was for more than merely food. I wanted breakfast but I also wanted contact, learning, love — all that my hermit-like existence had been denying me for so many years. I was both frightened and excited to realize the scope of my hunger. Whatever lid had been nailed on this box of yearnings had been completely pried off. I wanted growth, I wanted sharing — I wanted every one of the human elements absent from my isolated world. I had no idea how to get them, but I knew for certain that staying alone in my apartment wouldn't help. So I mustered my nerve, dressed, and stepped toward the Lincoln Street Cafe.

It was an expedition through a jungle of new stimuli. A black lab barked and growled behind a rusty chain-link fence, noisy birds fought for space in a ripe date palm, the scorched smell of burnt rubber assailed my nose near a deserted street corner. These were so much more urgent and richer than I remembered. I felt as though my life could consist of nothing more than the mundane events encountered on a walk — that would be enough.

Of course life refused to limit itself to this circumscribed script. No sooner had I settled into enjoying the morning than a new, twisted scenario greeted me at the cafe. My ex-wife Susan sat by herself in all her glory and I didn't notice her until after I'd been seated two tables away.

She waved her beauty queen wave — I'd always hated that mannerism — and flashed her twenty-thousand-dollar dental work. My sensory acuity vanished; it was as if the world had faded to black and white.

"Susan," I acknowledged from my seat. "I thought you were in North Carolina."

She gestured at the chair across from her and I dutifully carried my menu and battered bulk over.

"I'm just in town for a visit. How nice to run into you."

If there was ever a poster girl for incongruent speech and facial expression, Susan would be my pick. Her voice was honey; her eyes were loaded howitzers. As usual, when faced with her in the moment, I couldn't imagine why I'd ever been attracted to Susan. I never remembered the massive projection, fantasy, and self-conning that I'd inflicted on myself in my younger days.

"How have you been?" I asked.

"Fantastic. Never better. Jeff sold the company and then promptly dropped dead. You look like shit. Were you in a car wreck?"

"Something like that. I'm sorry about Jeff."

"I'm not. He was a treacherous son of a bitch. Worse than you."

Her glare would've frozen me fifteen years ago. Now I was almost amused. She was an absurd character — someone from a fifth-rate film noir. One second she was all smiles, a second later her mood might swing all the way to its polar opposite, complete with violence.

Physically, Susan was too overweight to be starring in any stylish movies and her tightly permed blond hair framed a face that hadn't aged well. What had been cute at twenty-two was now grotesque at forty-four simply because it was essentially the same. She was older but no more mature emotionally and her features reflected that. It was pathetic.

Mustering compassion for post-divorce Susan had always been a tough task for me. As I sat and realized the poisonous thought train rumbling through my head, I consciously strove to derail it.

"I guess you just haven't had much luck with marriage, but they say three's a charm. Maybe Mr. Right is going to be next."

"I think I'm going to become a lesbian, actually. Licking pussy is bound to be better than being shat on."

I reached the limit of my altruism. Without a word I rose and walked out. She knew perfectly well how I felt about that kind of language. It was abuse — a subtle variety of violence — and I wasn't willing to subject myself to it. I heard her laughing as I reached the sidewalk.

Breakfast choice number two proved to be much more congenial, and I was pleased to see that the local newspaper carried a story detailing the authorities' search for a new suspect in the serial killings. I did spend most of the meal hiding behind my paper from an ex-client, though, who I assumed would be uncomfortable encountering me since she'd stiffed me for a hundred and twenty dollars. Instead, she stopped by my table and whipped out her checkbook. Life could be good.

Chapter 26

I called Aileen Van Der Voot between clients and made an appointment for the next morning. For once, the rest of the day and evening were relatively uneventful. The spectacular visuals and startling soundtrack didn't reappear, but that was fine with me. I actually watched an old Peter Sellers film on television and caught up on my professional reading. Well, it was just *Psychology Today*, but it was better than nothing. Someday I might need to know why men who don't love enough often raise sons who love too much. Or something like that.

Aileen's office was very different from mine. For one thing, there were no chairs, tables, or desks — just a light green carpet, large Balinese pillows, and a series of black and white photographs of an old man's hands.

"My father," she told me, noticing my curiosity.

"Was there something special about his hands?" I asked.

"No. I've just always been fascinated by hands. You have interesting hands, don't you?"

"Do I? Other than them being rather big, I've never thought so."

She took one of my hands in hers. We were standing just inside the doorway. "Oh I do. They're such a provocative combination of brawn and subtlety — like a boxer in grad school or a physicist farmer."

"Einstein in overalls. That's not exactly my self-image." I was flustered by my proximity to this attractive woman, as well as by her words, which could be construed as quite flirtatious. Her tone of voice, though, was matter of fact, and her body language further proclaimed her neutrality. It wasn't her fault that the scent of sandalwood turned me on, after all. And if she'd been wearing a conservative suit instead of a diaphanous teal dress, I might not have fantasized at all.

"Do you feel like an experiment gone awry or a small person lost in a big body?" Aileen asked.

"Both. Exactly. How in the world could you know that?" I settled down onto a pillow and stretched out my legs. Her insights had blasted the licentiousness out of me. Perhaps she'd intended just that.

"The way you hold yourself — your posture now and the way you sat on the bench downtown. All that's very revealing if you're trained to pay attention on that level and then trust your intuition. Now how can I help you?" She gracefully lowered herself onto a pillow near me and gently smiled.

"Well, I've got one main question," I began. "Why should I be involved in spiritual transformation?" I asked. "That's what I want to know. I've never focused on it. I mean I don't meditate or anything."

She sat near me and focused on my face. Once again I was struck by the roundness of her countenance. She displayed no right angles or planes, just curves and circles. The overall impression was of softness, but with resilience, like a ball that always regained its shape after being thrown, hit, or whatever.

"You raise a good question," she replied. "For some, enhanced spirit is a response to a certain kind of stress — difficulties that appear insoluble."

"It's a rising to the occasion, in other words?"

"Sort of. I don't mean something that brings out the best in you per se, though. It's more like something so traumatic that it breaks down the structures in you that normally inhibit moving up to the next level. So you experience it as misery, not rising to anything."

"I understand. You get so devastated that you have to change to deal with it."

"Exactly. I wish I'd said it that way to start with. Now tell me about this new perspective you've attained. What's it like?"

"I'm scared almost all the time but that seems to have more to do with my getting used to things than anything actually being dangerous. Basically the world looks overwhelmingly beautiful off and on, and my experience is much more direct — less filtered through my mind, I guess."

"That's wonderful."

"I guess. But I still have the same problems facing me that forced the changes. Nothing's really different."

"*They* may be the same, but *you* aren't. Are you as anxious about them?"

"No."

"Are you as paralyzed by them?"

"No."

"Then, to you, they're not the same problems now. Meaning only exists in relationship."

"Meaning is exactly what I'm after. What does what happened *mean*? I don't think I'm going to have peace of mind until I know."

"So as a less anxious, less paralyzed guy, are you better equipped to find out?"

"Certainly, but let me tell you about the last few weeks. I want to see if *you* can make any sense out of it. It's been extraordinary."

"Go ahead. I'm listening."

I told my story as briefly as I could manage. Aileen listened attentively, occasionally asking a question. "So what do you think?" I asked when I was finally through.

"I think you're a tough nut to crack."

"What do you mean?"

"Look at all the drama it took to goose you into changing. Some people would've been out of personal resources after just a tenth of all that."

"But what does it mean?"

"That's what it means. It's about you, not them. It means you needed something powerful and esoteric and it showed up right on schedule. The rest of the mystery is just details."

"But there are lives at stake," I protested.

"So?"

"So I need to do something."

"Who put you in charge?"

I thought about that one. Was I caretaking beyond the scope of my actual responsibility? Well, yes. Could I just let it all go? No.

"Look," I replied. "You've got a valid point, but I can't walk away now."

"I'm not suggesting that. I'm suggesting that you not identify with a specific role, whether it's mystery-solver or masked avenger, and also that you not be as attached to a particular outcome. These aren't ideas that impel anyone to walk away. On the contrary, they encourage clarity which, in turn, promotes the generation of solutions, not just in this situation, but in all of life."

"So you're saying that two general principles apply here, right?" Aileen nodded. "One is that over-identifying with a specific role keeps you confused and the other is kind of the same thing except it's about caring too much that things turn out a certain way."

"You got it. What do you think?"

"I think I don't have a choice about attitudes in that realm. I'm set up the way I am."

"Bullshit. If it was ever true, it isn't now." She smiled but her gaze was steel.

"That's easy for you to say."

"Of course. Your making that choice will require a lot of work, but it's worth it."

"Yeah?"

"Yeah." She smiled again and her eyes were softer now.

I reflected on our conversation thus far, ready to rest a bit. "I've never said 'bullshit' to a client," I told her.

"I do it all the time. I don't mind an honest mistake, but I'm not willing to listen to bullshit."

"How can you be sure you've properly differentiated between the two?"

"Bullshit feels icky."

"That's it?"

"Hey, it works for me."

I glanced at the clock; we were way over the hour. This was either very unprofessional or very generous of Aileen. Without commenting on which it might be, I paid and scheduled another appointment for ten in the morning in two days.

She gave me an Elvis Presley trading card on my way out and told me to study it. I agreed, stuffed the card in my back pocket, and promptly forgot about it. I was seeing a rather eccentric therapist, I realized, but I liked it.

Chapter 27

When Arundel called early the next day, I felt prepared to deal with him. Not only did I feel immeasurably better physically, my mood had stabilized as well. Whatever else had happened with Aileen, I now felt ground underneath me. I had a place to stand.

"Hello. Tom?"

"Hi George. What's up?"

"You sound different. Have you been drinking?"

"No. Would you like to schedule an appointment?"

"What do you mean?"

"I'm a therapist. Do you want my professional help?"

"No, no. I just wanted to congratulate you on securing the freedom of the girls. And it's been determined that I didn't kill anyone. I thought you should know."

"Thank you. I appreciate your courtesy."

Arundel was silent. I think he could sense that his Velcro hooks had no counterparts on me and whatever he had planned was now obsolete.

"Well, I have some things to do," he finally announced.

"Good-bye."

I was pleased with the tenor of the conversation, which embodied a professionalism that had gone AWOL on me sometime after I was arrested and before I met Credula. The uncentered Tom improvised inexpertly; the post-Aileen Tom operated within a sanctioned structure when it was appropriate — and it worked. The phone call had almost been normal. I felt better, not worse, after communicating with Arundel. It was a revolution.

*   *   *   *   *

About two hours later I was emerging from the grocery store with a sack under each arm. This was my first shopping expedition since my concussion. I was ready to take care of myself again, and I eagerly anticipated the home-cooked meal I'd planned.

As I reached the curb, a short man wearing a navy blue ski mask accosted me and gestured with a large handgun for me to climb into an old Toyota wagon. Five or six people witnessed the incident, but no one intervened.

"Can I keep the groceries?" I asked.

He nodded and pulled a black scarf out of his pants pocket, which he tied tightly around my eyes after I'd crammed myself and my grocery bags into the car. He drove for perhaps forty-five minutes with the radio blaring top-forty country music. I tried to notice any smells, exterior sounds, or turns that might help me determine our destination, but after the first few minutes I was thoroughly confused, as intended. Wherever we were headed, we negotiated a complex route to get there that yielded few hints. The only geographical certainty was that judging from our uphill climb, we were in the Santa Cruz Mountains somewhere.

The final stretch was definitely a dirt road so I wasn't surprised that when we finally halted I could smell dust and a few wildflowers. I tried to gather up my purchases, still blindfolded, but a hand on my arm stopped me and then shoved me towards the car door. Once I'd clambered out, the same hand grabbed my elbow and guided me several steps forward and then through a creaky door. As the door was being locked from the outside behind me, I removed my blindfold and surveyed my surroundings. I was in a medium-sized room containing nothing but straw floor mats and Peter Rabbit wallpaper. It was as if the regular inhabitants were five-year-old Zen students.

The kidnapper departed and I paused a moment to cement in my memory all the data that my keen investigative skills had acquired concerning the man. He was white, about five-foot eight, with a medium build. His ski mask was constructed of fabric, while his gun was metallic. He wore jeans, white running shoes, and a black sweatshirt. I think he had internal organs but this was just extrapolation.

For the next half-hour I explored my cell. There were two windows; both were nailed shut and covered with cardboard on the outside. An overhead globe was controlled by a rheostat on the wall beside the only door, which was solid pine. Underneath the Japanese-style floor mats was a concrete slab. Also, Peter Rabbit was a happy bunny and so were his fuzzy pals.

I was frustrated that I knew so little and I resolved at least to ferret out whatever information was available to me conceptually. I sprawled on the hard matting and considered my predicament.

I felt reasonably sure that I wouldn't be killed. All the victims had been stabbed where they'd been encountered and all the kidnappees so far had been released unharmed. Also, why go to the trouble of keeping his identity concealed if the guy was planning to murder me anyway?

Despite the logic of all this, waiting in the bare room proved to be a particularly challenging context in which to de-attach from outcome, as Aileen had recommended. Were all the potential futures inherent in my incarceration okay with me? Hell no.

I was scared — scared to be locked in a strange room and flooded with dread about what might come next. Torture? Deprivation? Hot dogs? It may sound ridiculous, but the thought of those hot dogs became a symbol of my loss of control. I had planned a meal of vegetarian lasagne, garlic bread, and fruit salad. Would some maniac make me eat hog rectums?

Eventually Mr. Ski Mask returned, heralded by the rattling of the padlock on the door. I briefly considered hiding and then flinging myself on him before I remembered that there was nowhere to hide. Once inside, my kidnapper kept the gun trained on me and spoke for the first time. His voice was vaguely familiar but nothing like the phone caller who had purportedly held Dizzy and Zee. This man was much better educated, for one thing.

"I'm taking my mask off now," he said. "Don't try anything."

My nominal reserve of poise shrunk dramatically. The concept that his anonymity ensured my safety had served a bigger emotional crutch than I'd realized. In one quick movement, he whipped the fabric over his head and revealed himself. It was the chiropractor from the tower protest crew.

So much had happened since I'd met him that it felt as though we'd been in fourth grade together. What was he doing in my present-tense world? I was mystified. This guy wasn't a psychotic killer or even particularly abnormal.

I couldn't remember his name and told him so.

"Emory," he informed me. "And I owe you an adjustment."

"I'll settle for an explanation."

"That comes next and not from me. Now put your hands behind your head. We're going to walk over to the dining hall."

"Dining hall? What is this — a summer camp for serial killers?"

Emory smiled. "You'll see. Now let's move it."

He positioned himself a few feet behind me, gun in hand, and I moved forward on shaky legs. I was very frightened; how could he let me go now that I knew who he was?

Outside, I found myself on the fringe of a grassy meadow surrounded by a redwood forest. Approximately a dozen small cabins similar to the one I stood next to were arranged in a wheel around a larger, barn-like structure. All these wooden buildings were painted white and gleamed in the sun as though they'd just been washed and waxed. There was no sign of anyone else, although well-worn dirt paths criss-crossed the meadow.

We embarked on the widest of these on our march to the central hall, and my trepidation grew with each step. I felt as though the hell of the last few weeks was reaching a crescendo and suddenly hell looked a lot better than whatever was next.

Chapter 28

The interior of the dining hall was well lit and luxuriously appointed with antique Persian rugs, rosewood paneling, and elegant hand-carved tables and chairs. It was also full of familiar faces — Dizzy, Zig-Zag, Jessica, and all the environmental protesters. They sat amongst several dozen others in rows facing a small raised stage. None of them would catch my eye or even acknowledge my presence as I was led down an aisle beside them. In the front of the long room, on the stage, Arundel sat in a plain wooden chair next to an ornate gilt throne. His eyes were closed and his face was placid. He wore a brown robe that was cinched at the waist by a silver cord.

Emory directed me to a vacant seat in the front row between two men I didn't know, although one wore a policeman's uniform. There was a strange silence then. After a moment I realized that everyone in the hall except me was breathing in unison — long, slow, effortless breaths. I tried it but immediately felt nauseated and returned to my own rhythm. When the chanting began, any doubts I may have still harbored were banished. This was a cult. I was in the midst of forty or fifty fanatics, at least one of whom was a murderer.

I reviewed the recent cast of characters in my life who weren't present and decided that Roberta the therapist, Aileen the transpersonal healer, Susan my ex-wife, and Sadie the dog were all extremely unlikely cult leaders. That left Ferguson, whom I could just barely picture perched on a throne. Of course, the actual leader could've been a complete stranger, but I had a strong hunch he wasn't. My money was on Ferguson.

When an elderly dark-skinned man in a beautiful white robe slowly hobbled in and lowered himself onto the throne, I was very surprised. The cult was led by a dead man — Krishnanda. Who was buried in his tomb, I wondered? I'd seen the holy man's photograph in *Newsweek* during his week-long funeral ceremonies several years back. Were there a lot of obese, bearded Indians to select from? Were thousands of Hindus visiting the white marble tomb, paying homage to a homeless man or a wax dummy? My mind seized on this issue instead of any of the more intense, all too relevant questions that faced me.

The first thing Krishnanda did was smile at me and I must admit that receiving his direct attention was a powerful experience. His dark brown eyes were backless and bottomless — an entrance to a void. It was as if no one was in there, but unlike the vacant quality of catatonia or dementia, his eyes conveyed something more, not less, than that which had been replaced. I felt that I could fall into him forever.

His mouth indicated that he knew everything. At least that's what it seemed like. I have no idea how a mouth could convey this, but his did. The expression was wise, compassionate, and above all else knowledgeable. Clearly he was a teacher, even if his current curriculum was death.

Despite his weight, Krishnanda's posture and bearing, all the way down to the way he held his fingers, was aesthetically perfect — a living work of art.

Overall, his smiling scrutiny hit me as though it were a gale force wind. I actually blew backward in my chair in reaction to his psychic energy or whatever it was. The cop next to me grinned and placed a hand on my upper back to stabilize me. Arundel seemed to be enjoying my distress as well. He was leaning forward in his chair, devilish delight blooming on his face as he watched me closely.

Then Krishnanda began speaking quickly in a heavily-accented voice. It took me a moment to realize he was addressing me.

"Thomas, we need you amongst us. We need your strength and we need your love. Most of all we need the power that sleeps inside you. You have passed every test and proved yourself worthy of us. We are also worthy of you. Our work is most important. The world depends on us, although it knows this no more than it knows the other simple truths which are there for all of us to see."

There was a hypnotic quality to the fast rhythm of his speech. The words flowed out and poured over me, washing me in *his* mood, *his* ideas. It was unpleasant, perhaps because I fought it. Some part of me knew that if I relaxed my vigilance against him, Krishnanda would conquer and claim me as he had the others in the room.

"I am now going to answer your questions," the fat old man told me. "I will begin with the ones in your eyes and later we will address the ones that emerge from your mouth." He paused and then coughed deeply before continuing. "I am not dead, of course. It was necessary for our organization to become less public. This, I know, is only one very small way we have tricked you, although all in all, ninety-nine percent of the information presented to you by those you met was accurate. Misrepresenting the truth is a more effective form of deception than transmitting that which is simply fallacious. I do not apologize for what we have done, for it needed doing. The ultimate responsibility for this work will always rest with those who see the most clearly and I never shirk such tasks, however repugnant. I know, however, of the difficulties you have faced and overcome. It has not been easy for you, nor has it been easy for us. Lying, kidnapping, killing — these are not activities that are inherently spiritual, however necessary they might be in this case. Thus our members have agreed to mortgage their personal karmic futures for the benefit of all. This is no small thing." He coughed again. "Now I am ready to hear your questions."

I didn't know where to begin and I was conscious of the audience that was witnessing our interchange.

"Do you believe I'm an angel?" I finally asked.

"There are no angels. In the realm beyond the physical there is no hierarchy. We are all equal participants in consciousness when we do not wear bodies. However, as a simple conceptual representation of your potential role in the change... an angel is no less accurate than any other familiar label. That is why we introduced the idea to you."

So a guy sitting on a golden throne says there's no hierarchy. Great. And the rest of his answer was about as clear as mud. What did "no less accurate" mean, anyway?

"Are you going to murder more people?" I asked next, my hostility radiating toward the stage.

"We have no plans to do so. The forces of demonic inertia — that which maintains the status quo — have been vanquished within the bounds of the sacred circle. If further measures will be required, however, we will do whatever is necessary to nurture the change."

"How can you possibly justify taking lives?"

"Suppose someone had assassinated Hitler before World War II. Don't you believe that millions of lives would have been spared? Wouldn't such an action be justified and quite intelligent if one were armed with enough information concerning future world events? This is the position I found myself in several years ago. The change that is coming — the beginning of the so-called New Age — this can be a bloody civil war or a gradual awakening. We are working to ensure the latter."

"That only makes sense if you're right. Maybe you're wrong. How can you be so arrogant that you kill people based on your point of view?"

"You misunderstand. This is not a point of view, a prediction, a theory, a guess, or anything else that is open to debate. I *know*. I know more surely than you can trust your own senses. This is not braggadocio or arrogance. It is fact. If you say 'I have large feet,' and you do, are you being arrogant?"

"Knowing the size of my feet and knowing the world's future are two completely different things."

"Not to me. Lifetimes of spiritual study have prepared me to receive information from realms that are not available to you. I am simply an expert in an arena in which you are not. By the same token, I would not question your diagnosis of a patient."

"You should. Psychology is a very inexact science."

"My field is not. Not to me. What other questions can I help you with?"

"Why me? Why isn't my neighbor or a colleague standing here?"

"This is harder to explain. I'll begin at the energetic level. Your configuration fits the pattern of our needs, or seen the other way around, we are missing that which your being supplies. Of course, energy configurations also manifest on less esoteric levels — in personality, occupation, experience, et cetera. You are also a necessary cog in the cosmic machine in these terms, although it would require a great deal of time, which we don't have, to explore this in detail. Suffice it to say that I am patiently explaining myself to you because of our discovery of who you are. Do you remember the hatchet incident you witnessed fifteen years ago?"

I nodded, although it took another moment for me to recall Levine, the poor murder victim I'd been following.

"This was when your inner configuration first came to our attention. You were a bystander at an event we were orchestrating; such is the way we are all led to one another. As you see, we have planned long and carefully."

"You say you need me, but why do I need you?" I asked.

"We have a lot to offer you as an individual, which is still what you believe you are. We are a community with all the benefits and strengths of a community. We stand by each other, we love each other. Love is healing — something you need, Tom. I can also help guide you on your unique spiritual path. Do you want to live several thousand more lifetimes or do you want to move on to the next plane? You cannot accelerate your journey without help. Also, in terms of personal satisfaction, there can be none greater than the feelings derived from directly participating in the transformation of our world."

"That's something else I want to know. Just what is this transformed world going to look like? Are we talking about the dead rising up, no more diseases, or just more New Age churches? I think this is a key element here. I'd condone killing Hitler maybe, but not Wayne Newton. The stakes don't justify it. Do you see what I mean?"

"Absolutely. This is indeed a key element, although I don't know who Wayne Newton is. I presume he is a minor annoying figure?"

I nodded.

"Let me describe the world after the change. The dead will stay dead, some diseases will remain, but war will gradually fade away. All things exist to serve a purpose and when that purpose is no longer needed, neither is the phenomenon itself. In other words, war will end because the world will change into an entity that no longer needs war.

Spirituality will return as the everyday priority it once was. Science and technology will be demoted, along with personal goals. In greater harmony, the people of the world will cooperate to solve problems such as hunger, pollution, and mental illness. How does that sound?"

"Pretty vague."

"Would you like sports scores or perhaps stock quotes?"

Krishnanda's followers laughed.

"No thank you," I responded. "I guess I get the idea."

"Good. I am growing weary — my energy is not what it once was. Perhaps you could direct your remaining inquiries to my assistant." He gestured gracefully at George, who pulled himself erect in his seat and gazed at me expectantly.

"You're like the vice president, huh?"

Arundel nodded. "How may I help you?"

The way he said it, the phrase sounded like even more of a cliché than it was. Perhaps the cult members asked if they could help each other all day long.

"Are you a multiple?" I asked.

"Yes, but my alters communicate freely with each other. My presentation to you was misleading."

"Is Zig-Zag really his daughter?"

"Yes. As you were told, most information you were given was true."

"The birthmark?" I asked, cocking an eyebrow.

"An exaggeration. I'm not going to defend that which needs no defense. Whether you understand now or not, you will. The means in this instance definitely justify the ends. As you become more familiar with who we are and what we're doing, your doubts will fade."

"Perhaps. But for now I need to know more — to ask more questions."

"Go right ahead," Arundel offered.

"If there really aren't any angels — if they're just a symbol like Krishnanda said — then what about demons? Why kill people with demon names if there aren't any demons?"

"That's a good question," Arundel answered. "Technically, demons don't exist. But these souls *are* serving the purposes of darkness and their names are significant clues to their identities. Believe me, their deaths were necessary — vital — to the welfare of everyone on this planet."

"What was the point of the fake kidnapping?" I asked next.

"There were several. One, the police were closing in on me and we needed to divert their efforts. Two, we needed to keep you busy and confused — in overwhelm mode. Otherwise, your old configuration of personality would reassert itself and this would serve no one, least of all you."

"That's not arrogant? Listen to yourself, George. It's dripping off of you."

"I *am* arrogant. I freely admit I'm as full of human foibles as anyone else and I'm definitely unworthy of my job. Krishnanda, however, is gloriously qualified to make such judgments and he has, for his own reasons, designated me to be his assistant. I am at least evolved enough not to second guess an incarnation of God himself."

"What about the weird alters — Credula and the guy in the woods?"

"They're real. They work through me as Krishnanda commands," he replied.

"Were my legs really paralyzed?" I asked next. "You know — in the coffeehouse?"

"We have a member who is a pharmacist. The effect was perfectly safe and the dosage ensured you would only undergo temporary discomfort. The substance is used as an anesthetic for certain types of surgery. This highlights an interesting feature of our group. Many of us are specialists. Jessica, for example, devised the intricate plot line you have been living. Frank, the policeman on your left, keeps us informed of law enforcement activities. We function as an aggregation of skills and personalities. Together, we are a force to be reckoned with."

"I'm sure you are." I glanced at Krishnanda, who appeared to be sleeping. As if he sensed my examination, though, his terrifying eyes blinked open and he began speaking again without preamble.

"Emory? It's time to escort our guest back to the nursery. Tom — I want you to feel, intuit, and think about what you've experienced here."

"I couldn't avoid it if I tried," I told him.

"Good. Emory?"

Krishnanda closed his eyes again and everyone besides Emory, myself, and Arundel bowed their heads. I departed in a daze, shuffling back to my cell. I was very apprehensive about being alone. Only I could lose myself — give myself away to the cult — and a part of me wanted to. Would I do it?

Chapter 29

It all boiled down to Krishnanda. Was he the sort of being who legitimately transcended conventional morality? Was his purported prescience sufficiently accurate to warrant extraordinary measures?

I needed to evaluate who this extraordinary man was, but I was woefully ill-equipped to do so. My only experience of gurus had been Matthew Ferguson and perhaps Aileen Van Der Voot and they were the equivalent of kittens to the Indian's sabre-toothed tiger. Anyway, how well had I known Ferguson when only minutes ago I had expected him to be the mystery man occupying the vacant throne?

Certainly Krishnanda was charismatic and powerful. And a whole array of people, some of whom impressed me as being reasonably substantive, believed in him enough to break the law. On the other hand, how could a holy man endorse murder — no matter the circumstances? That I knew one of the victims and she had been in no way demonic strengthened my resistance.

When I could momentarily shake off Krishnanda's influence, it all sounded as crazy as ever. But the impact of my time with him was profound; I wasn't the same Tom Dalziel I had been an hour ago. The new Tom was much more open to outlandish spiritual possibilities, and even seemed to be more comfortable sitting on straw floor mats. Part of me could watch myself be different, while another part merely became lost in it. It was an odd sensation. My sense of self had certainly been taking a battering lately.

I don't know for sure where my ruminating was heading, although I'd like to think I'd have spurned Krishnanda's overtures. As it happened, I didn't get the chance. A tapping at one of the covered windows interrupted my latest internal debate.

"Tom?"

I knew that mellifluous baritone immediately. It was Ferguson.

"I'm here, all right. Be careful. They've got guns."

"Right."

I didn't hear from my rescuer again until he'd popped the hasp loose on the door and swung it open into the fading daylight.

"Ready to go?" he asked. He was smiling and wearing old denim overalls and brown hiking boots. I was elated to see him.

"Absolutely," I replied. "Let's get out of here."

I couldn't run — my knee still hurt too much — but he led me at a fast walk toward a narrow trail behind an adjacent building.

"There's a guard at the main gate," he told me. "I parked about a half-mile back this way."

"Great. How'd you know they had me?"

As we entered the dimly-lit redwood forest, Ferguson explained.

"Several witnesses reported the snatch to the police with a description of the victim. How many huge guys with scarred faces are there? Then I heard that the K-Lovers were having an emergency all-members meeting and I put two and two together. I've been monitoring the group for a while now; it's clear that they're on the verge of something big."

"The K-Lovers, huh? Well, here's a piece of news. Krishnanda is still alive."

"Really? Wow, that explains a lot."

"And he's been ordering his people to kill so-called demons — the serial murders in town."

"Shit," he exclaimed. "Pardon my French."

Dogs howled back at the compound.

"Shit," we both said this time.

"They've got dogs," I pointed out unnecessarily.

I tried to pick up my pace as the baying and barking grew closer, but I just couldn't run properly.

The redwood-dominated ecosystem we were moving through contained very little undergrowth or even other varieties of trees since redwood droppings distribute a substance that's poisonous to other plants. Unfortunately, this created longer lines of sight that would enable our pursuers to find us sooner.

A crook in the trail aided our cause, but soon after changing directions, an area damaged by fire revealed us again. This blackened landscape was Bosch-like in its utter strangeness. I felt we were speedwalking on another planet until we'd entered living forest again.

"I think it'll be close," Ferguson pronounced. "If we have to fight off the dogs, go for either their noses or their balls."

I pictured a pack of Rottweilers, Dobermans, or all the other breeds I was afraid of. If we didn't make it to wherever Ferguson had parked, I wasn't optimistic about our chances.

As the silver sports car came into view about fifty yards ahead of us, I heard paws pounding the trail behind us and pivoted just in time to see the four canines that were about to catch us. Two were small gray terriers, one was a golden retriever, and a portly Basset hound brought up the rear, baying with excitement. Ferguson bent down to pet the tail-wagging crew and they licked him into submission for a moment before we continued.

"I guess the dogs were more for locating us than subduing us," I said.

"Apparently."

All four of them ran ahead, playing with each other. The Basset tripped comically over a root once and his own ears twice.

"The one with no legs is kind of cute," Ferguson commented. "Maybe we should keep it as a hostage."

"Please. Just get us out of here."

We reached the low-slung sports car, piled in, and Ferguson roared away. Although it was a hard-packed dirt road, he drove at breakneck speeds. Each time we hit a curve, I was positive we were going to flip over and I braced myself accordingly. I'd never ridden in a car that could do what this one could. We sat a few scant inches above the ground in firm leather seats that transmitted every contour in the road via very stiff shocks. There was a great deal of leg room but a scarcity of headroom, and no back seat at all.

"What is this torpedo?" I asked.

"Lotus. Turbocharged," Ferguson managed to reply while downshifting into yet another hairpin curve. "Don't worry," he added a moment later. "I used to race."

I worried anyway. "Where are we?" I asked a few moments later.

"Between Boulder Creek and Saratoga off of Skyline Boulevard."

"Don't you think you can slow down now? There's no way they're going to catch us."

"Motorcycles. Crotch rockets. I saw them in the parking lot. If I was thinking, I would've disabled them. They're even faster than this thing."

"Oh God."

Ferguson was right. We reached a paved country road and turned south just ahead of two gaudily painted bikes, which sprinted lustily after us.

"I don't think these guys are going to kiss us," I said, remembering the dogs.

"There's a gun in the glovebox," Ferguson answered, accelerating up into the nineties in third gear.

It was a twelve-shot Glock pistol — a nice gun and fully loaded.

We surpassed a hundred and ten on a short straightaway but the motorcycles still gained on us. The Lotus' handling was rock solid, even as its turbo shrieked at these higher rpm's. Ferguson really was an expert driver, too. He squeezed everything he could out of the exotic car, but the bikes leaned through the corners more efficiently and were quicker off the mark when the highway momentarily straightened.

On the other hand, I reasoned, what could someone guiding a motorcycle at a hundred miles an hour do to you? Shoot a gun? Maybe — I didn't think so. At least not accurately. Could they cut us off — force us off the road? No. We were the threat to them in that department. So why was I anxious? Maybe it was the sheer speed, my anticipation of using the gun, or just the recent accumulated stress of being kidnapped and escaping. Any of those would do it, I decided. In the meantime the riders closed in on us.

Ferguson began swerving on the deserted two-lane road to prevent the bikes from overtaking us, but the strategy seemed hopeless. If he blocked one, the other gained ground. Sooner or later, we would be vulnerable to whatever the motorcyclists were planning.

Maybe God *was* involved in my life. Certainly the appearance of the Highway Patrol car at that point was an injection of classical Grace into the situation. It was the exact moment in my forty-some odd years that I most needed the law, and there it was. What are the odds?

The black and white cruiser was heading north, but as soon as the driver passed us, he made a skidding U-turn and gave chase. His car was out of sight behind us in seconds.

"I doubt he'll catch us at these speeds," Ferguson shouted to me. "We can slow down for him or trust he'll radio ahead and there'll be a roadblock later."

"Roadblock," I called back.

"Right."

Ferguson gunned the motor and we leapt forward even faster. The bikes receded a bit in the narrow rear window as we roared through a long straightaway at over a hundred and forty. At that speed, everything but a point directly ahead of us on the horizon was a blur. I couldn't imagine how Ferguson was steering in response to the road. Did he know it well? Were his reflexes superhuman? And what were the chances that my rescuer would be a former race car driver? If I got out of this mess alive, I vowed to rethink the whole question of spirituality.

Gunshots pulled my attention back into the moment. Realizing that they might not get a better chance now that the cops were involved, the bikers were firing handguns from behind us. It seemed unlikely they'd hit either of us, but I realized that if a bullet struck any vital part of the car, we were as good as dead anyway. At a hundred and forty miles an hour, even a flat tire could kill you.

Ferguson began swerving again, this time to make us a more difficult target. But as he changed directions coming out of a tight curve, the rear wheels lost traction and we began spinning wildly.

I figured we were in the process of dying and I was surprised to discover that I wasn't afraid. There was a matter-of-fact quality to the mosaic of sensations and impressions, as though I was experiencing them from a place deep enough not to care how it all turned out.

After an eternity, we stopped spinning and we found ourselves just off the road, facing the wrong way. The car stalled and Ferguson couldn't get it to start again. I was dizzy and nauseated, but very calm.

The bikes had overrun us and were revving their way back. I handed the gun to Ferguson, reasoning that anyone with a Glock in his glovebox was bound to be a better marksman than I was. The motorcyclists parked their bikes a good distance from us, dismounted, and drew their pistols. I was beginning to duck when the cop car came screaming around the curve facing us and jammed on his brakes. Skidding with only a small semblance of control, the highway patrolman shot by the entire tableau as the bike riders hopped back on their machines and tore off the way we'd come. Apparently the cop was satisfied with bagging the Lotus. He parked behind us and a minute later we were out of the car, our hands in the air in response to his drawn gun.

Chapter 30

By the time the state cop sorted through all the laws we'd broken, and we'd explained why we were justified in breaking them, the entire cult had cleared out of the K-Lover's compound, but over the next few hours various members were nabbed, including Zig-Zag. She couldn't bear to leave the area without Sadie, who was visiting her veterinarian.

Neither Zee nor any of the arrested cult members would talk to the police, but physical evidence at their homes and the compound linked the group to several of the killings. In Dizzy's medicine cabinet police even found a sophisticated designer drug that generated hallucinations and could be dissolved in water. Apparently she had drugged me in the Fall Creek woods when I'd used her water bottle; the vision/dream hadn't been entirely self-authored, after all. My tumble off the rocks must have disrupted whatever plan they'd concocted that particular day.

It also turned out that Dizzy's "devil name" had been concocted for the purpose of manipulating me and her real name was Kirala Jenkins. She was wanted in several midwestern states for various scams, including a fraudulent dating service. The black angel paintings had been crafted by someone else in the group, whose notoriety subsequently propelled his career upwards in the art world.

Over the next few weeks, more members were corralled and finally someone I didn't know broke down and spilled the beans about everything. Arundel committed the murders personally, at Krishnanda's direction, but almost everyone in the group participated in the planning and logistics. Charges of first degree murder, conspiracy to commit murder, kidnapping, criminal conspiracy, and a host of firearm and controlled substance violations were filed against all the members in jail and the ones still loose. A nationwide dragnet garnered more fugitives, but Arundel, Dizzy, and Krishnanda were never found.

The press speculated that perhaps the trio of cult leaders had committed suicide, but I don't think that was their style. I picture them relaxing in hammocks in a remote cabin in Idaho, scheming and planning their next campaign to save the world.

Another popular theory advanced by the media was that the cult members were merely victims, brainwashed by their evil overlords and thus not responsible for their illegal acts. Fortunately the authorities didn't see it that way and pressed ahead with prosecution. Although the trial is dragging on, watched daily by an alarming number of television viewers, it appears that most everyone concerned will do at least some prison time.

As for me, I learned that one reason I had been chosen by Krishnanda was simply because they needed a psychotherapist in the cult. As the stress of maintaining such a vast conspiracy mounted, more and more members were cracking up. I was the loneliest therapist in town — the one who was least connected to family and friends, which rendered me the most suitable recruit. Like nine-tenths of the messy aftermath, this news was rather anticlimactic.

*   *   *   *   *

These days I'm pleased to report that I spend a lot less time stuck in my head. In the five months since the mass arrests, I've encountered dozens of excuses to retreat back in there, but for the most part I've managed to expand the proportion of my waking hours lived in the moment. I never really liked it up in my mind, anyway. I was just too far out of balance to acknowledge my capacity for choice. Developing or even sampling the alternatives had been beyond my awareness and far beyond my fear threshold, so I filtered all my experiences ad nauseam until sensory input was reduced into the thin gray gruel I found safe. Of course I still wimp out and settle for gruel more than I'd like. But I'm working on it. It helps a lot that when I can truly focus on the present, I see and hear so clearly that my world transforms into something quite beautiful. The intensity of this experience engenders large doses of fear, but it sure looks and sounds wonderful as long as I can stand it.

Ironically, after the drug-induced vision, the angel wing phenomenon, and even my audience with Krishnanda, it was my near-death experience in the sports car that emerged as the most transformative episode. I suspect that this impression of momentousness is somewhat illusory since I know that permanent change is a gradual process and there certainly was no dearth of lid-loosening events leading up to the wild ride with Ferguson. His racing experience, by the way, consisted of two days of guiding go-carts as a teenager. At any rate, whenever I become anxious now I remember that at least I'm not spinning in a Lotus at a hundred miles an hour with fanatical gunmen on motorcycles closing in. And even when I was, it wasn't so bad. Unlike my earlier disfiguring car accident, the recent experience with Ferguson served to open me up, not shut me down.

I can see now that part of my inability to comprehend what had happened to me was that I had conceptualized everything in starkly dichotomous terms. The spiritual element of the experience was either fake or real. Arundel was either evil or good. I was either an idiot or a savior. I periodically swung the pendulum of my flawed judgment from one polar extreme to the other, never allowing it to rest in the middle where the truth lay.

I believe now that the crazy and the profound commonly coexist — are even drawn toward one another — and that accommodating paradox is a skill I dearly need to learn. There were numerous non-manufactured synchronicities — meaningful coincidences — woven into the K-Lovers' hoax, for example, but I couldn't appreciate them for what they were. Lies can't kill spirit, after all — it's everywhere. I experienced the explicit appearance of the spiritual realm in my life as an intrusion; then I analyzed it as though it could be a barometric reading on reality. I hope I'm behaving more sensibly now, but I'll probably look back on what I'm doing these days and find it just as ridiculous.

I've been studying with Ferguson, trying to expand my understanding of how the world really works, and I see Aileen Van Der Voot once a week, too. Both of them have been extremely helpful in processing the tremendous backlog of feelings that surfaced once my crisis mode had receded. Perhaps I could've worked with a mainstream therapist, but I'm very comfortable with people who understand exactly what I've been through. My consultants help keep me from becoming too serious or self-important, too. I still wallow shamelessly in these self-indulgences whenever my mood and the opportunity intersect.

My practice is thriving and my clients seem to have benefitted from my adventures as well. With more of me in the room — as a person, not just a therapist — our relationship has become a much more powerful tool. Our interaction itself — not talking about it, but simply doing it — seems to embody a healing quality that promotes the clients' goals. It's quite satisfying.

What else?

I'm scheduled for plastic surgery on my face next month. I'd like to feel more poised in public now that my girlfriend Marcia and I are attending a lot of concerts and shows. I met her on a movie line and was profoundly attracted by her authenticity and long, lithe legs.

*   *   *   *   *

Marcia and I were watching television together the other night when the penguins reappeared on the nature show. The same dopey male was toting his small black rocks to the same fussy female.

"I wonder how she knows which rock is a good one?" Marcia asked.

"Beats me," I replied. "Does it matter?"

"I guess not." She kissed me for a long time before finishing her response. "No, it definitely doesn't matter at all," she affirmed.

Have I left anything out?

Oh yes. Sadie lives with me. I ransomed her from the pound when it became clear that her reputation as a cult dog was hindering her adoption. Ferguson took the basset hound and spoils him terribly.

Life isn't so bad.

Aw hell, life is *good.*

The bio page of Marc Darrow's previous book, *The Santa Cruz Guru Murders*, squandered all his good material, such as that he is a married psychotherapist living in Santa Cruz. However, the following unrelated facts are at least all true, which is a desirable quality in this sort of undertaking.

The author's grandfather was the youngest of twenty-three children and one of his great grandfathers was in *Ripley's Believe It or Not* because he worked seven days a week for sixty years without missing a single day. On several occasions as a toddler, Marc was patted on the head by Albert Einstein. He barely missed being blown up by Mt. St. Helens and then several years later was trapped in the middle of the Mexico City Earthquake, 8.1 on the Richter. A guru in Australia convinced him to switch from briefs to boxer shorts, and then later to abandon his entire life and start over from scratch.

While in Italy playing professional volleyball, Marc wrote *Nightmares Are Caused By Bad Dust Bunnies* and brought back to the States a stray dog named Boober, who had the decency to answer to "Buddha" in public.

As Verlin Whisk, Marc made singing radio commercials and wore a western suit with big notes sewn on it. Although he takes no pride in it, he was probably the only songwriter ever to rhyme halitosis, osmosis, and multiple sclerosis.

Mystery in the Monterey Bay Area Series

The Santa Cruz Guru Murders — Marc Darrow
Shrinking The Truth — Marc Darrow
Hole in the Heart — Mark Mosca

The following Patrick Riordan mysteries, written by
Roy Gilligan, also take place in the Monterey Bay Area:

Chinese Restaurants Never Serve Breakfast
Live Oaks Also Die
Poets Never Kill
Happiness Is Often Deadly
Playing God... and Other Games
Just Another Murder in Miami
Dead Heat from Big Sur
Stab in the Bach

Novels with Monterey Bay Area locations:

Green Bananas — Michael Drinkard
A Much-Married Man - Robert Sward
Gig — James D. Houston
Gasoline — James D. Houston
Mordecai of Monterey — Keith Abbott